REIGN

USA TODAY BESTSELLING AUTHOR

ROXIE NOIR

FROM THE AUTHOR

Even as a kid, I wanted to be the villain in the Disney movies: Maleficent, who turned into a dragon. Ursula, who could do *magic*.

The heroines are pure of heart, but the villains are *real*. They're driven by jealousy, anger, envy, spite — all the unpleasant emotions. And despite myself, I get that.

This is all to say: I wrote a prince who isn't charming, and I wrote a heroine who's not pure of heart. I wrote them that way because I'm not charming and I'm *really* not pure of heart. I think most people aren't.

We're all messy and complicated, but fuck it. We deserve a love story too.

Here's a not-fairy-tale for the rest of us.

NOTE

Sveloria, its cities Velinsk and Tobov, its royal family, its history, and its geography, are all completely and totally made up.

I don't speak Russian. Not even a little, though after writing *Reign*, I can very, *very* slowly sound out words written in Cyrillic. By some miracle, my lovely editor Jess minored in it in college.

When the Russian is correct, it's her doing. When it's not, it's mine.

The State Department, U.S. Foreign Service, and the politics of Eastern Europe as a whole are probably misrepresented to some degree, and I'm sorry.

But don't let any of this stop you from enjoying the story.

CHAPTER ONE
HAZEL

Something clangs right above my head, and I wake up with a snort.

"Passport!" the uniformed man says.

He's very loud, very gruff, and staring down at me with the sort of flat, serious irritation only an Eastern European can muster. His accent is so thick that it takes me a moment to figure out what he's saying, and I just stare up at him, mouth partly open.

The customs officer puts his hand on the luggage rack above my head and leans in, just a little.

"*Passport*," he says, very slowly.

"Right," I say. "Yes. Of course. *Da.*"

He steps back, I stand, and the papers that were on my lap slide to the floor.

"Shit," I mutter, but everyone else in the compartment is totally silent. "Sorry. Sorry. *Prosti.*"

The uniformed man takes another step back, this time to the door of the train compartment, and just stares at me. Totally stone-faced. The compartment is full, but no one moves to pick anything up.

Thanks, guys, I think. I'm starting to sweat.

First things first. I need my damn passport so Mr. Ice Carving over here can move on with his rounds, *then* I can pick up my shit.

I grab my frame pack, sling it onto the seat, open the main compartment and slide my hand into the slim inner pocket. Then I fish around, feeling for the skinny booklet.

It's not there. I shove my hand in further. Nothing. I push my entire arm into my backpack, my hair falling in front of my eyes, sticking in the velcro fasteners.

"Sorry," I say. "*Prosti, prosti...*"

Still nothing. My heart is doing flips, and I'm frantically trying to remember the last time I saw my passport.

I had it when I got to the Ukraine four days ago, I think. *I had it when I checked into the hostel in Kiev.*

Jesus, did I leave it there?

Now I'm pulling dirty clothes out of my backpack and piling them onto my seat. The woman sitting next to me, who somehow still looks just as fresh and put together in hour thirteen of this train ride as she did at hour one, glares.

Everyone's glaring, but I don't care, because I *need my passport*.

Finally the bag is empty, and I peer into the entrance. My heart's hammering, because not only is it *very bad form* to leave your passport god-knows-where, my mom might actually kill me if she has to bail me out of this.

She'd be justified, though.

"No passport?" the man says. His facial expression doesn't change at all, but I smile at him desperately, my best *I'm irresponsible, not a terrorist* smile.

"It's here somewhere!" I say brightly.

My fingertips brush over a small cylinder at the bottom of the bag, and my smile gets even tighter. I look in the bag, praying that it's a cigarette that wandered in there somehow.

Nope. That's a joint.

I guess I did lose that one in Amsterdam, I think as my fingers go cold with fear.

I have no idea what the drug laws are like in Sveloria. Lax, I hope.

The man waiting at the door shifts, crossing his arms in front of him, and I pretty much stick my entire head into my bag.

At last, I see a corner of something that looks *very* passport-like poking out of a hole. I jam my hand into it and pull out the little blue book, nearly collapsing to the floor with relief.

I turn around, holding it out, but the guy is crouching on the floor, looking at the papers I spilled everywhere. Very carefully, he picks up a photo of Sveloria's royal family — king, queen, and crown prince — by the edges.

Then he picks up a stack of papers, thumbing through them slowly. Finally, he turns over the folder with the seal embossed on the front.

"What's this?" he says without looking at me.

The train rolls from side to side just a little. I grab onto the luggage rack to keep my balance while I try to think of the simplest explanation for this very official-looking file with photos of the royal family and a surprising number of charts.

"I'm visiting Sveloria for the first time, so I was reading a brief on the country," I say. "I like to be prepared."

A couple people in the compartment glance at me then, and it's dead obvious no one believes *that*.

The man starts gathering my documents back into the folder, and I kneel on the floor, trying to help, but he cuts me off.

"No," he says, holding up one hand. "Put your laundry back in your bag."

It's not really laundry, it's my clothes, I think, but that doesn't seem like a good point to make right now. I stuff all my things back into my backpack and cinch it shut.

The customs officer is standing now, my briefing in his hand.

"Passport," he says, and I finally hand it over.

He glances at it briefly, his eyes flicking from the photo to my face, and flips through the pages, looking at the stamps. Finally he closes it. I hold my hand out, but he doesn't give it back.

"Come with me," he says, and steps out of the train compartment.

I take a deep breath. Everyone else in here is still looking at me in total, stony silence as I hoist my backpack onto my back. For a moment I have the stupid urge to give them all a thumbs up as I leave, but instead I take a deep breath and follow the agent through the train.

Get a grip, I tell myself. If there's one thing I've learned from watching my mom, it's that cool, calm, and collected gets the best results.

We walk through four more cars, heading for the back. Through the windows to the left I can see the Black Sea, cliffs plunging down toward deep blue water, forested rolling hills to the right.

I definitely understand why the Svelorian royal family has their summer palace near here, because it's gorgeous.

The officer keeps looking back at me, like he's making sure I haven't tried to escape or something. I want to point out that *we are on a train*, but I keep my mouth shut.

Once the initial panic wears off, I'm not actually all that worried. Not only am I an American citizen, my mom's the American Ambassador to Sveloria.

So it's not *ideal* that I'm about to be questioned by Svelorian customs, but I'm pretty sure it's gonna turn out okay. As long as they don't find the joint at the bottom of my bag.

I say one last prayer that Sveloria is cool about marijuana and follow the agent into the last compartment on the train. This one has a metal folding table in the middle, and two other customs officers are smoking and playing cards on it.

They both stub their cigarettes out when we come in, and the officer I'm with says something harsh-sounding to them in Russian. No one makes a facial expression, but they leave and he cracks the window, then slaps my folder onto the table.

We both sit, and he points to the folder.

"What is this?" he asks.

I take a deep breath, lick my lips, and make sure that I speak as clearly as possible.

"My mother is Ambassador Eileen Towers," I start. "I'm visiting Sveloria because my parents invited me to spend the month with them at the royal family's summer palace."

No reaction, but he flips open my passport again.

"I have my father's last name," I explain.

"You're Chinese?" he asks.

I'm tempted to sarcastically reply *no, I'm American, just like my damn passport says*, but I know better than to be a smartass to a foreign customs official. Especially when there's a joint in my bag.

"My grandparents immigrated to the United States from South Korea," I say, because I know the question he's really asking.

He just grunts. I take that as an invitation to continue, so I explain that my mother might be the most thoroughly prepared person on earth, and she sent me this brief on Sveloria so I could learn something about the country before I came.

She also doesn't believe in doing things halfway, so it's complete with photos of the royal family, several members of the king's small council, photos of the summer palace where I'll be staying, and even a map of Velinsk, the nearest town.

And of *course* it's printed on high-quality paper, carefully organized with a table of contents, came in an official State Department folder, and was hand-delivered to my hostel in Kiev by a courier.

I finish, and he doesn't say anything. Even though the silence makes me nervous, I force myself to sit there, poised, and wait for him to finish going through the papers. He flips past a couple of pages on proper manners, Svelorian traditions, cuisine, and traffic laws.

At the end, he gets to the photos and spreads them out on the table.

"Lots of Prince Konstantin Grigorovich," he says.

I look down. There's four of him, which is more than anyone else, but it's not a *lot*.

Honestly, I think one of my mom's assistants has a crush, and I do *not* blame her. Konstantin looks like the model for a prince in a Disney movie if Disney princes also dripped raw, rugged sex appeal. He's got dirty blond hair and gray eyes, and in every photo he's glaring at the camera with the hottest glare I've ever seen.

I don't even *like* the serious, brooding type, but I didn't mind the extra pictures of the prince. I didn't mind them at all.

I look back at the customs officer and shrug.

"The documents were put together by a woman," I say. I don't know if it's true, but the more he thinks I'm just some silly American girl, the better.

For the first time, he cracks a smile. Just barely, but he does.

"The prince is very popular with women," he says, and I raise my eyebrows just a bit.

"I can see why," I say, and smile back at him.

He just grunts and collects the photos back into the folder, then places my passport on top of the folder and pushes both toward me across the table. I take them, relieved.

"Apologies for the inconvenience," he says, stone-faced again.

"It was no inconvenience," I say, nodding my head at him.

We both stand, and he gestures at the door of the compartment.

"We will arrive in Velinsk in thirty minutes," he says.

"Thank you," I say.

I walk back through the train, taking deep breaths. I can't *wait* to get off this thing. I've been riding it for thirteen hours, and I'm pretty tired of being in a metal tube.

Before I go back to my seat, I go to the tiny bathroom. I splash my face off, brush my hair, and pull it into a bun since it's obvious I haven't washed it in two days.

I wonder if I should change my clothes, since I'm wearing leggings, an oversize tunic, a sweatshirt, and sneakers, but everything else I have is dirty. Besides, I'm not formally meeting the royal family until my welcome dinner tonight, so I'll have time to change, bathe, and feel human again before that.

Then I go back to my seat and study the briefing like *mad*. I probably look insane, muttering names and phrases over and over to myself, but the people in this compartment have already seen me at my worst, so I don't really care.

Finally, the train pulls up to a small train station. I shoulder my enormous pack, straighten my spine, and get off the train at last.

The air is summery but slightly cool, and it smells salty and fresh. I take a deep breath, glad to be off the train full of human smells.

I start walking, and as I do, my phone goes off in my pocket.

Texts from my mom start pouring in, all time-stamped at least an hour ago. We must have been out of range, or something. I stop in my tracks and read them all quickly, my heart sinking. I start chewing on one thumbnail, something I always do when I'm stressed.

The gist of the texts is: *the royal family will be meeting you at the train station, so you should look presentable.*

I look around for a bathroom, where I can frantically change into dirty clothes that at least aren't *these* dirty clothes. Instead, I see my parents waving their arms. I stare for a moment and then hesitantly wave back, then walk over to them.

"Welcome to Sveloria, sweetie!" my mom gushes as I hug her, then my dad.

Then she smiles her polite-but-slightly-worried smile.

"Did you get my texts?" she asks.

"They came through about twenty seconds ago," I say. "I guess I was out of range, but I've got some other clothes with me. They're kinda dirty, but I can go change right now if that's better?"

A black limousine pulls up to the sidewalk outside the station. Two men in black suits step out, and the other travelers step out of the way. A few point and whisper.

My mom puts one hand on my arm. She doesn't look thrilled.

"Don't worry about it, sweetheart," she says.

CHAPTER TWO
KOSTYA

I exhale and squeeze the trigger three times in quick succession. Three neat holes.

I inhale, exhale again, and squeeze the trigger three more times. Three more neat holes, this time in the chest. Between gun shots it's dead quiet and almost perfectly still out here, the dewy calm of the early morning on the coast.

Inhale. Exhale. Right shoulder, left shoulder, right shoulder. At the royal residence in Tobov, the capital city, the shooting range has the full setup. The targets move back and forth, up and down. They can duck in and out of cover, and while it's not exactly thrilling, it's a little more interesting than the setup here.

At the summer palace, I've got a paper outline on a hay bale in a disused horse paddock. I breathe in and out again and shoot the paper outline through the liver and then once through each lung.

It's not as soothing as the range at home, because there's less to concentrate on. Shooting a hay bale isn't hard, but as I keep punching holes through paper, I can finally feel the knot inside me start to loosen.

I exhale again. Steady my hands. I shoot the paper's right shoulder so perfectly through a hole that's already there that I can't even tell, then I do the same thing to the left shoulder. *Now* I feel in control, finally, after waking up at four in the morning again, the sheets soaked in sweat.

There are some problems that the shooting range solves better than a four-mile run or a brutal hour-long workout, and this is one of them.

I lower the gun and step back a few paces, but before I raise it again, I see someone standing far to the side, respectfully waiting. The other palace residents only had to learn once what a bad idea it was to tap me on the shoulder while I was at the range, particularly when I've got hearing protection on.

I nod at him, shoot my last two bullets into the paper target, then put the safety on and put the gun down, taking the earmuffs off. He finally walks over.

"Your father requests your presence in his study," Niko says.

I look at my watch. It's eight in the morning, and I'm wearing a sweat-soaked t-shirt and track pants.

"I'll see him at the small council meeting in an hour," I say. "He needs me before that?"

Niko shrugs.

"He sent me to request your presence," he says. "You know he'd never give me more information than strictly necessary."

I almost snort. My father isn't in the habit of giving anyone more information than strictly necessary, and that includes me. The Crown Prince. The next in line for the throne.

The kind of person who should have some damned information sometimes.

"Thanks," I say. I eject the magazine from the handgun

and pull back the action, checking that there isn't a bullet in the chamber.

"Has he said anything about the reports from the north?" I ask, still looking at the gun. I speak quietly, even though I'm certain it's just the two of us.

"Kostya, if you hadn't told me, I wouldn't *know* there were reports from the north," Niko says, his quiet tone matching mine. "Your father hasn't even mentioned them in my presence."

"Of course he hasn't," I mutter.

My father, King Grigory II of Sveloria, is also suppressing them from the state-run media, which is the only media in our tiny country. After a year and a half, the guerillas are emerging from the mountains again. There's going to be fighting, maybe bad fighting, and we haven't warned our people.

Niko says nothing, but we share a long look. I know perfectly well that I'm one of the few people who can criticize my father, and even in private, it's a good idea for others to keep their mouths shut. But Niko and I go all the way back to boot camp, then to Five Hundred Squad, and then to the Svelorian Royal Guard.

The Royal Guard is an old, old name. They don't guard the royal family any more. Now they're an elite military force. More like the Green Berets than actual guards.

After Niko got hurt, I convinced my father to hire him as an aide. Partly because Niko is sharp, experienced, and lowborn — the kind of voice the palace desperately needs. Partly because I wanted to have a friend around.

"He's expecting you," Niko says, and inclines his head, just barely.

"Thank you," I say.

Niko walks away, shoulders straight, his limp very slight these days.

I don't even change before I go to my father's study. He wanted to see me now, he can see me before I'm presentable.

In the antechamber to his study, his secretary sits, straight-backed. Anna has worked for my father since his coronation nearly twenty-one years ago. She wears her gray hair in a bun at the nape of her neck, has cat-eye glasses, and if she's ever smiled, I wasn't around to see it.

All the same, I think there's a speck of fondness for me in there, somewhere.

"Good morning, Anna," I say, nodding at her.

"Good morning, Konstantin Grigorovich," she says, using the most formal version of my name.

I've told her a thousand times to call me Kostya, like most people do. She's known me since I was a child, after all, but Anna is old fashioned and I know she never will.

"Is my father in?" I ask.

She inclines her head slightly, the line of her mouth perfectly straight.

"You're to go right in," she says.

"Thank you," I say.

I step through the door to my father's study, and he looks up. I close the door behind me as he sits behind his massive, ornate wooden desk. It's one of a handful of furniture pieces that survived the nearly seventy years of Soviet rule.

I clasp my hands in front of me, the sweat on my shirt cooling against my skin. He gives me a long look, his face nearly unreadable, but I think there's a hint of disapproval there.

"You asked for me, father?" I say.

He finally looks up at my face.

"Yes," he says. "The Queen and I are receiving Ambassador Towers's daughter at the train station, and you'll be joining us."

For just a moment, I stare at him. It's not that he calls my mother, his wife, *the Queen*. That's what he always calls her. It's probably what he calls her in private.

But why are they going to a train station to greet the ambassador's daughter? And why the hell do I have to go with them?

"Father, I have a fairly busy schedule today," I say. I try my best to sound respectful.

He just looks at me, then looks back at the papers on his desk.

"After the small council meeting, I'm being briefed on the situation in the north by several of the outpost leaders there, and then I've set up a meeting with General Vladov to talk about the most appropriate response—"

"The United Svelorian Front likely has Russian backing," he says, cutting me off. He's still looking at the papers on the desk. "If we want to stand a chance against that kind of threat, we need the Americans on our side. We have extended every courtesy to Ambassador Towers, and we will do the same for her daughter."

"Father, I'll be meeting her at the formal dinner tonight," I say. I try to keep my voice flat and neutral, but I can hear the irritation creeping into it. "Surely it's more important that I understand the threat that the USF poses than meet some American girl on her arrival."

I want to say, *we're not still doing things the old way. We don't broker treaties and trade agreements over vodka shots in back rooms any more.*

"I'll have Anna reschedule all that," he says, barely glancing up at me.

I can tell from his tone that this isn't up for discussion, but I can't stand the way he's treating me like a child. I'm not whining that I'll miss my birthday party.

I'm trying to protect my country.

"The American government isn't going to care that I met this girl at the train station when they're deciding how many guns to send," I say.

"Yes, but they'll care about what Ambassador Towers has to say about you," he says. He's writing something, his voice going vague. "You're coming with us, Kostya."

He still doesn't look at me, and the black anger inside simmers to a boil. Lately, more than ever, he's seemed obtuse and old-fashioned, like he's ignoring reality in favor of the way he wishes things were.

But he's the king. I'm not. And if I want to be, I do what he says.

"Yes, father," I say, and turn for the door.

"Kostya," he says.

I turn, my hand on the knob.

"I've taken the liberty of asking Yelena Pavlovna to accompany you to the dinner tonight," he says. He looks up at me again.

I don't say anything. It's not as if protesting will change his mind.

"It's more than time, Kostya," he says. "A prince needs an heir, and for an heir, you need a good Svelorian wife."

Lately, he's been going on more and more that I need to get married and have a son, though my love life is the last thing I want to discuss with my father. When I find someone I think I can spend my life with, I'll get married. It's that simple.

Yelena Pavlovna, even though she's a sweet, pretty, well-bred girl, isn't that person.

"Yes, father," I say.

Then I open the door and leave, nodding at Anna as I walk past her desk.

My mother, the Queen, pats my hand as we sit in the limousine.

"Yelena is such a sweet girl," she says. "Her grandmother bore twelve children, you know. Her mother bore six. It bodes well for her suitability."

"I don't wish to marry someone because they can have a litter of children," I say.

Her face changes for a split second, and something like relief crosses it. She herself only had two, and we were ten years apart with plenty of strife in between.

"She's lovely and charming, all the same," my mother says. "You should give her a chance, Kostya."

Yelena's father is also in charge of the state-run oil company of Sveloria. The company belongs to the crown, but he's still a wealthy man, someone we'd like to keep happy.

"I think Yelena is a very nice, lovely woman," I say, trying to sound neutral.

It's true. Yelena is sweet, nice, lovely, well-bred, and perfectly mannered. There's nothing at all wrong with her, but I don't think we've ever had a meaningful conversation in the years we've known each other.

It's a bit like talking to a puppy: she's sweet, and she wants very much to please everyone, but she doesn't quite have the mental resources to give me what I need.

"Kostya, you don't need to be in love to marry," my father says. The limo goes over a bump, and my mother's gaze flicks to one side.

I *hate* how casually cruel he can be to her sometimes.

"Just marry," he says, and the limo comes to a stop.

The driver comes around, opens the door, and gives my mother his hand. She climbs out, followed by my father, and finally me.

We stand on the sidewalk in short row, and I try to fight my irritation again that I'm here, meeting some American girl, rather than doing my job back at the palace.

After a moment, three people emerge from the train station and begin crossing the plaza. Since two of them are Ambassador Towers and her husband, I assume the girl in between them is their daughter.

As they come closer, I straighten up a little, suddenly conscious of the way I'm standing.

The Ambassador's daughter is *pretty*.

No. She's *beautiful*. Gorgeous, in a way I've never even seen before, in a way I didn't even imagine a woman could *be* beautiful. Black hair in a high bun, latte-colored skin, narrow brown eyes and freckles across her high cheekbones.

Her mom says something to her and she laughs loudly, showing her teeth. The sound *almost* makes me smile.

Next to me, my mother makes a small sound of disapproval. I know without looking that she thinks Americans are too loud and jovial.

To make matters worse, the American girl is wearing leggings, an oversized sweatshirt, and sneakers, an outfit so casual that no Svelorian woman would be caught dead wearing it. The spandex pants in particular don't leave much to the imagination, but I don't mind.

I don't mind at *all*. She may be a tasteless American, but I can still enjoy the view.

When they're finally standing in front of us, Ambassador Towers begins the introductions. My father is first, and despite her attire, the American girl comports herself very well: she pronounces his name flawlessly, and even says *honored to meet you* in near-perfect Russian.

She does the same for my mother, and my mother manages to be gracious.

Finally the American girl is standing in front of me, and

she's even more beautiful up close, in a make-me-forget-my-own-name kind of way. Her sweatshirt slides over one collarbone, and I have to fight the urge to lean forward and plant my lips on her skin.

"Your Highness, may I present my daughter, Miss Hazel Sung," Ambassador Towers says to me.

"Miss Sung," I say, inclining my head slightly, offering my hand.

Hazel, I think.

"Hazel, may I introduce the crown prince of Sveloria, His Highness Konstantin Grigorovich,"

"*Priyatno poznakomitsya*, Konstantin Grigorovich," she says, and shakes my hand firmly, looking me right in the eye.

"I'm honored as well, Miss Sung," I say.

I hold her hand for a beat too long, then let it go. My mother is already making small talk with her in her accented English about the long train ride, and one of our bodyguards is loading her enormous backpack into the trunk of the limousine.

Hazel climbs into the limousine, and when she bends over, I can't help but stare at the half-globes of her ass before she disappears into the car. I wonder what they'd feel like if I could squeeze them. How they'd look *without* the leggings on.

"Kostya," my mother says, very quietly.

She's giving me a gentle-but-disapproving glance. Then we all get into the car.

CHAPTER THREE
HAZEL

There are ways that could have gone worse. I could have been wearing cutoff jean shorts and stripper heels. There could have been *two* handsome, sexy, suit-wearing princes.

Someone could have dumped an entire bottle of cheap cologne on me before I got off the train. I could have accidentally said something like *your mother is a famous giraffe-fucker.*

See? Plenty of ways to make a worse first impression than the one I actually made.

I sit in the rear-facing seat and squeeze my knees together, trying to be as demure as humanly possible while wearing spandex. Polite as they were, it doesn't take a genius to realize that the Svelorian Royal Family doesn't really approve of being met by someone wearing a sweatshirt and pants with an elastic waistband.

Plus, it turns out that pictures don't do Prince Konstantin justice. Not even close. He's hot in pictures, yeah, but *way hotter* in person.

Pictures don't get across just *how* tall and built he is. They don't properly communicate that when you're in front of him, and he's sexily glaring *at you*, you feel like an insect pinned to a board, but in a good way.

I'm still amazed I remembered what to say to him. For a second there I wasn't sure I could even manage *hi*, which is ridiculous.

I've met attractive men before, for fuck's sake. I've met some *really* attractive men, and I've never had *this* reaction.

The limo door darkens again and the prince climbs in, hesitating for a moment.

Not next to me, I think. *I smell like weird coffee and those Ukrainian cigarettes they sold on the train and stranger sweat and God only knows what. Please sit somewhere else. Please.*

My heart thuds against my ribcage. I clamp my arms to my sides like I can seal the odor into my armpits.

Konstantin sits across from me, settles himself, and looks at me again. I feel pinned, but less than the first time, and a tiny bit disappointed that he didn't sit next to me, despite my *Eau de Thirteen Hours On A Train.*

"Did you have a good trip?" he asks.

His English is perfect, and he barely even has an accent. That was in the brief, of course, but I'm relieved all the same that I won't be spending a month trying to overcome a language barrier.

"Yes," I say. "Beautiful and uneventful, just the way travel should be."

I've set U.S.-Svelorian relations back enough already without telling everyone about my passport debacle.

"The ride from Kiev is quite lovely, if long," he says, his face still stony.

My dad gets in and sits next to me, and the limo starts moving.

"I started feeling like cattle after about eight hours," I say. "And, judging by the smell, I think the guy across from me was smuggling goats in his luggage."

I smile at the prince, waiting for him to laugh politely. He frowns. Now the king and queen are also looking at me, and it's very, *very* clear that my stupid joke didn't land.

"I would love to take that ride someday," my mom says, saving my ass. "Without the goats, naturally, but it's supposed to be the best way to see some parts of the Black Sea coast that are difficult to reach otherwise."

I take a deep breath. I'm tired and more than a little loopy. My dad pats my knee affectionately.

"Glad you made it, Freckles," he says quietly. "Goat smells and all."

I wrinkle my nose but laugh anyway.

"I wish that was everything," I say.

He raises his eyebrows.

"Later," I say.

Prince Konstantin is still glaring at me, his wide shoulders squared, his spine very straight, his hands clasped in front of him. I smile just a little, out of nervous habit, and he doesn't return it.

Okay then. Guess we won't be friends after all.

I give up and pay attention to the conversation my mom is having with the king and queen.

At least one of us is in her element right now, I think.

THE CASTLE IS massive and beautiful. Even in person it looks like something that's been put together by the Svelorian Tourism Committee: stone turrets, towers, and ramparts, all perched on a cliff overlooking a white sand beach that stretches down to the perfect, blue waters of the Black Sea.

If you told a kid *draw me a castle*, they'd draw something like the Summer Palace. It's not the first castle I've stayed in — my mom's a diplomat, after all — but it's definitely the most castle-like.

My parents and I have a whole wing to ourselves, in two towers at either end of a hallway, and both of our suites are *glorious*. I've got a giant four-poster bed facing tall, iron-framed windows. Outside there's a balcony that's more like a patio, complete with an outdoor sitting area.

Inside the bedroom is another sitting area, complete with a big TV, two couches, and a miniature kitchen. A quiet, solemn man carries my bag for me and ceremoniously places it on a luggage rack, nods once at me, and leaves.

"This is *nice*," I say to my parents. "How did any of this survive the Soviet occupation?"

"It was a backwater," my mom says. "If this had been closer to Moscow, or strategically important, it wouldn't have. Sveloria is lucky it didn't find out that it had oil until the late nineties."

Some backwater, I think.

"Try to enjoy yourself," my dad says, smiling at me.

"I had most of your clothes shipped over from Boston," my mom says. "They're in the closet, along with some other things I took the liberty of getting you."

She glances at my outfit again, and I cross my arms in front of myself.

"You don't think I impressed them?" I ask. "Oversized sweatshirts are *the thing* right now in Paris, you know."

My mom just laughs.

"Svelorians are very serious," she says. "It takes some getting used to, but underneath, they're very kind, warm people."

"Way, way underneath," my dad says, adjusting his glasses. "But that's why they've got vodka. So they can smile sometimes."

"Tom, stop it," my mother says, playfully.

He shrugs, smiling.

"I'll let you unpack and get some rest, sweetheart, but come to our suite an hour before dinner. We want to hear *everything*, and we've got a bottle of the finest South Svelorian wine."

I raise my eyebrows.

"Is it good wine?" I ask.

"It's wine," my father says evenly.

I laugh. They both hug me again, tightly.

"I'm glad you're here," my mom says, still squeezing me. "I know you've had a rough year."

Yeah, I think.

My dad hugs me too, and then they leave and shut the big wooden door behind them.

I set my alarm, then get in bed without even washing my face.

AFTER A LONG, deep nap I shower, do my hair, and venture into my closet. A tiny portion of it is taken up by the clothes I left at my parents' house after my fiasco this spring, but most of it I've never seen before. Hell, most still has the tags on it, and I wade through it piece by piece.

There's a couple designer things, but it's mostly nice-but-normal clothes. Lots of J. Crew and Banana Republic, the kind of thing a diplomat's daughter should be wearing when visiting foreign royals. It's a good thing that my mom picked all these out, because I'm clueless about this stuff.

Still wearing a towel, I pick out a V-neck black cocktail dress. Miraculously, there are bras and panties in a drawer, and they even fit. Thirty seconds later I've gone from towel-wearing mess to perfectly respectable, and I look in the mirror and take a deep breath.

Definitely better, I think.

Then I put on a pair of black heels, touch up my eyeliner, and head for my parents' suite. They're both in their sitting area, drinking glasses of red wine and looking ready for a formal dinner.

When my mom sees me, she sighs and crooks one finger at me. I try not to laugh as I walk over. She reaches up, beneath my hair, and pulls a price tag off my dress.

"Thanks," I say.

They pour me a glass, and I take a seat on a velvet couch.

"Tell us everything," my mom says. "Start at the beginning."

I tell them about the past two months of backpacking across Europe: London, Dublin, Paris, Amsterdam, and Copenhagen. I met a friend there and drove through to Switzerland, then through the Alps to Italy, where she immediately met a Florentine man and decided to go to Capri with him.

After Italy, I traveled the Adriatic coast. I meant to go to Istanbul but that train was sold out, so I went to Vienna instead, then Prague and Berlin before it was time to head east. I went through Poland, the Ukraine, and finally to Kiev and then here.

I stayed in hostels and cheap hotels, for the most part, though I did spring for a room with its own bathroom a couple of times. I slept on a lot of trains and busses. I asked a lot of strangers for help or directions and I tried to do it in the local language, though most people answered in English.

Most of the time, I was alone. I went on the trip alone, and I traveled with other people sometimes, but I was mostly by myself, and I *loved* it. When you travel alone, there's no one else to hurry you along or make you stay behind somewhere. There's no one to say *haven't we eaten enough gelato?* or *I don't really want to see the catacombs,* or *let's just hang out in the hotel room today.*

There's also no one to help carry things or walk next to you when it's three in the morning and your train just got in, but I thought the tradeoffs were worth it.

"Then I got on a train, and now I'm here," I finish, shrugging. "Ta-da."

"Goat smells and all," my mom says, teasing me.

"I showered," I say, laughing.

"I'm glad we could convince you to visit this terrible place," she says.

"You did have to blackmail me," I say.

My mom sighs good-naturedly.

"Hazel, I told you," she says. "This was *bribery*. Blackmail would be if I said *visit us in Sveloria or I'll post your old diaries on the internet*."

"Do you still have those?" I ask, tipping back the last of my wine.

"Refuse to visit us sometime and find out," she says, and stands. "Ready to make a better second impression?"

"You tell me," I say, and turn slowly for her inspection.

"Yes," she says. "Come on, let's salvage this diplomatic mission."

"When the inevitable conflict starts, they'll call it the Spandex War," I say, dryly. "Future historians will debate what might have happened had I gotten your texts in time to change clothes this morning."

"Get moving," my dad says. "You can be late or you can be a smartass, but you can't be both."

I stick my tongue out at him. He laughs, and we leave the suite.

CHAPTER FOUR
KOSTYA

"I do hope they use the old china pattern for the dinner and not the newer one," Yelena says, standing at my side, her voice high and soft. "I love those pretty pink roses on the old dishes. The ones rimmed in gold leaf?"

"Yes," I say, nodding down at her, even though I'm not quite listening.

I think Yelena knows more about the palace's china patterns than I do. No: I *know* she does, because I'm not really sure what she's talking about. Apparently we own plates with roses on them.

"There may not be enough of those for this dinner," she says, worrying at her lip. She seems concerned, like it's her fault that the palace staff might have used a different china pattern.

"It's no loss if they use the other china," I say, because I'm sure the other china is just as nice.

She just sighs, her wide blue eyes flitting around the drawing room, taking in everything and nothing. Finally she looks up at me and takes my arm.

"Of course not, Kostya. You're right."

The double doors open and a footman precedes my parents in.

"May I please present—" he starts.

"It's just our son," my father growls. "He knows who we are."

The footman ducks his head and backs out of the room, pulling the doors closed, and my parents walk toward us. Yelena curtsies to them, and I nod.

"You're well, I expect?" my father asks Yelena.

"Yes, your highness," she says. "We were just discussing the palace's china."

I try to make eye contact with my father, but he ignores me.

"Yes, it does need updating," my mother says, her hand on my father's arm. "It could use a woman's touch, and I'm afraid that I haven't the fashion sense or taste to do it justice."

This isn't a conversation that requires my input, so I let my mind wander. A waiter comes by with a tray of wine, and we each take a glass.

I take a long sip and look out one of the tall paned windows. This one looks onto the gardens. Today, they're beautiful and well-kept, full of rosebushes in bloom, walking paths, everything neat and orderly and green.

The first time I saw this palace, I was five, and the gardens were bare dirt. It was the February after an ugly winter, and my mother and I had been sent here because the opposition forces were closing in on Tobov, the capital city.

The palace was freezing and miserable. My mother worried constantly, desperate for any scrap of news about my father, fighting for his life. I spent my days exploring secret, unknown wings of the palace until it was time for dinner, putting the prizes that I found — a bat skeleton, a scrap of gold cloth, a child's spinning top — into a box in my bedroom.

My mother wasn't the queen then. I wasn't a prince, just a

kid whose ancestors had sat on a throne once. We were always cold and usually hungry, and twenty-odd years later, here I am talking about china patterns.

"Don't you think so?" Yelena says, looking up at me.

"Of course," I say. I have no idea what I think, but I doubt I have an opinion.

"That would be very stately," my mother agrees.

The doors open again, and the same footman steps through.

"May I present United States Ambassador Eileen Towers, her husband Mr. Thomas Sung, and their daughter Miss Hazel Sung."

He steps aside, and the three of them walk past him. Each thanks him, because they're American, and Americans love thanking people who are simply doing their jobs. The footman looks slightly confused.

Hazel nods her head slightly as she thanks the man, her long black hair shining in the light. Then she walks toward us, looking around the room as she does, taking in the portraits on the wall, the heavy wooden furniture, the overstuffed chairs.

She even *walks* like an American: shoulders back, head high, hips barely swinging even though she's wearing heels. Nothing less than confident, even though we're royalty who saw her in a sweatshirt earlier today and she's a loud, brash commoner.

We all exchange pleasantries again, I introduce Yelena, and her parents start talking with mine. Something about architecture, but I'm not really listening, I'm looking at Hazel. She's got on a black cocktail dress that's curve-hugging yet tasteful, with a deep V that just *barely* hints at her cleavage.

Now that she's rested and polished, she's nothing short of *breathtaking*.

The waiter with the wine comes back, and Hazel grabs a glass and takes a sip.

"It's nice to see you again, Konstantin," she says.

"Likewise, Miss Sung," I say.

"You can call me Hazel," she says, with a little half-laugh. "We're going to be seeing each other for a month."

I don't know why she's laughing, but I nod.

"Then please, call me Kostya," I say. "Konstantin is far too formal."

She nods again and looks around the room.

"This is a beautiful palace," she says. "I've never seen anything quite like it, and I've certainly never stayed anywhere like it."

"It was built five hundred years ago to withstand barbarian attacks from the Black Sea," I say. "The walls are five feet thick at the base."

"Wow," she says.

"Many of the interior passages still have murder holes in the ceiling," I go on. "They've been plastered over, but if you know what to look for, you can find plenty."

She takes another sip of wine.

"Murder holes?" she asks, politely.

"If the gates were breached and enemies got past the walls, the defenders would boil water or oil, and pour it through grates onto the attackers," I explain.

"Did that ever actually happen?" Hazel asks.

"Once," I say. "During the reign of Maksim the second, the castle was left undefended while he was fighting across the country, near the Russian border. But when he returned, he took the castle back and mounted the head of every man who'd taken it from him on spikes outside the walls."

Hazel's got both eyebrows up, her mouth partly open.

"All of them?" she asks.

I just nod.

"It was a simpler time," I say. Then I lift my hand with my wine glass in it and point at a portrait. "That's him," I say.

Maksim the second stares out of the frame, his gaze intense five hundred years after his death. I've never had a problem believing that he would execute hundreds, maybe thousands, and display their heads on spikes.

Hazel looks from the portrait to me, then back again.

"I see the family resemblance," she says.

"I've been told we have the same chin," I say. "Though I've never put a head on a spike. I understand that's frowned upon."

Hazel just looks at me uncertainly for a long moment.

I guess that's what I get for trying a joke.

"Maksim was a third cousin twice removed to Vlad Dracul," I go on. "Known better as Vlad the Impaler."

Her eyebrows go up again.

"Does that mean you're related to Vlad the Impaler?" she asks.

"Very distantly, of course," I say.

"I assumed," she says, and takes another sip.

"Why?" I ask.

"Because he's been dead for hundreds of years?" Hazel asks.

To my left, Yelena is absently examining her manicure. She's probably heard about Maksim the Second a hundred times, and I doubt she ever cared to begin with.

"Of course," I say to Hazel.

I'm getting the sense that I'm not being a very good conversationalist right now, and god knows Yelena isn't helping in the least.

"Your parents told me you were traveling through Europe for the past two months," I say. "You had no commitments in America?"

Hazel looks quickly into her wine glass. I can see her take a deep breath, the hollow of her throat expanding as she does it.

For just a moment, I wonder what it would taste like if I

licked it there, then ran my tongue along her collarbone to the point of her shoulder—

I'm getting hard. I force myself to stop.

"No, I didn't have any commitments," she says, looking back up at me. "I dropped out of med school this spring, so I was pretty commitment-less."

"Was it too difficult?" I ask. "I've heard that becoming a doctor takes a great deal of work."

Her face stays perfectly neutral.

"It was very difficult, but I left because I realized I didn't want to be a doctor any more," she says. "There were a lot of reasons. It's a long story."

"I enjoy stories," says Yelena, in her soft high voice.

Her English is very good, but she hasn't spent much time abroad and doesn't understand nuances well. Hazel takes another deep breath.

"What was your favorite city to visit?" I ask, trying to steer this conversation back into pleasant waters.

"Rome," Hazel says instantly.

The doors open again, and the footman comes in.

"Dinner is served in the Emerald Dining Room," he says.

Hazel looks relieved.

THE EMERALD DINING room is the third-largest in the palace. Since it's summer, the sun is still setting, and the view through the west-facing windows is spectacular.

My father sits in the center of the long table, my mother on one side and me on the other. While I was telling Hazel that I've never impaled anyone's head on a stick, other dignitaries and important Svelorians trickled in, so the party now numbers about sixteen.

A small, intimate party, at least by our standards.

Servants refill wine glasses and lay out the first course, a small plate of pickled smelt and new potatoes. I'm sitting directly across the table from Thomas Sung. On one side is his wife, the Ambassador, and on the other is Hazel.

The room goes quiet, and my father taps his spoon against his wine glass, even though no one's speaking.

"I propose a toast," he says. In English, of course.

The door at the end of the room opens, and servants with chilled vodka bottles walk out and begin pouring a measure of vodka into our aperitif glasses.

"I would like to welcome the Ambassador's lovely, engaging daughter to Sveloria," he says.

Hazel nods once, smiling politely.

"To another generation of continued American-Svelorian relations," he says, holding up his glass.

"*Nah zdrovya!*" everyone at the table says, including Hazel.

We drink. I down the glass as I see Hazel glance around quickly, like she's making sure she's doing the right thing.

Then she does the wrong thing and swallows the vodka in one gulp, the only woman at the table to do so. The other women sip their vodka, putting their nearly-full glasses back on the table.

Hazel is beginning to flush a pale pink, but she uses the correct fork as we begin the first course.

I don't think she knows that it's customary to begin *every* course with a toast. She certainly doesn't realize that she isn't obligated to drink a full shot of vodka each time, and it isn't as if I can correct a guest's manners at this formal dinner.

I eat my first course and make small talk with Yelena, who is telling me a charming story about a time when she went fishing with her father as a child. I've heard it before, more than once, but I don't tell her that.

That course is cleared and the next laid down. Our vodka glasses are refilled. Hazel watches hers like she's concentrating very, very hard, then thanks the waiter for doing his job. Americans.

My father holds up his glass.

"To the sunset over the sea," he says, a traditional Svelorian toast.

I try to make Hazel look at me, as if I can tell her *just take a sip*. She doesn't, her eyes just skipping past me like I'm not even there.

"*Nah zdrovya,*" everyone says again, and then we drink, Hazel tossing hers back just like a man.

"The American girl is getting drunk," Yelena says to me, quietly, in Russian.

"She doesn't know better," I murmur.

"She should learn," Yelena says.

Hazel flushes a brighter pink and continues avoiding my eyes.

CHAPTER FIVE
HAZEL

The table is starting to wobble in front of me as we begin the next course. This one is grape leaves stuffed with some sort of spiced rice. It's very good, or at least it would be if I weren't quickly getting hammered just to be polite.

Is this going to be what my whole month is like? I wonder, very carefully cutting a slice and lifting it to my mouth.

I make it. Success!

It's not like I'm a teetotaler. Fuck no. I went through a bottle of whiskey in a week after the shit hit the fan and I dropped out of school, but I'm a total lightweight.

Sveloria might be the death of me, I think. I successfully get another forkful into my mouth, and I just hope that I don't look like a barbarian eating. I don't want my head to end up on a spike.

The way Kostya keeps *glaring* at me, it's starting to feel like that might be my fate. I'm not even doing anything, just trying my hardest to fit in here, be polite and demure, and not fuck anything up.

Partway through the course, my father leans over to me and speaks in a low voice.

"Your mother wants me to tell you it's perfectly polite to sip the vodka, particularly for women," he says.

I look at my empty glass, then glance at the queen's glass. Mostly full. Yelena's glass is also mostly full, as are all the other women's glasses at the table.

Fuck, I think. *How was I supposed to know this was gendered?*

I nod once.

"Thank you," I say.

"Hang in there," he says, then leans away again. His face is beginning to flush pink.

I take a deep breath and keep eating. I make as much polite conversation as I can with the middle-aged man on my other side, but he's much more interested in the other people, and that's fine. I'm just trying to keep my shit together over here.

They clear plates. They fill glasses, and this time I watch the clear liquid fill the little glass triumphantly.

Not today, motherfucker, I think at the vodka. *Not today.*

The king raises his glass.

"To the grass in the fields," I think he says. I mutter *nah, froyo*, and take the tiniest possible sip of vodka, then put the glass down.

Across the table, Kostya is still staring at me. Glaring at me. Stare-glaring.

There's probably a word for that in Russian, I think. *Or they don't have a word for "looking," only "stare-glaring."*

I look away first, because I know I'm not handling myself well, and I *know* he disapproves of me. Plus, I can feel my Asian glow out in full force, so I'm bright pink.

But I've cracked the secret to not getting super drunk at this formal dinner, and it's gonna be fine. From here on out I can only get *less* drunk.

The waiter puts a very small bowl of soup in front of me. The second the steam hits my nose, I know it's got kidney in it.

I cannot *stand* the smell of kidney, even sober, and my stomach lurches.

I take a deep breath through my mouth and focus on a salt shaker.

You're fine, I think. *You're not gonna throw up from four drinks. No one does that.*

I catch another whiff of kidney and have to grit my teeth together, because it's abundantly clear that *I am about to do that.*

"Excuse me," I manage to say.

I stand and somehow, through sheer force of will, I walk out of the dining room in my high heels. I have no idea where I'm going, but I *have* to get out of that room, filled with vodka and kidney smells.

I walk into some sort of passageway. The windows over-looking the sea are open, and the fresh breeze feels *good*. I take a deep breath, and some of my nausea dissipates instantly. I take another, and another.

There's a bench along the wall, facing the windows, and I sit on it gingerly. I lean my head back against the wall and keep gulping air. Maybe if I can stay like this for a few minutes, the soup will be gone, I won't puke, and I can go back in there like nothing's happened.

A few minutes pass, and I'm almost feeling better.

Then I hear footsteps coming down the hall.

My eyes pop open, but before I can stand, Kostya comes into view.

Great, I think. *The very last person I want to see.*

I swallow hard and lean forward to stand, but he holds up one hand.

"Sit," he says, like he's commanding a dog.

I glare, trying to give him a taste of his own medicine. He seems impervious to it.

"I'm fine," I say.

"You're drunk," he says.

I close my eyes and lean my head back.

"I'm sorry. Don't put my head on a spike," I say.

"You didn't invade. You're a guest," he says, and I feel his weight settle next to me on the bench.

"I'm still a barbarian," I say, eyes still closed.

I hear something rip, and open my eyes just enough to look down. He's got a bread roll in his hand, and he's torn a chunk off of it, holding it in front of me.

"You need bread," he says. "It soaks up the vodka."

"That's not how digestion works," I say.

His father must have sent him to do damage control with the drunk American girl, I think.

"Eat," he says. I take the hunk of bread and put it in my mouth, chewing it slowly.

This is way, way worse than the train station. I look better now, but rushing out of a formal dinner because I'm so drunk I think I might vomit is beyond the pale. Hell, I should just pack my things and go home *now*, before this dinner is over, so I can't ruin anything else.

My stomach stirs, and I lean my head against the wall, closing my eyes. Kostya presses another bite of bread into my hand and the tips of his fingers brush my palm. They're warm and surprisingly rough for a royal.

I eat the bread. I swallow. I don't open my eyes. He presses another bite into my palm, and we repeat this over and over again.

After a few minutes, I *do* start to feel better. I take a deep breath and open my eyes. He's stare-glaring at me. I just blink.

"Better?" he asks. His expression stays flat.

"I think so," I say. "You should go back. I'll be okay."

"It's fine," he says, and presses the last chunk of bread into my hand. "That vile soup will be gone when we return."

I eat the last chunk of bread and try not to smile at *vile soup*.

"My mom gave me a brief on Sveloria, but I guess I skimmed the part about toasts," I say.

"You're not the first foreigner to be duped," he says. "According to legend, that's why we have so many of them."

"To get foreigners drunk?" I ask. "Is Sveloria the frat party of Eastern Europe? You get outsiders drunk so you can get lucky?"

He frowns slightly and looks at me. I open my mouth, only to realize that I can't possibly explain that dumb joke right now, so I just shake my head.

"We have an excellent tolerance for alcohol," Kostya says. "In the old days, rulers would negotiate over a meal. In Sveloria, it was traditional for that meal to include a number of toasts, and anyone who refused to drink was committing a grave social sin."

He still looks dead serious, but I start smiling.

"And your king would keep his head while the other guy got *wasted*," I say.

"Precisely," he says.

"Tricky," I say. "You Svelorians are fucking crafty."

I shut my mouth, because I probably shouldn't call the crown prince *fucking crafty*.

"Times have changed," he says. "Now it's also considered polite for guests to sip their vodka. We can't even put heads on spikes any more, even when we wish we could."

I lean my elbows on my knees, take a breath in, and then look at him. He's not smiling, but for the first time, he's not exactly glaring, either.

"That was a joke," he explains, and looks at the windows. "I don't wish to put heads on spikes at all."

I pinch the bridge of my nose between my finger and thumb and start laughing. I'm still drunk, so it seems *extra* ridiculous that the heir to the throne is here, feeding me bread and trying to be funny.

I'm sure his father sent him to check on me, but I have a feeling his father didn't ask him to try to make me laugh.

"I think you may not be laughing at my joke," he says, and stands.

I take a deep breath, trying to get control of myself, and look up at him.

"I think I may not be," I say.

He offers his hand. I take it. It's warm and strong and rough, and even though I wobble a little getting to my feet, he's got me.

"Thank you for the bread," I say.

"It was my pleasure," he says, and offers me his arm.

It's a formality, Hazel, I tell myself.

I take it, and he escorts me back to the dining room. As the doorman starts opening the heavy doors, we look at each other. I slide my hand out of his arm, and we walk back into the dining room.

As I sit, my dad leans over to me.

"You okay?" he asks.

"Fine," I whisper back.

I'm just in time for the main course, a heavily spiced lamb dish with some sort of thick red sauce. I inhale, and my mouth starts watering.

The bread worked, I think, even though I know perfectly well that it shouldn't have.

I glance across the table. Even though I'm pretty sure Kostya was sent as damage control, and even though he just gave me bread and tried to be friendly, I have the strange urge to keep what just happened a secret.

My stomach squirms again. I tell myself it's the vodka.

Yelena, Kostya's pretty, blond, blue-eyed date, is speaking to him softly. He leans toward her, nodding intently, focused on whatever she's saying.

He was being polite to you, I think, and a sliver of disappointment slices through me, even though I don't know why. It's not like I thought I was going to date a foreign prince. For starters, I'm the ambassador's daughter, and I can only imagine that's frowned upon.

For the thing that comes after starters, he's a prince. He lives in a palace and stuff, and someday he's going to be in charge of a whole country. A country where I don't even speak the language.

Yelena smiles and touches his hand, her big blue eyes exploring his face. Kostya nods, not smiling, but I'm not sure he *can* smile.

Just appreciate the hot prince from afar and spend your month reading books and really finding yourself or some shit, I tell myself.

Then, as Yelena's still talking, Kostya raises his head a fraction of an inch and looks at me.

I get that pinned bug feeling again. For a split second, I forget to breathe.

Kostya's mouth twitches, just a little, for just a moment. I look back at my plate.

I think he just smiled at me.

CHAPTER SIX
KOSTYA

For the rest of the dinner, the vodka level in Hazel's glass doesn't change. At every toast, the waiter pours a few more drops in, but she's only pretending to drink now.

Good. I'm glad she can learn.

As soon as the main course is over, Yelena wraps her hand around my forearm and gazes up at me, fluttering her long black lashes.

"What did you think of the lamb, Kostya?" she asks.

I hardly thought anything of it. I was busy keeping my eyes down, on the table or on my food and not looking at Hazel.

It feels like we have a secret, but I'm at a loss. I've got nothing to hide. There was no impropriety. She's our guest, and I was hospitable.

"The lamb was excellent," I tell Yelena.

"It was my mother's recipe," she says. She tilts her head just a little, looking almost like a pretty bird. "The chef asked her for it last week."

"Your mother is an excellent cook," I say, but my half of this conversation is on auto-pilot.

I'm just agreeing with whatever she says because my mind

is back on the bench. I'm thinking of Hazel saying *I'm a barbarian*, of the strange electric jolt that passed through me when she took my hand.

"She's taught me everything she knows," Yelena says. "I could make you that lamb dish in my sleep."

I'm so distracted that it takes me a moment to realize that Yelena is flirting with me. Or, if not flirting, trying to sell herself as my wife. She's telling me that she's a good cook, and if I'm not careful, she might move on to listing the number of children all her foremothers have had.

"What did you think of the soup course?" I ask, trying to steer the conversation.

She blinks, and I can almost see the gears turning in her blond head as she thinks back to the soup course. I missed it, of course, because I was taking a bread roll from the kitchen and finding Hazel in the hallway.

"I think it had a bit too much kidney in it," she says, after a long pause. "It was very well spiced, though."

"How would you have made it?" I ask as dessert comes around. It's baklava and ice cream, and Yelena hardly touches it as she gives a long explanation of how *she* would have made the soup.

My father gives another toast. I drink again, finally starting to feel the effects of the vodka.

I glance over at Hazel, but she doesn't look at me, instead carefully eating the baklava, doing her best not to get pastry flakes everywhere. Next to me, Yelena is eating neatly, delicately, with small bites.

I keep my eyes down and finish dessert.

AFTER DINNER, Yelena suddenly wants to take a stroll through the rose garden. It's a beautiful, warm August night, and she takes my arm as the two of us walk around and she talks about which flowers are the loveliest.

How does someone who thinks so little say so much? I wonder, then feel bad immediately.

Thinking bad thoughts about Yelena is like being annoyed at a puppy.

Besides, she's not the first girl who's tried to win my interest. She's not even the most aggressive. When you're the crown prince, women just *throw* themselves at you in the most unattractive ways. Half the time I feel like a trophy to be won, like I'd simply be these women's ultimate accessory.

Yelena, at least, is here at her father's urging, and probably my father's too. She's genuinely pleasant and kind, even if there isn't much going on upstairs.

"Don't you ever wish it was the olden days?" she says, gazing up at a tower. "When ladies wore those beautiful dresses and men were so dapper, and the whole castle would have been lit by candlelight? There would be fancy dinners every night and balls each week, and everything would be lovely."

"How long ago do you mean?" I ask.

"Oh, before all the bad things," she says.

I know that she means before 1919, when tiny Sveloria was swallowed up by the U.S.S.R., but I can't help thinking *there was never a time before bad things*.

I also can't help being taken aback at the last hundred strife-filled years being reduced to *the bad things*.

"No," I say. "I've never wished that."

She smells a rose, then blinks at me.

"Why?" she asks. "You would still be king someday."

I look up at the windows of the palace and imagine beautiful women swirling around, dancing with men dressed to the nines. The warm orange glow of a thousand candles.

"No, I wouldn't," I say.

"Of course you would," she says. "Your family has ruled for hundreds of years."

"It's not that simple," I say.

I think of Maksim the second, glaring out from his portrait. I want to say *this castle has murder holes for a reason*. I want to say *the barbarians were always at the gates*.

I want to say *right now the barbarians are attacking villages in the north, only now they call themselves the United Svelorian Front, and my father insists on pretending that everything is okay.*

"You're of royal blood," she says. "It isn't complicated, Kostya."

Everything is complicated, I think.

"When I was seven, I wandered into a part of the castle that was under construction," I say. "And I stepped on a nail that the workers had accidentally left on the floor, sticking up through a discarded board."

Yelena's turned her mouth down at the corners, and she puts one delicate hand over it.

"I was so humiliated that I hadn't been watching where I was going that I didn't tell anyone. My foot turned bright red and swelled up, and I didn't tell anyone. I didn't want them to know I'd done something wrong, that I was anything but smart and capable, even at age seven. It wasn't until my governess saw red streaks going up my leg that anyone realized I'd gotten blood poisoning," I go on.

I pause a moment, wondering if Yelena will connect the dots on her own, but she just looks at me.

"If that had happened in the olden days, I'd be dead," I finish. "But we have antibiotics, so I'm still here."

"What a stubborn child you were," Yelena says, shaking her head. "I would never allow my child to be so stubborn."

I think she's forgotten what we were talking about. She takes my arm again and we continue walking.

"My dress for the ball is deep red," she says. She's already forgotten that I nearly died twenty years ago, or that every-thing was never perfect.

Dear God, there's a masquerade ball next week. It's on my calendar, but I'd completely forgotten about it.

Probably because I have thousands of better things to do than attend the ball Yelena talked my mother into hosting, I think.

"Oh?" I say, because I don't care and don't know why she's telling me.

"Deep red with rhinestones on the bodice," she says in her soft, sweet voice. "Your mother helped me choose it. It will look lovely with your uniform."

FINALLY, we go back inside. As sweet and kind as Yelena is, I've had more than enough. I tell her goodbye very formally, and she leaves the palace with her parents.

Hazel disappeared long ago. She's probably asleep by now, and I don't blame her.

Everyone else leaves slowly, and then it's only my mother, my father and I in the formal drawing room, standing stiffly. My father looks at my mother and nods once, severely. She nods back.

"I'm going to retire for the evening," she says, kissing my father on one cheek.

"Good night," he says.

"Good night, my dear," she says, and then kisses me on one cheeks. "Sweet dreams, Kostya."

"Sweet dreams, mother," I say, and she leaves the room.

As soon as the doors close behind her, my father turns to me. I'm a half-inch taller than him, but we have the same eyes and similar faces, though I got my mother's hair.

"I will not have you chasing after that unmannered Amer-ican girl again," he says, his voice deadly quiet.

Something clenches inside me at *unmannered*, even though he's technically correct.

"I was being hospitable," I say.

"You chased her down, leaving Yelena Pavlovna alone at the dinner table," my father says, his voice coming close to a growl.

That's what this is about.

"I thought you wanted us to have close relations with the Americans," I say, even though I know full well that arguing with my father has never gotten me anywhere.

"Don't you disrespect me," he says.

Anger flares inside me, sudden and hot. That's what he says when he doesn't want me questioning him. When he's being stubborn for the sake of being stubborn.

But he's the king. He can be as stubborn as he wants.

I step forward and lower my own voice. I want to shout, but I can't shout what I'm about to say.

"The USF burned a dozen houses to the ground yesterday," I say. "And today, you forced me to accompany you to the train station to meet *that unmannered American girl* instead of doing something about the threat."

"Meeting her at the train station was a formality," he says. "Ignoring a good, well-born Svelorian woman to chase after a strumpet who can't hold her liquor is pure folly, Kostya."

"You can't ignore the USF forever," I say.

He looks me hard in the eyes, not backing down. I'm probably making this worse by pushing him on the matter, but I can't help it.

I spent years of my life fighting against them. I crawled through dirt and slept in mud to defend my country. I watched men who were like my brothers die at their hands.

And now, when I could *really* be doing something about it, my own father is more concerned with my love life than the fate of his country.

"I'm not ignoring them," he says. "They're a small threat, and small threats burn themselves out. But you need a wife and an heir, Kostya. A *Svelorian* wife and a *Svelorian* heir. And don't think I'll give permission for anything else while I'm still drawing breath."

Then he turns on his heel and walks out, leaving me alone and furious in the drawing room. Maksim the second glares down at me from the wall, and I glare back at his portrait, my hands clenched in fists.

A FEW DAYS PASS. My father doesn't budge, even though the reports keep coming, and they keep getting worse. Houses and farms burned. People killed. Good, hardworking people whose only crime was living in the wrong place.

It's small-scale, yes. But this is like a few drops of rain before a storm. I was on the ground there for a long time. I can *feel* it.

He refuses to let the news channel or the newspapers report on the deaths and destruction, saying *it's only a few people*, or *we'll take care of it*. I meet endlessly with generals and people who've come from the north. I try to send a battalion, organize *some* kind of protection for the people under threat.

My father says he'll consider my suggestions.

I hardly see Hazel. She and her parents are being whisked around Velinsk, a picture-perfect coastal town, full of charming stone houses that line the cliffs, cobblestone streets, outdoor cafes, and beautiful white beaches. There's no wonder the summer palace is here, and no wonder that other wealthy Svelorians come here to get away.

I avoid her. Not because of what my father said. A bride and an heir are the last things on my mind right now. For either to matter, there needs to *be* a Sveloria.

No, I avoid Hazel because I can't stop thinking of her ass in those ugly spandex pants. Because I can't stop thinking about what she might look like naked. I can't stop wondering whether she's got freckles everywhere or just her face.

I can't stop wondering what she *tastes* like, or what she sounds like when she comes.

Two nights in a row, I jerk off thinking about her body underneath mine, her breath coming in short, soft gasps.

I've had women before. I've been in relationships. I'm a prince, not a monk.

I just have things besides pussy to worry about, and I've never met a woman incredible enough to be worth the distraction.

There's never been a woman I *had* to be with.

Still, it's been a long time since I jerked off thinking about anything besides porn. Worse, jerking off isn't helping at all. Usually it releases some pressure, gets my mind off sex for a while, but not now.

I'm still watching her for too long across a room. Still watching the shapes her lips make as she talks, listening for her loud American laugh.

It's a problem. I'm the head of my father's small council. I'm his advisor, Minister of Military Affairs, and Lord of the Realm. I'm an important state figure.

I *cannot* sleep with the daughter of the American Ambassador, and I *especially* can't now.

CHAPTER SEVEN
HAZEL

I manage to behave myself for several days. It probably qualifies as a miracle.

It helps that my parents and I don't attend any more formal events with the royal family, so at least I can't embarrass myself in front of Kostya any more. He's already had to rescue my drunk ass once, and even though he was very polite about it, the fact remains: I made a spectacle of myself, and his father sent him to do damage control.

We only catch glimpses of each other. Walking down hallways in opposite directions. On either end of a big room. Him in the garden, me on my balcony, enjoying the sun. I do my best to ignore the way my insides twist when we make eye contact.

The king seems intent on making our stay at the Summer Palace as pleasant as possible, and his office arranges outing after outing for us.

We stroll through the beautiful seaside town of Velinsk, which is almost impossibly charming. Like the palace itself, it mostly went without being noticed by the Soviet Union, so it's still quaint and lovely, unspoiled by the brutalist architecture that so many other towns sprouted during that time.

A friendly, English-speaking tour guide takes us up and down the coast, past beautiful cliffs filled with sea caves, past pristine white-sand beaches unreachable except by boat. We have champagne picnics and cook fresh fish over a fire.

Another day, we visit the roman ruins in the town. It was only ever a small outpost, but the Romans maintained a presence there through the fall of the Byzantine Empire. Now the ruins are stark and beautiful, no more than a few low walls, columns without a roof.

I ask how much archaeological work has been done on them, and the tour guide just shrugs. Behind a low wall, I find a single empty wine bottle lying on its side and wonder if the ruins were cleaned up for our benefit.

Velinsk isn't big, and we cover most of the town in a few days. The people seem bright, happy, and wholesome, and they all speak excellent English.

One evening, sitting in a cafe and sipping strong Turkish coffee, I look at a map of town. Once, it was split into quarters — the Russian quarter, the Svelorian quarter, the Roma quarter — but they've done away with that.

All except one sliver of town. On the outskirts, to the northeast, away from the coast, is the Shadow Quarter. The tour guides haven't taken us there. They haven't taken us anywhere *near* there, though we've been to nearly every other part of town.

I take a sip of coffee and frown at the map.

"What's over here?" I ask the tour guide, tapping *the Shadow Quarter* with my index finger. He looks at it, and I see a frown pass over his face quickly.

"That's the old industrial section of town," he says. "It was built up under Soviet rule. They wanted to make Velinsk into a fishing town, so they built a few sardine canneries on the outskirts. But they were abandoned when something else closer to home drew their attention away."

He smiles, but it's not a smile that reaches his eyes. It's a learned smile.

I don't let it bother me, because it's obvious by now that smiling doesn't come easily to the Svelorian people, and it's nice that he's trying.

"The Svelorian people did not exactly clamor to get Soviet attention back on themselves, so the canneries remained abandoned. It's a very tedious, boring part of town. There's nothing to do there," he says.

"Can we go?" I ask.

"Why?" he says.

"I'm curious," I say. "I haven't learned much about the Soviet occupation here."

"Frankly, we'd rather forget it happened," he says evenly.

He takes a sip of his coffee. My parents have both finished theirs, and they're listening politely.

The tour guide and I look at each other. I can't tell if he's hiding something or if I just can't read his expression.

"It's also the most dangerous part of town," he says, finally. "The unsavory element tends to congregate there, and I can't have the U.S. Ambassador getting mugged, can I?"

I lean back in my cafe chair. It hadn't even occurred to me that Velinsk *had* an unsavory element, it's so charming and picturesque.

"I see," I say, and smile. "That makes sense."

I'm still curious. Tell me I can't go somewhere and it's the first thing I want to do, but I drop it. For now.

A calm silence settles over the four of us for a moment, and a gentle, salty breeze blows through. My father leans forward over the table.

"Who laid out the streets in Velinsk?" he asks, always an

academic at heart. "Was it the Romans, or did they follow pre-existing pathways?"

The tour guide launches into the history of city planning in Velinsk, and I finish my coffee. It's actually pretty interesting.

WHEN I GET BACK to my room late that afternoon, the first thing I see is my empty backpack, very neatly propped on top of the dresser. Instantly, I know that the housekeepers at the palace have taken my dirty laundry to be washed.

I hate being waited on, and I've been trying to avoid it. The first day I was here, I left some dirty clothes on the floor, only to return to my room to discover that they were in the hamper, my shoes neatly tucked away in the closet, my used towels replaced with fresh ones.

That was the last time I left anything out of place, *especially* dirty underwear, because the thought of someone else picking *that* up after me actually makes me a little nauseous. But I thought that my backpack was safe in the closet, joint hidden at the bottom and all. Honestly, I kind of forgot about it. I've been wearing the clothes that my parents had shipped from Boston.

There it is, though. Empty and on top of the dresser.

Well, I'm not arrested yet, I think. *So that's a good sign.*

Not that they're going to arrest the Ambassador's daughter, I think.

I grab my backpack and look inside. Nothing. I stick an arm in and fish around for a while, explore the hole into the lining where the passport got lost, but there's still nothing.

Maybe the joint got stuck in my dirty laundry, I think, half-shrugging to myself.

Hopefully the women who do the laundry are having a great time getting high, not getting into trouble.

Feeling guilty that someone else did my laundry, I open the dresser drawers. Everything is very neatly organized, even my underpants, which makes me feel a little squirmy inside.

When I open the last one, there it is. Sitting on top of the t-shirt my best friend gave me before I left for my Europe trip that says:

GOOD GIRLS GO TO HEAVEN
BAD GIRLS GO EVERYWHERE

Maybe they thought it was a hand-rolled cigarette, I think.
Well, why'd they hide it for me then?
In any case, crisis averted for now.

I've GOTTEN into the habit of having happy hour with my parents in their suite before dinner. The dinners aren't formal now. There are still more courses and forks than I'm used to, but the other people there are others who work in the government or at the palace, not actual royalty. I don't think they're even highborn.

When I knock on the door this afternoon, it's just my dad, because mom's off somewhere in a meeting about exports and tariffs or something.

"It's good for her to have something important to do," he says, handing me a glass of wine. "She's starting to get a little stir-crazy."

I roll my eyes.

"Be nice, she's your mother," he says.

We both drink.

"But between me and you, she could stand to learn to relax," he says, with a smile. "We don't need an itinerary for going to the beach."

"Did she really make you a beach-going itinerary?" I ask. "When? This trip?"

My dad puts one elbow over the back of the couch where he's sitting, opposite me, and sighs.

"She's gonna give me hell if she knows I told you this," he says.

"My lips are sealed," I say.

"This was a couple years before you were born," he says. "We drove up to Maine from Boston for a weekend getaway, just the two of us. I pick her up outside her apartment, help her put her bags in the trunk, and when we get back in the car, she hands me a sheet of paper."

I start giggling.

"How old were you?"

"About your age. Maybe a year or two older, twenty-six or twenty-seven," he says.

"So she's always been this way."

I couldn't be less surprised. The level of organization that my mom's achieved *has* to be inborn.

"Your mother has actually loosened up some, believe it or not," he says. "Anyway, the title of the itinerary was *Relaxing Beach Vacation*. Underneath that, she'd included the objective *enjoy ourselves*."

I laugh so hard I snort.

"Did you achieve the objective?" I ask, between giggles. "Did you hit all your relaxation benchmarks in a timely fashion?"

"I believe we vacationed to her satisfaction," he says. "It helped that large chunks of each afternoon were simply scheduled as *unstructured free time*."

"Oh, my God," I say, still laughing helplessly. "God, of course they were."

We sit there, laughing and drinking, for a few more moments. Then I remember what I wanted to ask him.

"Dad," I say. "Quick question and you can't tell Mom."

"The tooth fairy isn't real," he says, and I roll my eyes. That's his standard answer when I say I've got a question, even though it hasn't been funny for about fifteen years.

"How illegal is pot in Sveloria?" I ask.

He raises his eyebrows.

"Asking for a friend," I say quickly.

He gives me his I-can't-believe-you're-asking-this look, tipping his head a little to the side and looking exasperated through his thick-frame glasses.

I smile innocently and shrug.

"I believe it's technically illegal but not really enforced," he says.

I nod. He looks into his wine glass.

"I've also gotten more than a few whiffs of it walking around outside at night," he says.

"So, if my friend maybe accidentally found a joint in her bag, she doesn't necessarily need to flush it down the toilet and waste perfectly good Amsterdam weed?" I ask.

"*Your friend* probably doesn't need to flush it," he says. "Particularly if *your friend* can be discreet, and if she's a guest of the crown."

I nod.

"I'll pass that on," I say.

"Did *your friend* happen to carry this weed through customs in a dozen different countries?" he asks.

I grimace at him and shrug. He gets up and pours himself another glass of wine.

"This is why parents drink," he says.

CHAPTER EIGHT
KOSTYA

For the third night in a row, I'm awoken by a *boom* and a flash of light and I open my eyes still gasping. The screams in my ears fade, the bedsheets clenched in my fists.

I stare at the ceiling, whispering to myself.

"Summer palace, Velinsk, Western tower," I say.

I swallow.

"Summer palace."

Slowly, my hands unclench.

"Velinsk," I whisper.

I take a deep breath.

"Western tower," I say, and exhale.

It's not always the same dream. My subconscious has plenty of horrors to choose from, but I always wake up the same way: soaked in sweat, every muscle in my body clenched tight.

It's silly, but telling myself out loud where I am helps. It reminds me that I'm not deep in the mountains, fighting someone I can't see. I'm safe at home: Summer palace, Velinsk, Western tower.

I walk to the big windows in just my boxers and look out,

over the Black Sea. The moon is behind me, so the tower is casting a shadow to the front. It's not more than half-full, so everything out there looks silver-blue and dreamlike.

A far cry from the vivid reds and greens of the war dreams. They'd been getting better for a long time, right up until about a week ago when the USF started attacking again. Just reading the reports and knowing what was going on triggered something again, something that gets me out of bed at one in the morning and won't let me sleep again for an hour or two.

I cross my arms and look out. Military service is mandatory in Sveloria: everyone is required to do two years of service by the time they turn twenty-five. Most people do their two years stationed somewhere fairly pleasant and never have to fire a gun at another human, then get out and go on with their lives.

I joined at twenty-two, fresh out of college. My father tried to talk me into taking a cushy officer's position, one where I could be in charge of people and wouldn't have to do any of the dirty work, but I refused. When I insisted on going to basic training with everyone else, he tried to talk me out of it.

I didn't tell him I was trying to join the Royal Guard until I'd already made it in, after the most grueling three months of my life. If I'd thought I could keep it hidden from him, I would have.

It's hard to keep secrets from a former KGB agent.

He threatened to disown me if I didn't leave the Guard. He told me he'd make my younger brother Mikhail, all of thirteen at the time, the crown prince. He threatened to exile me and make me a refugee from my own country.

I told him to go ahead. It was the first time I really ever stood up to him.

I can still remember the way he *screamed* at me. At one

point I could hear my mother's voice, asking what was wrong, and he called her a stupid cow and told her to leave.

But I won in the end. All along, I knew my father wasn't stupid enough to disown me for serving my country. *His* country.

When my two years ended, I signed on for two more. This time, when I told my father, he didn't say anything at all, just hung up the phone. We didn't talk again until I finally left the military and took on duties at the palace.

My father's never been a nice man. He's never been a warm or loving man to either of his sons or his wife. I can't imagine a tender moment with him; I can't imagine him holding an infant or comforting a child.

I lean against the wall next to the window and look out at the sea. It's childish, but I always wonder if there's someone on the opposite coast, somewhere in Turkey, looking back at me.

I'm too hard on my father sometimes. He's had a hard life. Everything he's done, all the fighting, all the ruthlessness, all the iron-fisted ruling, I know he's done because he thinks it's right.

He grew up under communist rule and had to lie about who his family was just to survive, and he wants something different for me and Mikhail. For everyone in Sveloria.

I just don't always think he's going about it the right way.

I take a deep breath and exhale, the window pane fogging up for a moment. I'm not getting back to sleep any time soon, so I put on a pair of jeans, an undershirt, and shoes. I walk out of my suite and close the door softly behind myself.

Even in the dark, I know the way to the ramparts by heart. The wide stone walks stretch from tower to tower, and while they're technically off-limits for safety reasons, everyone in the palace knows how to get up there.

The moment I push open the heavy wooden door, I get the faintest whiff of pot smoke, and I frown.

It's not really uncommon for people, mostly the younger house and kitchen staff, to smoke. But they usually smoke out on the grounds, further away from the palace itself.

I've never seen them smoking up here. It's surprisingly bold of them, almost reckless. I shut the door softly and walk out onto the rampart, ready to give some young idiot some strong advice about *where* they should be smoking.

Then, near the far end of the stone walkway, a figure shifts, backing away from the waist-high wall and scratching the back of one leg with the opposite foot.

They've got long black hair, and they're wearing a t-shirt, shorts, and no shoes.

And even from here, I can tell they've got a really nice ass.

CHAPTER NINE
HAZEL

I take one more hit, then crush the joint on the stone wall of the ramparts. I don't want to be super high right now, but it's one in the morning and I can't sleep, so I'm getting a little buzzed.

If the people who work in the kitchen smoke sometimes, I figure I'm good.

I rub my hands over the waist-high stone wall, and it feels like I can feel every single grain in the stone. I can feel every single time someone's come up here and fired an arrow at the barbarians below, every single time someone's hoisted a boiling pot of oil to pour down over the side.

Right now, though, it's lovely and peaceful. Maybe even *idyllic*. There were a couple signs about how this area was off-limits on the way up here, but no locked doors. I figured the signs were more of a suggestion than anything.

Then there's movement off to my right. I snap my head around.

Someone's walking toward me.

Are you fucking kidding me, I think.

I slide the rest of the joint and my lighter into the pocket of my shorts, then lean against the wall, trying to look casual.

Just once, I want to stop fucking up, I think. *It would be great if someone caught me doing something impressive.*

Like a yoga handstand, or calculus.

Of course, I'd have to do either of those things to get caught doing them.

The figure gets closer, and I squint at it in the moonlight. Tall, blond, wide shoulders. Military bearing.

It's Kostya. Fucking of *course* it's Kostya.

I've been behaving perfectly well for days, and the hot prince catches me smoking up in my pajamas, I think.

I cross my arms in front of myself, because I'm not even wearing a bra. Not that I've got a ton going on, boob-wise, but I already feel half-naked around Kostya and his sexy glare.

He walks up, stops a couple feet away, and looks at me.

"The ramparts are off-limits," he says, straight-faced.

I look straight into his gray eyes, a knot gathering itself in my chest. Kostya's gaze doesn't waver, but why should it? It's his country, his castle, and I should just apologize and leave before I commit another dozen faux-pas.

Instead I think of my arm through his as he escorted me back to dinner the other night, and I think of how we separated ourselves before the doors opened. Like we had a secret that might come out if people saw us touching.

I swallow. My mouth feels a little dry, but that's the pot. I lick my lips.

"I won't tell if you won't," I say instead of apologizing.

I think his lips twitch upward.

"You don't have any leverage," he says, but his voice doesn't have that hard edge any more. "They'll take my word over yours."

"What are you going to say?" I ask. "'When I went up to the off-limits ramparts, the American girl was there too?'"

He probably doesn't have to say anything. It's not as if the staff is going to reprimand the crown prince.

"You should give me some credit," he says, crossing his arms in front of himself. "I'm craftier than that. I'm *fucking crafty*, actually. Like all my people."

I narrow my eyes at him, and for a long moment, we just look at each other.

"You're teasing me," I finally say, even though I'm not sure.

"I'm attempting it," he says. "Because the other day you said Svelorians were *fucking crafty* after I told you why we have so many toasts. I was referencing that."

I try hard not to laugh, and fail. Kostya sighs, turns his back to the stone wall, and leans against it.

"At least you find something I say funny," he says.

"I'm sorry," I say. "Thanks for coming to my rescue at that dinner, even if I felt like the world's biggest idiot and then told you your people were crafty, like you're foxes in a fairy tale or something."

"I've been called much worse than a fairy tale fox," Kostya says. "At least in our stories, the clever animals usually come out on top."

I lean my back against the stone wall as well, trying not to look at him. It's the first time I've seen him dressed so casually, in jeans and t-shirt, and it's... distracting, the way his sleeves hug his biceps, or the way his shoulders are just a touch too wide.

"Do they do it by getting the other animals drunk?" I ask.

"Only sometimes," he says, and I can *feel* his eyes slide toward me again.

For a moment, he's silent, just looking at me. My face heats up and my heart beats faster. Desperately, I think *it's nothing, it's nothing, it's nothing*.

"Did you get your shirt from a church?" he finally asks.

I look down at myself, because I've never gotten a shirt from a church and have no idea what he's talking about.

With my arms crossed, all that's visible of this dumb shirt is *Good girls go to heaven*.

"Definitely not," I say, and uncross my arms.

I use every ounce of my willpower not to shiver and pucker my nipples.

"Aha," he says, reading *Bad girls go everywhere*.

Then he looks at me, and something sparkles in his gray eyes. I think it's a smile. I *think*.

"Which are you?" he asks.

"The shirt was a gift," I say, not really answering the question. "My best friend gave it to me before I went on this trip, as sort of a joke, because I was going to a lot of places and I'd just dropped out of school."

"Was one of the places heaven?" he asks.

"Does the Vatican count?" I ask.

"Not even close," he says, and the corners of his eyes crinkle.

"I went to the top of Notre Dame Cathedral," I say.

"Closer, and beautiful, but not heaven," he says.

I look away for a moment. My back is to the sea, so we're looking over the stone work of the castle and the grounds beyond, all dimly lit and silver in the moonlight. I'm just buzzed enough that I can feel the moonlight on my skin, cool and liquid.

"I watched the sun come up on a train in the Alps," I say.

"Still not heaven," he says. His voice has gone a little softer and almost *growly*. Now that we're alone up here, just the two of us and the night sky, he sounds different. Not quite so harsh.

Fuck it, I think.

Flirt back. He started this.

"Kostya, are you trying to get me to say I'm a bad girl?" I ask.

"I'm just making polite conversation with a palace guest about her shirt," he says, and I swear there's just a hint of a smile in his voice. "Though it does seem you've been many places, and not one of them was heaven."

I swallow as warmth snakes through me, tightly coiled and writhing.

I'm acutely aware that I *should not* be doing any of the things that I'm doing right now: I shouldn't be in this off-limits area, I shouldn't be smoking pot, and I shouldn't be flirting with a future monarch.

"I wouldn't say I've been *everywhere*."

"You've got time to fix that," he says. "And I think *every-where* is much more interesting than heaven."

A slight breeze drifts over us and I hug myself tighter as I feel my nipples pucker.

Don't look, I think. I swallow.

Or do look, fuck, I don't even know.

Being near Kostya lights something stupid and dangerous inside me, something that wants to throw all caution to the wind and tell him I'm a *very* bad girl. Something that wants to do something ridiculous, like lean against this wall and lick my lips and *invite* him to sex-glare at me, nipples at full attention while I bite one finger like some kind of sexpot.

I don't do any of those things.

"Heaven's never sounded all that appealing," I admit. "I think I'd rather be on the goat train from Kiev than spend eternity on a cloud with one of those tiny harps."

"I believe they're called *lyres*," he says.

"Show off," I say, teasing him.

He opens his mouth, closes it, and frowns very slightly. Then the corners twitch a little.

"Because I know what a tiny harp is called?"

"I'm just kidding," I say, already wishing I could backtrack.

He kicks at a loose rock and it bounces across the stone blocks that make up the floor of the rampart.

"Did it work?" he finally asks. "Are you impressed?"

"That you knew the word lyre?" I ask, smiling.

"That I know more about heaven than you," he says.

"You're not going to convince me you're an angel," I say. "You snuck up here just like I did."

"It's my palace," he points out. "I don't have to sneak anywhere."

"So the palace guard knows where you are right now?" I ask.

"I just said I don't *have* to sneak, not that I didn't," he says. "Having your every move tracked can get tedious after a while."

"You're taking a pretty big risk being alone with me, then," I say. "Maybe I'm an assassin."

The second I say that out loud, I regret it.

"I'm not an assassin," I say quickly.

"Yes, that was a joke," he says, his eyes sparkling again. "I'm catching on."

"I just couldn't sleep," I say.

"Me either," he says.

He looks like he's about to go on, but doesn't.

I take a deep breath.

He came and gave you bread when you humiliated yourself, I think.

"You know what helps me sleep sometimes?" I say, reaching into my pocket.

"Is it smoking marijuana?" he asks.

"Shit," I say, and laugh. "I guess I wasn't very crafty."

"It's not what Americans are known for," he says.

"I've still got half a joint," I offer. "I smuggled it from Amsterdam by accident."

I pull out the joint and the lighter and offer them.

I have no idea if he's ever even smoked before. Everything

I've read about the prince makes him sound like a serious, straight arrow who toes the line.

I'm starting to realize that there's more to Kostya than the official reports, though.

"A medical school dropout *and* a drug smuggler," he says, taking the joint and the lighter. "Bad girl doesn't even start to describe you."

"It got lost in my dirty laundry," I say. I have no idea whether that makes me more or less of a bad girl. "I didn't *mean* to smuggle it here."

He lights it and takes a deep breath, then holds it in before blowing the smoke up toward the stars. Then he coughs a little.

"It's been a while," he says.

The crown prince of Sveloria takes one more hit off of my smuggled joint, then hands it back to me. I crush it out again on the stone wall. He exhales again and clears his throat.

"These stones are hundreds of years old," he says. I think he's trying to sound stern again, but I'm not falling for it.

"Then they've had worse things happen to them," I say, and put the stub and the lighter back in my pocket again.

"The ramparts were built so that archers could fire flaming arrows at ships coming ashore," he admits.

I stick my hands in my pockets, not bothering to cross my arms anymore. My nipples are definitely out, proudly declaring *I am cold and/or slightly aroused,* and trying to hide them is only making it more obvious.

I hope Kostya thinks I'm just cold.

"What's keeping you awake?" I ask.

He looks at me for a long moment. His eyes are slightly glassy.

I pray that I didn't get him too high. Even though he's over six feet of muscle, if he doesn't smoke much, two hits can screw a guy up.

"I'll make you a deal," he says. "If I tell you why I'm awake, you tell me the long story about why you dropped out of med school."

"It's not a good story," I say.

He shrugs.

"It doesn't reflect well on me," I say. "Not that I've made a great impression so far."

Kostya runs one hand over his hair, shakes his head a little, and then looks at me.

"Now, you worry about the impression that you've made?" he asks.

"Better late than never?" I say.

He smiles. Maybe it's the pot, but he actually, legitimately *smiles*.

"You're never boring, *zloyushka*," he says.

I frown. My very limited Russian doesn't include that word.

"*Zloyushka*?" I ask.

He just gives me a teasing look.

"I can't sleep because of the dreams," he says.

"What dreams?"

"From my time in the military," he says.

"I'm sorry," I say, softly.

I know he was in the Royal Guard, but beyond that, most of his activities are classified by the Svelorian government. There's been speculation that he was fighting in the north, but no one knows very much for sure.

"Can you keep a secret?" he says.

"If I can't, we're already in trouble," I say.

Well, mostly me. His kingdom, his palace, et cetera.

"We were fighting the separatists in the north of Sveloria, up in the mountains," he says, his eyes straight ahead, raking over the moonlit stone. "Guerrilla warfare, which means you're always fighting. When you're sitting in a camp, writing letters, you're fighting. When you're eating, you're fighting. When you're sleeping, when you're taking a shit, you're still fighting. All the time."

My eyes widen, and I stay perfectly quiet. A single shiver runs down my spine.

I don't know why, but I get the strong feeling that he's telling me something he's never told anyone before, and I have no idea why he's telling *me*, the awkward, loud, unmannered American girl, of all people.

"Any second, the shooting could start," he goes on, gazing into the distance. "While we were doing anything. We were shot at while sleeping, while scouting, while getting supplies in town."

He swallows.

"Once, we stopped at a hut that was far outside of a village. We could hear someone moaning in pain inside, and even though it was dangerous to stop, we did."

He swallows again. I wish I'd brought water up here.

"Inside there was a young man, not more than eighteen, lying on a bed. Both his legs were missing up to the knee. Infected, bright red, oozing pus. I ordered two more men into the hut, thinking that if we could get him somewhere fast enough, he might live. We thought maybe we could help."

My eyes are wide. I've got one hand over my mouth just imagining the scene. The knot in my chest tightens.

"I was outside, standing guard in the road while the others went in," he says, and pauses, staring at the stonework on the ground. "And suddenly, the hut exploded. It knocked me forward, onto my hands and knees, my face in the dirt, half my back covered in burns."

"Oh, my God," I whisper.

I've seen plenty of burns in med school and before that, as a volunteer EMT, and they're ugly.

"The kid had volunteered himself as bait for a trap," Kostya says. "We fell for it. *I* fell for it."

"You couldn't have known," I say.

He takes a deep breath.

"I lost four men," he says. "And I learned that trying to help people is dangerous. Two hard lessons."

"I'm so sorry," I whisper. "That's what you dream about?"

"It's one of the things," he says.

"Are the others similar?"

Kostya just nods. He looks so distant and *alone*, standing there with his arms crossed, his hundred-yard stare raking over the stone castle. I can't even begin to imagine doing what he did and not being able to even *tell* anyone.

I take a deep breath and reach one hand for his shoulder, because hugging the crown prince is probably off-limits, and I don't even know if he wants one.

He looks at me as my fingers hover over his shoulder. I pause and we lock eyes, his face somehow softer, almost vulnerable. I swallow and touch him, his heat radiating through his thin t-shirt, and stoke small circles on the hard muscles of his shoulder.

"What helps?" I ask. We're still looking at each other.

"Reminding myself where I am," he says, softly. "Coming up here when it's dark and the moon is out and I can be alone."

"I can leave," I offer.

"Talking to bad American girls helps too," he says.

I sigh, still rubbing slowly widening circles on his back, trying to ignore the way his body feels beneath my fingers and the effect it's having on me.

"I'm burning this shirt," I mutter.

He raises both eyebrows.

"Now?"

I stop rubbing for a moment, open my mouth to say *no*, blush, shut my mouth, keep rubbing, and swallow.

"Only if I can have yours instead," I say instead.

What the fuck is wrong with you? I think.

Slowly, Kostya smiles, and a teasing, challenging look comes into his gray eyes.

"I don't think you'll go through with it," he says.

"Is that a dare?" I ask, my fingertips tracing a circle around his shoulder.

"It's a challenge," he says. "I'll give you my shirt, but you have to burn yours. Right here, right now."

Laugh, say no, and leave, I think. *Just for once, try not to make a situation worse.*

I take my hand from his shoulder, take the lighter from my pocket, and set it on the stone wall. Then I look back at Kostya just in time to see his gaze flick up from my way-too-perky nipples.

Heat floods downward through my body, even though it's cool out. I'm pretty uncertain about a lot of things right now, but I know one thing for an absolute fact.

Prince Kostya wants to see me topless. He turns to face me, still smiling.

"No cowardice," he says, and I laugh.

"You mean, don't chicken out?" I say.

"Sure," he says. "No chickens."

"No chickens," I say.

My heart is hammering in my chest, and as certain as I was that I shouldn't have been smoking up on the ramparts, I am *super ultra really fucking certain* that I shouldn't be getting half-naked with the prince up here. I'm equally certain that telling anyone who catches us that it was *his* idea will be useless.

I hold out one hand anyway, the other on my hip, my bravest stance.

"Your shirt," I say.

He *dared* me, after all.

CHAPTER TEN
KOSTYA

When the hottest girl you've ever seen is standing in front of you, wearing short pajama shorts and demanding your shirt, there's only one option.

You give the girl your shirt.

"No chickens," Hazel says. "Your shirt."

I think she's laughing at me, but I reach behind my head and tug my undershirt off anyway, then deposit it in her outstretched hand, the soft white cotton crumpling. Her hand makes a fist around it.

Then she looks at me, her eyes traveling up from the waistband of my jeans. It takes a split second, but I can practically feel the burning trails that her gaze leaves behind.

It's been a long time since a woman saw me shirtless, and I cross my arms over my chest, hoping the half-dark hides some of the scars.

"Well, *zloyushka*?" I ask. "Feeling some chickens now?"

I know that's not quite the English phrase, but I'm too fucking distracted to remember idioms.

"It's *chickening out*," she says, the teasing look back in her eyes. "And I'm not."

She tosses my shirt on the stone wall, next to the lighter, and then turns her back to me.

I'm not surprised, but I'm disappointed. My cock twitches anyway, half-hard no matter how much I try to keep it down.

Hazel whips her shirt off, and suddenly she's half-naked on the palace roof, her black hair swishing over her shoulder blades. She's got those perfect dimples in her lower back, right above her shorts, and despite myself I go rock hard just looking at them.

I clench my fingers into my arms. I swear, it looks like those indents were put there so I could grab her by the hips and sink my thumbs into them, and it's all I can think about.

My hands on her skin, pulling her toward me. The *gasp* she'd make, the way the curve of her ass would rub against me.

I grind my teeth together, but I can't stop *staring*.

She tosses her shirt onto the stone wall, and as she does, I can just *barely* see the outer curve of one breast, and I clench my teeth even harder. As she grabs my shirt, she glances over her shoulder at me for one instant, as if to say *I told you I'd do it*.

Then she slides my shirt over her head, and I exhale. She sweeps her hair and and turns around, a triumphant look in her eyes, and I'm just praying she doesn't look down and see Mount Kostya practically exploding out of my jeans.

"Told you," she said.

My shirt is swimming on her, the v-neck coming almost down to her sternum, the slight curve of her cleavage visible in the moonlight.

That's not why I'm staring, though. I'm staring because it's a thin white shirt and her nipples are very, very prominently staring right back. She catches me, looks down, makes a face, and crosses her arms.

"It's cold out here," she says, but she won't look me in the eye.

"I don't even have a shirt," I say.

"Whose fault is that?" she asks, tilting her head to one side.

"Yours," I say. "You did demand the shirt off my back, *zloyushka*."

She grabs the t-shirt and lighter from the stone wall and dangles the shirt in front of her, looking at it one last time.

"Sorry, Courtney," she says. I assume Courtney is the friend who gave her the shirt.

Hazel flicks the lighter underneath the shirt and holds the flame to the hem. She holds it there for a long time, waiting for it to catch, glancing up at me every couple of seconds.

At last, it does, and she pulls the lighter away. Immediately, the shirt stops burning, the hem barely worse than scorched.

"Shit," she mutters.

"Remind me not to take you on a wilderness mission," I say. "We'd starve, then freeze to death."

She snorts.

"Were you thinking of doing that?" she says, flicking the lighter again.

In the tower behind me, I hear a *thump* as a heavy door shuts. Hazel freezes, her eyes going wide.

"Oh fuck," she says, not moving.

I point at the spot where there's a corner in the opposite wall. Behind it's a notch, black with shadows. She looks at it and then back at me.

"Your shirt," she whispers.

The footsteps in the tower get closer, and even though I'm beyond tempted to tell her that I need my shirt back, *now*, I have a little mercy.

"It's under control," I whisper.

"Won't it look worse if I'm hiding?" she whispers.

"Only if you're found," I whisper back.

Hazel scampers over, tosses me one last glance, then disappears. I turn toward the stone wall and look out over the ocean, breathing the cool, salty air deeply, pretending that I'm just up here to clear my head.

Hopefully whoever's coming won't notice my massive, aching erection.

Twelve times three is thirty-six, I think. *Twelve times four is forty-eight, twelve times five is sixty* —

The heavy wooden door opens and a palace guard comes out. The moment he sees me, he snaps to attention and bows his head slightly.

"Your majesty," he says.

"At ease," I say, the words almost automatic.

He doesn't relax.

"I heard voices and thought it best to investigate," he says.

"It's only me," I say. "I couldn't sleep, so I took a walk."

He nods again, brusquely. Then he pauses and sniffs the air slightly, his brow furrowing. It's obvious he's about to say something he doesn't want to say.

"I'm obligated to tell you that these ramparts are off-limits for safety reasons," he says stiffly.

I nod once.

"I'm being very careful," I say.

"Have a good night, your majesty," he says, then nods and disappears.

I listen to his footsteps fade down the tower stairs, then walk to the spot where Hazel's hidden in the shadows.

She's sitting with her back against the wall, elbows propped on her knees.

"Coast is clear?" she asks, her voice low.

I offer her my hand, and she takes it. I pull her to her feet so that she's standing just a little too close to me, just close enough that I can smell her, a combination of sweet floral shampoo and the bite of pot smoke.

"I should go," she whispers, but she doesn't try to remove her hand from mine. The air between us feels like it's sparking, charged with static, and it's all I can do not to press her against the stone wall and fit my fingers to the dimples in her back.

I'm hard again. The multiplication tables barely helped, and we're so close that it's a miracle if she can't tell. I should let her go and tell her to go back to her bedroom, forget any of this ever happened.

Instead I ask, "How much of Velinsk have you seen?"

Hazel blinks.

"Most of it, I think," she says. "It isn't very big."

I'm close enough to see the shape of every freckle, even though here in the shadows it's nearly dark.

"Do you want to see the real Velinsk?" I ask. "The parts the palace tour guide doesn't show visitors?"

Hazel hesitates, pressing her lips together and looking down.

"Why do I get the feeling it's something else I shouldn't do?" she asks, looking up at me.

"Because it is," I say, and half-smile.

"You know, Kostya, everyone thinks you're the perfectly upstanding, well-behaved prince, and here you are telling me to burn my clothes and asking me if I want to see the seedy parts of the city."

"It's a good reputation to have," I say, and I let my mouth curve up, just a little. "Do you think you believe it, *zloyushka*?"

"I think I need to find out what that word means before I say yes to anything else," she says, eyebrows raised.

"I'm sure you can figure it out," I say.

"So you're not going to tell me."

"Where's the fun in that?"

Her hand is still in mine. Neither of us has let go, and the warmth of her skin against mine is making electric ripples spread up my arm and across my chest.

"It must mean something bad," she says. "What is it? Loud? Mouthy?"

Now she's smiling up at me, the challenge back in her eyes.

"Déclassé drug smuggler," she guesses.

"We don't have a single word for that," I say.

"Rude foreigner," she goes on.

I put one hand on the stone wall above her head and lean over her, just a bit. She doesn't move or flinch, and it takes every ounce of self control I've got not to push her against it right then and there.

"Tomorrow night," I say. "The bench in the garden nearest the stone arch. Midnight. If someone sees you, say you can't sleep and you're taking a walk."

She cocks her head to one side and examines me. I can't remember the last time I was this close to someone else. The air between us is crackling and snapping, and it feels like I'm breathing in electricity.

I don't know how much is the pot and how much is Hazel, but I'm not that high. Barely buzzed.

"Does it mean something like *hot mess*?" she asks.

"No, but that's closer than *déclassé drug smuggler*," I say.

"You won't tell me where we're going, you won't tell me what *zloshka* means," she says.

"*Zloy-ush-ka*," I say, very slowly. "You've got to spell it right if you want to figure it out."

"Or you could tell me," she says, her voice low and quiet.

Somehow, her face is even closer to mine than it was before, and the urge to kiss her, to push her back against the wall and press myself against her is overwhelming.

This is stupid, I think. *This is impossibly stupid.*

"Tomorrow night," I say.

Then I finally drop her hand and step back. The electricity disappears. I almost feel like I can breathe again.

Hazel gives me another long look, and then the corners of her eyes crinkle, just a little.

"Maybe," she says.

Then she walks back to the door in the tower, still wearing my shirt and carrying hers, heaves it open, and disappears inside. I watch the door shut behind her, then walk back to the wall.

I look out over the ocean and force my breathing to slow. I force myself to stop thinking about the swell of her breasts, the dimples in her back, her nipples poking through my shirt.

Most of all, I wonder what the hell I was thinking, inviting her out tomorrow night.

CHAPTER ELEVEN
HAZEL

When I get back to my bedroom I sit on the edge of my huge four-poster bed, still wearing Kostya's shirt, and put my head in my hands.

What the fuck are you doing, I think.

I take a deep breath, grit my teeth, and remind myself that nothing actually happened. Yeah, we both got half-naked sort of in public, and now I'm wearing his shirt and my entire core is one feverish, hollow ache because he *does* things to me, but we barely touched each other.

I take another breath.

We didn't do anything, I think. *See? No international relations problems.*

Slowly, I lay back on my bed. I stare at the ceiling because every time I close my eyes, I see Kostya standing in front of me, shirtless, that massive bulge in his jeans.

Holy *hell*.

My eyes snap open and I stare at the ceiling, clenching and unclenching my fists.

Despite myself, I think about Kostya leaning over me, one

hand on the wall behind me. Still shirtless. So close that if I'd moved at all we'd have touched.

Zloyushka, I think. The memory of his voice saying it low and slow sends a shiver down my spine, and the ache inside me deepens.

I sigh and slide my hand under my shorts, unsurprised to find that I'm wet as fuck, my underwear pretty much soaked through. I squeeze my eyes shut and rub myself fast and hard, thinking of Kostya in the moonlight, until my toes are curling against the bedsheets.

I come *hard*, and as I do, I wonder whether Kostya's doing the same thing.

AFTER BREAKFAST — sardines, thick yogurt, and toast, which is actually much better than it sounds — I wander the palace halls for a bit. There has to be a library here *somewhere*, and that library's going to have a Russian dictionary in it.

I could probably just ask someone, but I have no idea what it means. I don't *think* Kostya is calling me a stupid gorilla vagina or something, but I still prefer to find out from a book, not someone who can make a face at me.

Zloyushka is a challenge, and I fully fucking intend to at least show Kostya that this loud, awkward, déclassé American can at least use a dictionary.

Well, after I find the library.

I walk around for twenty minutes, and start to wish that this place had a directory, like a mall or something. I've always had a good sense of direction, and I could find my way *back* to almost anywhere in the palace, but these doors aren't labeled, and I'm not about to be the idiot American girl who just walks about opening doors in a foreign ruler's house.

At last, staring a big double door in a stonework arch, I hear someone clear his throat behind me, and I turn around.

It's Nikolai, one of the king's aides.

"Miss Sung, correct?" he asks very, very politely.

"Yes," I say. I walk toward him and hold out my hand. "Please, call me Hazel."

He doesn't smile, but he does shake my hand.

"Are you lost, Miss Sung?" he asks.

Shit, I think. I'd been hoping he's remind me of his full name, because it makes me feel like a dick that he knows mine and I don't know his.

"I'm actually looking for the library," I say. "I wanted to learn a little more about Sveloria's fascinating history."

And also find out what the prince keeps calling me, I think.

He raises both eyebrows so slightly that I could be imagining it.

"It's on the ground floor," he says, and points down a corridor. "Down the main stairs, to the hall on the right. Heavy wooden door with a stained glass inset."

I nod once, very slightly, and remind myself not to smile.

"Thank you," I say.

He nods formally, and we walk in opposite directions.

The library is exactly where he said, and unlocked to boot. There are high, iron-wrought windows set in all the walls, and the place is beautiful and sunny. I'm practically humming as I grab a thick Russian dictionary, an English-to-Russian dictionary, *A Guide To The Svelorian Dialect For English Speakers*, and a pencil and scrap paper.

The first challenge is figuring out how to spell it in Cyrillic, the alphabet that Russian is written in. I'm not exactly sure what the difference is between some of the letters without someone here to guide me, but I give it a shot.

Then I crack open the dictionary to the end and scan the page, biting my lip.

Zloyushka isn't in it, and I sigh dramatically, leaning my chin in my hand. I consult the English-to-Cyrillic guide again. I look back at the Russian dictionary, scanning my eyes down the page.

This time, my gaze falls on *zloy*, and I almost laugh out loud.

Duh, Hazel, I think. *It's a root with some stuff tacked onto the end. You know, the thing languages do?*

ZLOY (ADJ). *Bad; wicked; naughty.* See also *ploho, neposlushnyy.*

I STARE at the word and think for a long second. There's a suspicion bubbling up in my brain, and I flip to the front of the Russian dictionary where the section on nicknames and diminutives is.

I read it, frown, stare at the wall, and think for a long moment.

Then I grab *A Guide To The Svelorian Dialect For English Speakers,* and flip through it until I get to the nickname section.

I read it. Then I read it again, just to make sure I've got it right.

I look at the word I've written in terrible Cyrillic on the scrap paper, and despite myself, I start smiling. The *-ushka* ending is a diminutive, something that attaches to a name to make it into a nickname.

Russians in Russia don't attach diminutives to adjectives to create nicknames, but Svelorians do. The most literal translation of *zloyushka* would be something like *naughty little female person.*

Bad girl. The crown prince is calling me *bad girl.*

That means I've got no choice but to meet him tonight, right? So I can tell him I figured out his stupid nickname?

It would be rude not to.

At least, that's what I'm going to tell myself.

THE REST of the day seems endless. I play some badminton with my dad, go visit the horse stables, and walk along the beach for a spell. Even though I was enjoying the break at first, I can feel myself start to get a little itchy at the inactivity, like there something I ought to be *doing*, but instead I'm hanging out at a palace being absolutely useless.

At eleven, I head back to my own rooms, because I feel like my face is one giant billboard that says I'VE GOT A SECRET.

I tear through my closet, and finally pick out ankle boots with a low heel, dark skinny jeans, a green tank top and a black, long-sleeve shirt. The shirt zips diagonally up the front, so it's at least a tiny bit stylish.

Not that I have any idea where we're going. It could be a black tie event for all I fucking know, in which case I'm wildly underdressed, a feeling I've already gotten a pretty good grasp on during my short time here.

The minutes tick by. I pace back and forth, flipping through TV stations on the TV, but they're mostly in Russian, though I think there's one where they're speaking Turkish. We're not far from Turkey, after all.

At 11:40 I give up and tiptoe to my door, and then I stand there with one ear to it, listening.

It quickly occurs to me that I'm being ridiculous. I'm allowed to leave the room, after all.

For that matter, I'm allowed to walk to the garden, and I'm allowed to have a conversation with Kostya. Hell, I'm *allowed* to go wherever he's taking me. I'm a guest, not a prisoner.

I just *probably shouldn't.*

With that in mind, I walk through the palace as casually as I can manage, like I've never even heard the words *clandestine meeting* in my life. I see a few staff members, but they just nod at me.

Finally, I'm there. At the bench, by the arch, the heavily sweet smell of roses trickling through the air. My stomach is tied in a million knots, or maybe it's one giant knot. Maybe it's a million knots that have formed themselves into one big knot, like some kind of anxiety Voltron. It doesn't fucking matter.

At exactly 12:00am, a dark form steps through the stone arch and looks around. I stand, adjusting my shirt, and step forward.

"Kostya?" I murmur.

The other person steps forward, and the second he moves, I know something's wrong — he's a little shorter than Kostya, and he's got a very, very slight limp. I stop short and hold my breath, but it's way, way too late.

Run! I think wildly. *He's got a limp, he won't catch you!*

I force myself to stand there. If I run, someone's going to think there was an assassin in the garden, the whole palace will go on alert, and I don't need to cause any more trouble.

"Miss Sung," a familiar voice says.

I exhale.

"Nikolai..." I say, trying desperately to remember his formal patronymic. "Sergovich?"

I'm almost positive that's not it.

He inclines his head very slightly.

Oh, my god, just tell me what your fucking name is, I think. *I already feel like an asshole.*

"It's a lovely night," he says, very formally.

"Yes," I say. "I couldn't sleep so I was taking a stroll through the gardens. They're very beautiful, and also relaxing and mesmerizing."

Mesmerizing? I think. *Moron.*

He just nods again.

"I frequently walk through them when seeking calm," he says. "Pleasure to see you again, Miss Sung."

"The pleasure was mine," I say.

He walks on, disappearing as he rounds a bend in the path.

Shit fuck shit fuck shit cock damn hellfire, I think.

I wonder if I should give up and just go back to my rooms, because now Nikolai knows I was expecting to see Kostya in the garden at midnight, and if that's not suspicious as shit, I don't know what is.

You haven't even done anything, I remind myself. *Besides get high on the roof, but there's nothing between you to keep secret.*

It just feels like there is.

More footsteps. I take a deep breath and turn to see *another* figure standing in the stone archway. This time I keep my mouth shut as the figure walks toward me, approaching until he's towering over me, so close I think I can feel the body heat radiating off him. I swallow hard.

"I was right," Kostya says, his voice low.

CHAPTER TWELVE
KOSTYA

"I figured out your nickname," Hazel says, looking up at me. She's always got this expression in her eyes like she's laughing, and I don't know whether she's laughing at me or at the world or whether I'm misreading, but there's something enticing about it. Like she and I share some joke, some secret from the outside world.

No one's ever looked at me that way before. I don't know what it means, but I know I like it.

"And?" I ask.

"It just means *bad girl*," she says. "I'm disappointed. I thought maybe you were more creative."

"Is that a request?" I ask. "I can send you to the dictionary every day if that's what you want."

"There's already enough here I don't know," she says. "I like at least knowing you're not calling me a squirrel scrotum or something."

"Squirrels are revered animals in Svelorian folklore," I say, keeping my face perfectly straight. "Their scrotums have a long, storied history in alchemy and magic here."

Hazel looks up at me and pauses, narrowing her eyes.

"That's a joke," she says, but she sounds uncertain.

I stare at her for another moment before I crack, letting myself smile.

"It's a joke," I say, and offer her my arm. "Would you care to stroll the gardens with me?"

She wraps her fingers around my forearm, and even through my leather jacket, I can feel her warmth sinking into my skin, sending jolts of electricity through me. We walk on between the rose bushes, the mostly-dark windows of the palace above.

"You still haven't told me where you're taking me," she says, keeping her voice low.

"We're going to the ugly part of Velinsk," I say.

"There's an ugly part?" Hazel says, then frowns. "Wait, the Shadow Quarter?"

God, what a ridiculous name.

"Do the English maps still call it that?" I ask.

"Don't tell me it's really called something else," she says. "*Shadow Quarter* sounds romantic and exotic, like it's where the brothels and opium dens are."

"Brothels and opium dens are romantic?"

She laughs softly.

"Wrong word," she says. "I just mean interesting and dangerous."

"You won't be disappointed, then," I say. "The gray district doesn't have brothels or opium dens, but it's both of those things."

Her hand adjusts on my arm, and we stroll under another arch, entering another section of the gardens, this one filled with willow trees.

"And yet I'm letting you take me there, no questions asked," she murmurs.

"You've asked quite a few questions," I point out.

"Sounds like I haven't asked enough," she says.

"We're meeting some friends of mine at a bar," I say, and glance over at her.

"That's it?" she says.

Then she frowns.

"Wait, I thought there were no bars in Velinsk," she says, her voice suddenly hushing.

"There are no legal bars in Velinsk," I say, dropping my tone to match hers. "My father shut them down when he re-opened the summer palace here. *There can be no hint of immorality in a ruler's surroundings*," I say, imitating my father's stern voice.

"I watched him down at least six shots of vodka the other night," she says.

"It's not the drinking," I say, wondering how the hell I can explain this to an American, the important difference between bar-drinking and home-drinking. "It's the rowdiness in a public place. The congregation of too many people all under the influence."

She looks at me very, very skeptically, even as her hand tightens on my arm.

"My father sees every opportunity for people to gather as a threat to his reign," I say softly.

"I thought Sveloria was stable," she says, her voice just above a whisper.

"It is *now*," I say. "But twenty years ago my father made it that way by blood and fire, and he knows that twenty years isn't very long. To him, every face he doesn't know will always be a threat. Soviet loyalists around every corner, communists, anarchists, all just waiting to put an end to everything he's worked for. So he still rules with a metal fist."

"Iron fist," Hazel says.

"A fist is a fist," I say.

I've been trying to get him to loosen his grip ever since I got back from the Royal Guard. Other countries have bars where people get drunk together and don't overthrow their governments. Other countries have a free media that reports on anything and everything, and power still transitions in an orderly fashion from one ruler to another.

But I know he's never going to change. There are lessons you just can't unlearn.

"So we're going to an explicitly illegal speakeasy in a dangerous part of town," she says.

"There's still time for you to feel chickens," I say.

"The phrase is chicken—"

"I know," I say.

"Sorry," Hazel says, laughing.

I stop. We're in the middle of a grove of willow trees, their long green branches waving around us in the same breeze that just barely moves Hazel's long black hair.

Skip the bar and stay here, something inside me whispers, something that doesn't give a shit about the stern talk my father gave me.

The ground is soft enough. No one would hear you. It's late, no one else is out.

Just once.

I nearly snort out loud. I can already tell that once would never be enough. I'm already being stupid and reckless, out here, alone, with the first girl who's ever made me feel like I can't help myself.

I'm playing with fire. I know it.

I also don't care.

CHAPTER THIRTEEN
HAZEL

Kostya stops short, right in the middle of the willow grove. I press my lips together, wondering if I've said something, or whether he's changing his mind about taking some dumb American to his secret hangout.

Then he looks down at me, and I swear his serious, smoldering gaze burns a hole right through me, even as I'm half-convinced that I'm reading all his signals wrong. Every time that I'm sure that this *tension* between us is real, a moment later he's Prince Serious again, and I'm wondering if I'm imagining things.

Right now, for instance. I almost can't tell if he's about to kiss me or reprimand me. Maybe both at once. It seems like something a Svelorian could do.

My insides start to twist anyway. I don't break his gaze.

Just kiss me or say something or do something, I think.

I'm gonna lose my mind if this keeps up for a whole month.

Kostya slips his arm from my grasp, then slides his hand into mine, warm and rough. He half smiles.

I swallow.

Then he pulls me between the curtain made by two willow

trees, their long green branches dragging over my hair as I duck. Behind them is a tall, dense green hedge. Kostya hesitates for a moment, scanning it, and then pushes into the small gap between two plants, still pulling me behind him.

Four feet of shrubbery later, we're on a paved asphalt road, a green field on the other side of the black ribbon. I look left and right, trying to figure out where exactly we are, because this part of the palace's grounds doesn't look familiar at all.

"The back route to the garage," he says, and we start walking down the road. He doesn't take his hand away and I don't either, even though we're right out in the open now.

You haven't done anything yet, I remind myself, over and over again. *Not yet. Not really.*

"I thought you didn't have to sneak," I say.

"I don't have to sneak to the ramparts," he says. "If my father caught me out in the gray district, it would be a different story."

He looks down at me, and we come around a curve, the big stone building coming into view.

"Particularly with the Ambassador's daughter," he says.

I swallow and pretend very hard that we're not holding hands, even though I don't let his hand go.

"You're just showing me some Svelorian hospitality," I say.

That's why you told me about your nightmares, and why you dared me to burn my shirt, why you gave me a nickname.

And why you still haven't let go of my hand.

He looks over at me, his eyes dancing, his face serious.

"Yes," he says.

He unlocks the garage, and once inside, he punches a code into a panel just inside the door.

The inside of the garage is huge, and it smells like grease and brakes, like rubber and new leather. We walk down the center of it, between rows of low-slung cars that gleam even in the dark, their headlights like the eyes of panthers, tracking us in the night. I wonder how fast they go.

Kostya hasn't let go of my hand yet.

"Do we get to take one of these?" I ask, looking around. The massive space swallows my voice.

I know as much about cars as anyone, which is to say I know about Fords and Hondas, and I drove my friend's Mercedes once when she got too drunk to drive herself home. But I think these are Porsches and Maseratis and Ferraris and I-don't-even-know-whats. Cars so nice I'm a little afraid to even touch them.

Kostya laughs, a deep-throated chuckle.

"Not tonight," he says. "I can't imagine what would happen to one of those if I took it to the gray district."

"So you'll take me and not a fancy car," I tease.

"I'm not planning on parking you outside and leaving you there," he says. "*You're* not leaving my sight."

His voice suddenly has a hard, almost protective ring to it.

There's a big part of me that wants to say *I can take care of myself, thanks*, but I press my lips together and swallow the words, because I know there's a good chance they're not actually true in a shady part of a foreign country.

"I wouldn't want to trigger an international incident," I say.

"*Zloyushka*, I'm not going to take you anywhere that I can't keep you safe," he says.

"I'm not worried."

"Good," he says, and we stop.

We're standing near a big black SUV. Even in the near-dark I can tell that the windows are tinted. It looks exactly like something a monarch would be driven in.

"Is that bulletproof?" I ask, letting my eyes slide along it. It's so well-polished that there aren't even fingerprints.

Kostya frowns. Then he follows my gaze, looks at the SUV, and snorts.

"*That* is," he says, nodding at the massive vehicle.

Then he points to an ancient-looking motorcycle, nearly hidden in the shadows next to the gleaming SUV.

"*This* isn't," he says.

"Does that run?" I ask.

He finally lets go of my hand and walks toward it, running one hand almost tenderly over the handlebars.

"It *purrs*," he says, and then half-laughs. "Like an old, asthmatic tiger with a bad cough."

It's big and bulky, anything but sleek. The paint's a little rusted, the headlight is so big it looks like it's from a locomotive, and it's got a sidecar that might have been riveted together from scrap metal.

"Soviet?" I ask.

He reaches into the sidecar, pulls two helmets, and hands me one. This, at least, looks new and not like it's older than I am.

"Of course," he says. "I found it in the back of an outbuilding when I was seventeen. My father wanted to scrap it, but I convinced him to let me fix it up instead."

He uses a thumb to rub some dirt off of a dial on the handlebars.

"He hates this thing," he muses.

"I didn't know you fixed bikes," I say.

"Even a prince needs a few practical skills," he says. "And I can't cook or clean for shit."

He puts the helmet on, and I follow suit, then look down at the sidecar.

It's not very big, and it might be the only thing in this garage that looks *more* beat up than the bike itself. I'm pretty sure that if we hit something, it'll crumple like aluminum foil.

"I've never ridden in a sidecar," I say, my voice sounding dubious even to me.

"I won't make you start now," Kostya says. "As long as you promise you can hold on tight."

I think of the night before, trying not to stare at him as he handed me his shirt, and I'm glad I've got this helmet on in the dark because I feel my face flush just at the thought.

"Of course," I say.

Kostya uncouples the sidecar, wheels the bike forward, and then gets on. He's wearing jeans, motorcycle boots, and a black leather jacket that fits *exactly* the way a black leather jacket ought to fit a man.

Watching him straddle a motorcycle, even with the helmet hiding his face, all I can think is: *it's completely unfair how hot he is.*

"Come on, *zloyushka,*" he says. "You're not having second thoughts, are you?"

"Not for a second," I say, sounding slightly braver than I feel.

I'm not nervous about going out with him, but I'm a little nervous about riding something that looks like it belongs in a museum.

Also, I can't figure out how to get on the back. The second seat is just high enough that I don't know if I can get a leg over it, so I stand there for a moment while Kostya holds the bike still, and I shuffle from foot to foot.

"Step there and hold onto my shoulder," he finally says, pointing at a bar sticking out of the back.

"It won't fall off?" I ask, poking at it gingerly.

"It's a foot rest," he says. "This is what it's for."

I put my weight on it and grab his thick shoulder, swinging my leg over the seat.

Kostya turns his head, and for just a second, his hand drifts to my knee and holds it, warm and comforting. I take a deep breath and then reach my arms around his waist, very determinedly *not* thinking about him shirtless.

He says something, but I can't hear him.

"What?" I say.

He turns his head and reaches back, sliding one finger along the underside of my helmet. There's a faint click, and then I hear Kostya's voice right in my ears.

"Tighter," he says.

I tighten my arms, and the bike roars to life, the noise echoing inside the big garage. We take off toward a big garage door, slowly opening.

I fight the urge to duck as we go under it, and Kostya points a remote back over his shoulder.

Royals, I think. *They use garage door openers just like we do!*

Then the bike's engine cuts out.

"Shit," I say into my helmet's intercom. "Did it break already?"

"I told you, this thing is indestructible," Kostya's voice says back. "The engine is too loud."

We coast through the palace grounds, past hedges and trees and old stone buildings until we're at the service entrance. Unlike the front gate, this is a simple iron affair, and it opens as we approach, then closes behind us.

Once we're outside the palace grounds, the bike roars to life again, and I tighten my arms around Kostya as we pick up speed. Soon, we're flashing past the dark windows of shops and restaurants, the warm summer breeze blowing my hair back.

Then we're past the Old Town, riding inland from the sea, and I can see the shadow quarter — or the gray district, whatever, I like my way better — looming in front of us.

There's no way to describe it except to say it's Soviet as hell, pure communist-bloc brutalist architecture. The buildings are huge, uniformly gray cubes. Some are perched on concrete legs, some have rows of windows looking out at the night glassy-eyed, but there's no mistaking any of it.

I'm not surprised that tour guides won't take tourists here. Besides apparently being dangerous, it's *ugly*.

Kostya drives us down a street that dips below, and suddenly we're next to a channel full of water. There's no guardrail or anything between us and the canal, and I turn my head so I don't have to look at it. The buildings here all have loading docks right on this street, at the level of the canal. Each had a streetlight at one time, but most of them are smashed or burned out now.

He lets off the gas and the motorcycle starts slowing. I haven't seen another person since we entered the gray district, and it's making me feel uneasy. Finally Kostya brakes, then puts his feet down and walks the bike into a dark, narrow alley between two huge industrial buildings.

When he cuts the engine, there's near-total silence. Not even the concrete-lined canal behind us makes noise.

"This is where the bars are?" I ask into my intercom.

"Illegal bars have a way of being quiet," he says.

Slowly, I release Kostya, find the foot rest, get off the bike, and get my helmet off, shaking out my hair and running my fingers through it, wishing I had a hairbrush. Kostya gets his off and runs his hand through his hair once.

"Why'd we park in an alley?" I ask, my voice low, glancing into the pitch blackness beyond us.

"How would it look to have a hundred cars parked outside an abandoned building?" he asks.

Good point.

"Like there was something going on inside," I say, glancing again at the dark.

"This way," he says, and puts one hand on my lower back, leading me out of the alley. Between the motorcycle ride, Kostya's hand on me, and the bad part of town that's *way* too quiet, my whole body is on high alert, tense like a tightrope.

Something crunches under my foot, and I look down. It's a syringe, needle sticking out, and I thank my lucky stars that I wore closed-toe shoes. Not that I haven't been plenty of places with syringes on the ground.

Kostya's hand lingers on my back as we walk along the canal on the dark, ugly cement path between the loading docks and the black water. I keep my back straight and walk my best don't-fuck-with-me walk, but I know full well that if something happens, it's not going to be me kicking anyone's ass.

We walk past a few buildings, and then Kostya walks up to one. He reaches up, knocks on a high window, then crosses to a door on the opposite end of the wall and waits.

I look up at him.

"Secret code?" I ask.

"Of course," he says. "Every good illegal bar needs one."

After a few more moments, the heavy metal door swings open a few inches and a very suspicious man with a thick beard and long, dark hair peers out and glares at Kostya.

CHAPTER FOURTEEN
KOSTYA

Looks like Viktor's on the door tonight. We're not great friends, but I've never punched him in the face, so at least he'll let me in.

Before he does, he takes a good, long look at Hazel. So long I start to tense up, my fist tightening on my helmet in my hand.

"She with you?" he finally asks in Russian.

I just nod.

"What is she?" he asks, still looking at her.

Hazel's looking at him, her gaze slowly becoming a glare.

"A human woman," I say, pushing on the door just enough that he notices. "You're familiar with the species?"

Viktor scowls, but he steps back and lets us in. I keep my hand on Hazel's back.

The inside is a massive industrial space, filled with thirty-year-old machinery around the outer walls. The makeshift bar is in front of a massive chimney, concrete and metal, that stretches up to a high ceiling. Pipes and catwalks run across it, and under our feet, there's sawdust on the concrete floor.

Hazel's taking it all in quickly, her dark eyes narrowing as she looks around.

"Was this really a cannery?" she asks.

"Is that what they told you?" I ask.

Hazel just nods, her eyes up toward the ceiling.

"Not at all," I say, and then I hear someone shout my name.

I turn, and Niko's waving at me from a long, beat up metal table.

"That looks like your father's aide Nikolai," Hazel says, sounding confused.

"That's because it is," I say.

"Someone who works for your father is here?" she asks, sounding suspicious.

I chuckle and lead her over. Niko's already half-drunk, grinning at me, his arm around his girlfriend Marina. He's at the table with a few other friends, and they all wave as we walk over.

"You *did* bring the American girl," Niko says in Russian. "I thought so."

Hazel's eyebrows go up at *Amerikanskaya*.

"This is Hazel," I say to the table in English. I know they all speak it perfectly. Niko just wants to rag me about this.

Hazel takes a deep breath, then nods.

"Hello again, Nikolai," she says.

Niko laughs.

"You can call me Niko when we're not in the palace," he says.

Hazel relaxes visibly.

"Thank God," she says. "I think Svelorian introductions are gonna kill me one of these days."

I go around the table and everyone introduces themselves: Marina, Niko's girlfriend, Sergei and Dmitri, who were in the Guard with me, and Dmitri's girlfriend Sofia.

We sit, putting the motorcycle helmets on the floor behind us. Two dark beers appear in front of us. Niko shouts a toast to pretty girls and dark nights or some nonsense, and we all drink.

"Did Kostya bring you around so we'd impress you with his war stories?" Sergei asks. He's flushed, his curly brown hair sticking up in every direction.

Hazel laughs.

"*Is* that why Kostya brought me?" she asks, leaning her chin on her hand and turning toward me, laughter in her eyes.

"If I wanted to impress you with war stories I'd tell them myself," I say. "These assholes will only tell you about all the times I made everyone get out of bed and into defensive positions in the middle of the night because I heard a squirrel."

"You know us too well," says Dmitri.

"True," I say, and everyone laughs.

I sneak another glance at Hazel. She looks a little confused, still, but she's laughing along with the group.

"The palace is stuffy and formal," I say, shrugging. "I thought you might want to escape for a while and go somewhere that you didn't have to remember your manners."

"Oh, come *on*," she says. "I'm not that bad."

"She met the king and queen in a sweatshirt and spandex pants," I tell the group.

Marina just puts her face in her hands, and Niko pats her back.

"I'd just gotten off a thirteen-hour train ride, and I didn't *know* I'd be meeting them," she says, but she's laughing. "And I never even told you what happened on the train."

"It can't be worse," Marina says, peeking through her fingers.

Hazel just takes a sip of her beer, then looks around. Everyone's waiting for the story, and she laughs awkwardly.

"You have to tell us now," Sergei points out.

"Shit," she says.

She exhales, blowing a strand of hair out of her face and looking into her beer.

"I'm visiting because my mom's the American ambassador," she starts. "She can be kind of intense, so before I visited, she sent me a full dossier on Sveloria, Velinsk, the Summer Palace, the royal family, everything."

She tells the whole story: almost losing her passport, finding the joint, Svelorian customs wondering if she was a terrorist, and then getting off the train to find out that she was going to meet the royal family wearing spandex.

My memory of her spandex pants is *excellent.*

By the time the story ends, everyone is laughing along with her.

"And they didn't kick you out?" Dmitri asks, his eyes dancing.

"Only because they don't want to start an international incident," Hazel says. "It's probably better to put up with someone who can't behave herself than piss off the American ambassador."

"What happened to the joint?" asks Sofia.

"I flushed it," Hazel says, twisting her beer glass between her fingers. "I figured it caused me enough excitement already."

I glance over at her, but she doesn't look at me. I force myself not to smile at the secret we're still keeping.

"I can't believe you didn't share," I say.

Now she looks at her, her eyes sparking.

"I thought you might toss me into the dungeons," she said.

"We haven't used those in a hundred years," I say.

"Only a hundred years?" she asks.

Niko and Sergei are grinning like idiots, watching Hazel tease me.

"She's got a point," Sergei says. "A hundred years isn't that long ago."

I lean back in my chair and give them all a good long look.

"Keep it up and you're going in there," I say.

"Everyone better shape up," Niko says. "His majesty has spoken."

"Can I have a cell with a window?" asks Marina.

"I think not," I say. "Rats, bread, and gruel for the next person who says something about the dungeon."

"But no heads on spikes," Hazel says, leaning back in her chair as well and looking over at me.

"You can't lock *her* up," Niko points out. "Hazel, ask him *how* big the rats are."

I roll my eyes, and Hazel laughs.

"Are there really dungeons in the palace?" she asks.

"Yes," I say.

"You skipped those when you were telling me about the murder holes and heads on spikes," she says.

Dmitri snorts, then reaches for the pitcher of beer. He refills Hazel's half-empty glass, then goes around the table, topping everyone off, ending with himself.

"Kostya really knows how to talk to women," Sergei says as Dmitri is pouring.

"His majesty doesn't have to talk to women," says Niko. "He's a prince, they present themselves at his feet."

"Is this because I haven't come by in a couple weeks?" I ask. "Is this how you tell me you miss me?"

They all laugh, and I can't help but smile as I drink more of my beer. I sure as hell missed *them*. Being royalty gets old after a while.

"It must be hard to have every eligible woman in the country make eyes at you," Niko teases me.

"Niko, have you *seen* the Summer Palace? I'd leave you if Kostya said the word," Marina says, laughing.

He makes a face.

"It's not that great," he says.

I steal a glance at Hazel, because I kind of wish the conversation hadn't taken this turn. It's true that being the crown prince has gotten me lots of female attention, but I could take it or leave it. I've got more important things to do than bed some rich man's daughter.

She glances at me quickly, then takes a very small sip of her beer. At least she's figured out that if she keeps emptying her glass, it'll keep getting refilled.

"Has your father bred you to Yelena yet?" Dmitri asks, totally oblivious.

Hazel makes a face. Dmitri laughs.

"Jesus, Dmitri," I say. "I'm not a show pony."

"*She* is," he says. "How many strong Svelorian children did her grandmother produce, again? Was it twelve?"

"I don't know," I mutter.

Hazel lifts her eyebrows.

"She was the woman you were with at that dinner, right?" she says, and there's something cool in her tone, suddenly a little standoffish.

I glare at Dmitri, who pretends not to notice.

"Poor Yelena," says Sergei. "She just wants to make you good meals and strong babies."

"Be nice," I say. "Yelena's a very sweet, genuine girl."

I trail off before I say anything mean.

"She genuinely wants your royal dick," Sergei says, and next to me Hazel nearly spits out her beer, laughing.

She closes her eyes and buries her face in her arm, still half-laughing and half-coughing. I grab her beer and put it on the table so she doesn't spill it, then rub her back until she's finally stopped coughing, her long black hair tickling my hand as I do.

Sergei looks *incredibly* pleased with himself. I glare.

"Oh, god, I'm sorry," Hazel says. "That wasn't even that funny."

"You laughed pretty hard," Sergei says.

"I was just surprised," she says.

Everyone's watching my hand still on Hazel's back. I pull it away and put it back around my beer. Hazel clears her throat.

"She seemed nice," she says, her voice cool again.

For a moment, I want to murder everyone at this table.

"Yelena is very nice," I say, making myself sound reasonable. "She's also the latest in a long line of rich, boring, empty-headed women that my father keeps pushing on me, in the hopes that sooner or later I'll break down and make myself an heir."

"You poor thing," Marina says, leaning her chin on her hand on leaning forward. "All those pretty, willing girls."

"They just want the title," I say. "I could bathe once a month, pick my nose at the dinner table, fart in public, and as long as I was next in line for the crown they'd still line up."

"Have you tried it?" Hazel asks. "I bet not bathing for a month might deter *some* of them."

"You think I should?" I tease her. "You're still here for three more weeks, aren't you?"

"You could start after I leave," she says.

Her eyes are laughing again, and something warm and happy winds through my chest.

"It was your idea," I say. "I think I start tonight."

I set my one-third-full beer on the table with a loud *clunk*. Hazel wrinkles her nose, and the rest of the table chuckles.

"How long until your father has his guards take you outside, strip you, and hose you down?" Sergei asks.

"Two weeks," Niko says. "Less if I tell him what you're doing."

To my right, I swear Hazel turns faintly pink.

It's the beer, I tell myself, even though she's hardly had half a glass.

"Careful," I say. "I know where all the murder holes are."

"No showers, murder holes," Marina teases. "Line up, ladies."

"I didn't *make* the murder holes," I say. "I'm just descended from the crazy-eyed bastard who did."

CHAPTER FIFTEEN
HAZEL

None of this is what I was expecting, not at *all*. When Kostya said we were going to a bar in the gray district, I thought we'd probably drink vodka near a bunch of other quiet, serious people in a concrete room.

I didn't realize we'd be meeting his friends, or that when it's just them and they're drinking, they're friendly, and warm, and funny, and *love* giving Kostya shit. I feel at home for the first time in a week, and it's at this speakeasy in the worst part of town.

"Careful what you threaten," Niko says. "I think your father might like me more than you right now."

"I think my father likes everyone better than he likes me right now," Kostya says, shaking his head. "I'm the only one who'll argue with him."

"Sounds dangerous," Sergei says, but Kostya just shrugs.

"His other option for the crown is seventeen and failing his way through a Swiss boarding school," Kostya says. "So we argue."

Niko lets out a low whistle.

"Misha failed out of another one?" he says. "How many Swiss boarding schools are there?"

"He hasn't actually been kicked out of this one yet," Kostya says. "But it turns out there are quite a few."

"See, your brother's doing it right," Dmitri says. His glass is empty, and he pours beers for everyone again before he pours his. "If you're gonna be a prince, smoke lots of weed, party all the time, and bang lots of French heiresses."

I raise my eyebrows and look over at Kostya, who frowns. Then I put my elbows on the table.

"Tell me more about this brother," I say.

"He's too young for you," Kostya says, only half-teasing.

I wrinkle my nose.

"Ew," I say, and everyone laughs.

"Mikhail — Misha — has failed out of two boarding schools, gotten kicked out of one for drug use, and *allegedly* charmed his way into half the panties in Europe," Niko says.

If he's as good-looking as his older brother, that part wouldn't be hard, I think.

I look over at Kostya, who's halfway to a glower.

"And this is *your* brother who's charming," I say. From the corner of my eye, I see Niko grin.

Kostya just takes another drink.

"The family resemblance is quite striking," offers Sergei. "Just think, if things had gone differently, Kostya could have been really *fun*."

I laugh. Kostya huffs.

"So Misha is bizarro-world Kostya," I say.

Everyone at the table looks at me, frowning slightly, and blinks.

I realize I have no idea how to explain what bizarro-world is to a group of people only vaguely familiar with Superman.

"It's from a superhero comic that's really big in the U.S., but it just means the opposite—"

Suddenly there's a huge *bang* at the entrance of the bar. The heavy metal door flies open, and every head turns toward it.

The guy who was standing there shouts something, but he's already tripping over his own feet, hands in the air, walking backwards from the door where as a man wearing a uniform and carrying a huge gun shoves his way in.

I glance over at Kostya quickly, hoping he knows what's going on, because I sure fucking don't. I don't even know if that guy is holding up the bar's cash register or whether he's police.

Does that distinction even matter here? I wonder. I'm frozen in place, completely and utterly out of my element.

Two more men come through the open door, pointing their guns around at the customers, mostly frozen in place.

Then a third man comes in. He's wearing a different uniform, more official, and he stands in the doorway, looks around, and shouts something in Russian.

There's pandemonium *instantly.* Everyone at the table but me jumps to their feet, though I follow a moment later as Kostya grabs my arm. Now *everyone* in the bar is shouting.

There are *more* men with huge guns walking toward the center of the room from the sides. The bartenders are just standing there with their hands in the air, but the bar patrons are scattering.

Everyone but me is shouting back and forth in Russian. Niko's pointing in one direction, Sergei's pointing in another, Dmitri's waving his arms around, and they're all looking at Kostya like this is *his* decision to make.

The men with guns move through the crowd in our general direction, and I feel like my stomach is trying to strangle me.

Are those machine guns? I think, trying not to panic. I half want to sprint away and half want to get on the floor and cover my head.

Just fucking once I want to be sitting at home and knitting or something when shit goes down, I think, still staring at the uniformed men as my heart hammers in my chest. Kostya, Niko, and Sergei are all still shouting at each other, and I'm standing there uselessly doing *nothing*.

People in the crowd start getting to their knees. We're still just standing there, and panic spikes through my chest just watching the uniformed men walk, pointing those huge guns around like they barely notice that they're holding them.

Finally Kostya nods at his friends, shouts something, and then points at the back wall. Everyone scatters and leaves the two of us standing there, Kostya's hand still on my arm.

He leans down, grabs the motorcycle helmets, and hands me mine, totally cool, calm, and collected.

Are we getting out of this because he's the prince? I wonder wildly.

"Come on," he shouts over the din.

He moves his hand off my arm and takes my hand, then pulls me toward a huge piece of machinery against one wall. As we disappear behind it, I see one of the men — soldiers? Policemen? Thugs? — look at us and shout, but then we're behind the thing and through a hole in the wall that opens into a wide, dark underground space.

Suddenly it's much, much quieter and darker. Kostya's hand is still in mine. The air is damp and it smells like dirt in here, so different from the room we were in moments ago that my head spins.

"What the hell is going on?" I whisper.

"This way," Kostya whispers back, and pulls at my hand. The ground feels springy and damp under my feet, but I follow him, the motorcycle helmet in my hand banging against a wall.

I'm excruciatingly aware that I'm completely out of my

element. If he left me here, I'd probably be fucked, not to mention lost as hell, so I stumble along, trusting him blindly.

I mean that literally. It's so dark I can't see a thing.

We turn right, then left, then right again. Then we stop. The noise of the bar has completely faded. I can't hear anyone following us. There's no sound but my breathing and his. I squeeze Kostya's hand, trying to keep my panic under control, even though I'm underground in a foreign country being pursued by men with very large guns.

Kostya squeezes back. Then he lets my hand go.

A moment later, there's a bright light, and I turn my head away.

"Sorry," he mutters. "This part's tricky."

Blinking, I look up. He's using the flashlight on his phone. I think we're in some kind of vaulted storm drain, the concrete roof arched over our heads, three enormous pipes leading out of the room.

"Almost there," he says, and turns the flashlight off.

For a moment, we're silent.

"Sorry the night ended this way," he says, his disembodied voice echoing off the walls.

"It's okay," I say, but my voice sounds shaky. "It's an adventure."

He takes my hand again, and we start walking. Now the floor is solid, and my shoes echo along it.

"Usually, we have a few drinks and then leave through the front door," he says.

"Seems like this happens often enough for you to memorize tunnels," I say, my voice just above a whisper.

We seem to spend a lot of time whispering in the dark, I think.

"I have an excellent sense of direction," he says. "It only took me a few tries."

"You sure you're not the bad brother?" I ask.

He chuckles.

"I'm clean as a snowdrift," he says. "Utterly above reproach."

"You mean pure as the driven snow?"

"I like my way," he says.

"That's why you're running from the police in a storm drain, towing a trashy American girl along?" I ask.

We stop again, and he lets my hand go.

"Light," he says, and I narrow my eyes as it flashes on.

We're standing twenty feet from a wall, and against the wall is a mishmash of furniture, all ancient and half-broken.

"You aren't trashy, *zloyushka*," he says, a smile lighting his eyes. "You're just a bad influence."

We walk toward the furniture against the wall, and he puts his phone on top of a dusty, old dresser, light facing up so we can still see.

"Help me move this away from the wall," he says.

I grab my end and lift. The dresser's light, and we move it a few feet from the wall no problem. There's a hole in the concrete and a dim light shining through.

"You were running from police in speakeasies long before I showed up," I say, moving toward the hole.

"No one is perfect," he says.

He puts his hand on my lower back and guides me through the hole, into a concrete room with one dim bulb lighting it. In one corner is a metal staircase, and he leads me up it, his hand in mine, then pushes open a heavy metal door at the top.

Now we're outside, the constant smell of the Black Sea fragrant in the air. I close my eyes and take a deep breath, because at least I'm not going to get left behind in a storm drain tonight.

"Thought you got lost," says a voice, and I turn to see Niko standing ten feet away in the shadows.

He walks forward, and for a moment, he's looking at my hand in Kostya's.

"Where are the rest?" Kostya asks. He doesn't let my hand go.

"Gone already," he says. "Sergei's taking Marina home. I wanted to stay behind and be sure you made it. Can't have the crown prince perishing in a subterranean maze."

He looks at me.

"Or the Ambassador's daughter," he says.

"Thanks," I say.

He just nods.

"See you tomorrow, your majesty," Niko says, and starts to walk away, listing faintly to one side with his limp.

"Do you want us to walk you to your car or something?" I call out.

This is a dangerous place, I think.

Niko turns, looks at me, and grins.

"I can take care of myself," he says. "But thank you, Miss Sung."

"It's Hazel, for fuck's sake," I say.

Both of them chuckle.

"My patronymic's Bogdanovich, by the way," Niko says, still walking away. "You had some trouble with it earlier."

"Shit," I mutter.

Then he waves back at us and walks around the corner of a building.

"Come on," Kostya says to me. "The bike's not far."

WE DON'T SEE many other people as we walk between huge, hulking gray buildings to get back to where Kostya parked his bike. I'm completely lost, because not only is it hard to have a sense of direction underground, but everything here looks the same to me. Every time I catch a glimpse of the canal I try to make a mental note of it. If I really have to, maybe I can find my way out using that.

And then, we round a corner into yet another dark alley, and there's his hulking, boxy, ugly motorcycle and I'm so relieved I start laughing.

Kostya looks at me like I've lost my mind, and I remember that laughing for no reason must make me seem like a lunatic to him.

"I'm glad we found it," I say.

"It was never lost," he says. "You don't trust me, *zloyushka?*"

"It's been a night," I say.

Kostya looks down at me, but then two men walk by the entrance of the alley, just barely lit by a faraway street light.

They glance toward us. We look at them.

Then they stop, still staring. I try to stop, but Kostya keeps walking.

All of my alarm bells are going off right now, every nerve in my whole body on high alert.

Just get on the bike and leave, I think. *Just leave. Just go. Please, God, please.*

"*Dobre dehn,*" Kostya calls out. *Good evening.*

"*Dobre dehn,*" one of them says back. It's clear he doesn't mean it in a friendly way.

He takes a step toward the alley, then crosses his arms in front of him. He says something in Russian to his comrade, and both of them chuckle in a way that makes all the hairs on my neck stand up.

Kostya and I are almost up to the bike. Both of the other guys start walking toward us, but Kostya doesn't let my hand go, even as he sets his helmet on the seat of the bike.

My helmet is still in a death grip in my hand, and the closest of the two men says something to us in Russian, his voice nasty and mocking.

I take half a step back, involuntarily, and Kostya lets my

hand go. I swear to God he *smiles* as he says something back, his voice low and calm and quiet.

Kostya takes off his jacket and tosses it onto the bike, then cracks all the knuckles on his right hand. He's still half-smiling, just wearing a black t-shirt and jeans. The two men say more in Russian, something snarling and threatening, and I'm just trying to stay as still as possible.

Maybe this is just how Svelorians have conversations, I think wildly, even though I know it's stupid.

Then he says something to them and shrugs. The first guy walks up to him until they're almost chest-to-chest, and even though Kostya's got a couple inches on him, there's two of them, one of him, and I am *freaking out*.

"Guys, calm down," I say, but no one even looks at me.

They exchange a few more words in angry, snarling Russian, and I feel like I should *do* something but I don't fucking know what. I don't even know what they're saying, for shit's sake, and then the guy takes a swing at Kostya.

I gasp, my hands over my mouth, but Kostya dodges it and hits the guy in the ribs. The second guy shouts and grabs for Kostya as the first guy grunts and stumbles, but Kostya steps backward and knocks him off-balance, just as the first guy recovers.

"Stop *fighting*!" I shout.

It's useless, obviously, but I can't just stand there, and joining in would just be stupid.

They rush him both at the same time and this time I yelp. Kostya elbows one in the side of the face and I cringe and hold my breath, because that looks fucking *painful*.

Maybe he has this under control, I think, even though I still feel like I can't breathe.

Then someone grabs around me from behind.

I *scream*, struggling hard against the arm that's around my chest, dropping my motorcycle helmet. Kostya looks over and one of the guys clocks him in the chin.

"Fucking get off me!" I shout, but the guy who's got me just laughs and tightens his arm, saying something I don't understand into my ear.

I grind my teeth together and force myself to take a deep breath, even though I'm shaking so hard I can barely stand up straight, and I will myself to remember something, *anything*, from all those self-defense classes I took in college.

I stomp the heel of my shoe down as hard as I can, right on his toes.

The guy behind me *roars*. He doesn't let me go but I thrash and manage to get away from him at last. He's screaming at me in Russian, one hand on the wall, his foot in his other hand.

I just made him angrier, I think.

Fuck fuck fuck fuck.

He looks down at his foot, and in that split second I grab Kostya's helmet off the bike and swing it at his head as hard as I can.

It connects with a dull thud before glancing off, and the guy's head snaps to one side but it doesn't knock him out like I was hoping it might. He's still screaming, his face turning purple with anger, and behind me I can hear Kostya still fighting the other two.

The guy I hit lunges toward me, and I scream again. His face is inches from mine, and for some reason, I notice that his top teeth are straight and his bottom teeth are really fucked up as he grabs me by the front of my jacket and shakes me.

I drop the helmet. He swings me toward the wall, nearly lifting me off my feet, and I do the last thing I can think of.

I knee him as hard as I can in the balls.

His eyes go wide and he makes the worst sound I've ever heard a person make, the veins in his forehead popping out.

I do it again.

Then I back away. My foot catches something and I nearly go down, but then the wall's at my back and I put my hands on it for support. My heart's thundering and I'm breathing so hard I feel like I've run a marathon, my eyes glued to the guy whose balls I just kicked.

He stares at me, agony written all over his face.

Then he falls to his knees, both hands cupping his crotch. I just stand still. My whole body's shaking so hard with adrenaline that I feel like there's an earthquake inside me.

"Hazel," Kostya's voice says, and I snap my head up.

He's still standing in the middle of the narrow alley. One of the guys is on the ground, curled around himself, and the other is against the wall, holding his nose, both eyes purpling.

"Hey," I say, like an idiot.

He glances at both the beat up men, then walks toward me and grabs me by the arm.

"Are you okay?" he says, his voice low and serious. His eyes bore into mine.

I just nod wordlessly. I'm afraid that if I try to say anything else I'm going to start sobbing.

CHAPTER SIXTEEN
KOSTYA

I'*ll fucking murder them*, I think, looking down at Hazel. *If they fucking hurt her I'll fucking murder them, I swear to God.*

"I'm fine," she whispers at last, and even her voice is shaking. I can tell she's trying not to cry.

I pull her to me and hold her tight. She's trembling and my heart is still beating wildly. Sweat's pouring down my back, and I'm practically jumping out of my skin with adrenaline, but Hazel's okay.

I'll kill them, I think, over and over. *I swear I'll kill them.*

"I'm sorry," Hazel whispers.

"Shh."

"I'm sorry, I'm sorry, I'm fine," she says. She's babbling. "I'm okay."

The guy on the ground coughs, and I tighten an arm around Hazel, her head against the hollow of my throat. She takes a deep breath, and I can tell she's trying to get a grip on herself.

"Can you hold on?" I ask.

She nods shakily.

"Then we're gonna leave," I say, and let her go.

The asshole against the wall with the black eyes is looking at me like he's thinking of trying again, and the guy on the ground is on his hands and knees, still breathing funny, but he's looking at me with murder in his eyes.

The guy Hazel kicked in the balls is down for the count, on his knees, head bent. I fight the urge to kick him in his goddamn face and break his skull, because I've got enough honor not to hit someone when he's down.

I grab my jacket and hand it to her.

"I'm fine," she says, shaking her head.

"Take it," I order her, and she does.

I pull on my helmet and straddle the bike, watching the three guys while she climbs on behind me and buckles her helmet. I can't *actually* kill them, at least not if they stay down.

"Pig," one of them says to me in Russian.

"You want more?" I growl back at him.

He glares, but he doesn't do anything. If I were alone I'd happily go another round, but I just want to get Hazel out of here.

I can't believe I took her here in the first place, I think. *What the hell is wrong with me?*

Hazel gets on behind me, swimming in my jacket, her hands disappearing into the sleeves when she reaches around me.

"Hang on," I say into the intercom.

Then I start the bike with a roar, leaving the three of them behind and zooming along the canal as fast as I dare. Neither of us says anything until the hulking gray buildings are disappearing behind us, but I can hear Hazel's breathing over the intercom, slowing and evening out.

Once we're in a better neighborhood, I slow down a little, then take one hand off the handlebars and slide it into the sleeve of my jacket, finding Hazel's hand.

"What was that about?" she finally asks.

"The bar got busted by the military police," I explain.

"Is that why they had machine guns?" she asks.

"All police have machine guns," I say.

"Oh."

"The men in the alley recognized me," I say. I zoom around a little white hatchback. "They were drunk and decided it was my fault that their good time got ended tonight."

There's a long pause.

"It seems pretty dumb to beat up the crown prince," she finally says. Her voice is starting to sound like her again, with just a sliver of that laugh, and I'm relieved.

"It is," I say. "At least, it's dumb to try."

"Are *you* okay?" she says, and squeezes my hand. "I didn't even ask."

Inside my helmet, I smile.

"I'm fine," I say.

I get off the highway and take the road toward the palace, turn off it onto the service road. The back gate opens for us and I cut the engine, letting the bike coast to the garage. I don't let go of her hand until I guide the bike into its parking spot.

We dismount and toss our helmets into the sidecar, and before I know what I'm doing, I'm pulling Hazel against me and wrapping my arms around her.

"I'm fine," she says. She's not shaking anymore, at least.

"I'm sorry," I say. "It's my fault. I shouldn't have taken you."

"I had a really good time until the end, actually," she says. "Even the tunnels weren't so bad. Your friends are..."

She trails off.

"Assholes?" I offer.

Hazel laughs.

"I was gonna say *fun*," she says.

"You sound surprised."

"I *am* surprised."

"Am I that bad?" I ask.

Alone and out of danger, her body pressed against mine in the dark garage, I'm acutely aware of *everything*. The way her chest expands against me when she breathes. The way her voice hums against my chest. The way her hands are locked around my waist, the way she fits against me perfectly.

"Not at all," she finally says.

After a long moment, she pulls out of the embrace to take off my jacket.

"Here," she says, looking up at me. "You're — shit, Kostya, you said you didn't get hurt."

She touches my chin so lightly that I can barely feel her fingers. I toss my jacket onto the bike behind her and shrug.

"I've been hurt worse," I say.

One of the guys managed to land a glancing blow on my chin, just hard enough to bruise and split my lip on one side, nothing major. It's not bleeding anymore, and barely even swelling.

"You should put ice on that or something," she says.

Her fingers run underneath my lip, skimming the surface of my skin, and I swear her touch tingles. She's examining my face, concern in her eyes.

"I'm fine," I say, as her cool fingers run over the lump on my chin.

She just frowns.

"*Zloyushka*, I'll be good as new in a couple days," I say, and take her hand in mine.

"I don't think you get to beat up two guys outside a speakeasy and call *me* the bad girl," she says.

Her eyes drop to my knuckles.

"Your hands are fucked up, too," she points out.

"What's that English phrase?" I ask. "The one that means the person I fought is worse?"

"*You should see the other guy*," Hazel says. "And I did."

Now she's got both her hands on mine, examining my bruised knuckles, feeling along the bones and tendons, making sure nothing's broken.

I know nothing is, but I could stand here forever and let her touch me, in this vast dark garage, surrounded by fancy cars bought with Sveloria's oil money. I feel like time has stopped, like the outside world stopped mattering.

This is stupid. I know this is stupid, and I'm perfectly aware that I'm careening toward something much, *much* more stupid, but I don't care.

If I cared, I wouldn't have followed her out of that dinner when she was drunk. I would have turned around and left the roof last night. I would have left her at the palace tonight and gone out alone.

But I didn't do any of that. For the first time, I've met a girl I feel like I can't stay away from, and I dove headlong into idiot decisions.

"At least I didn't kick him twice in the testicles," I say.

Hazel just wrinkles her nose, and I realize that was probably the wrong thing to say in the moment.

"Give me your other hand," she commands softly.

I do it, and her light but firm fingers work it over, checking for damage.

"I've gotten in fights before, you know," I say. "I've made it this far."

"Kostya, shut up and let me do *something* after you probably saved my life," she says.

"That's no way to speak to a prince."

"Then throw me in a dungeon," she says, and her eyes flick up to mine, a teasing smile around them.

"I told you, we don't do that anymore," I say.

I let her hands go and slide my thumb along the line of her jaw, completely unable to stop myself.

"Now, we let the barbarians come through the front door and smoke pot on the roof," I say.

Her hand is on my side now, her eyes wide and deep brown.

"I'm civilized," she whispers.

"Are you sure?" I ask, letting my voice drop. "I like barbarians."

I bend down and kiss her before she can respond, and her mouth underneath mine is warm and pliant and she kisses me back, her fingers curling against my side. My heart is slamming against my ribs, her silky hair between my fingers, and I run my other hand down her back.

After a moment I end the kiss and just barely pull away. I'm breathing hard and my whole body is buzzing with desire.

I want to kiss her harder. I want to fit my fingers to the notches in her back. I want to hear the sound she makes if I kiss her neck, I want to lift her up and I want her to wrap her legs around me as I push her back against the bulletproof SUV.

Instead, I wait for a heartbeat, her lips millimeters from mine. I'm afraid I'll spin completely out of control if I don't.

But then Hazel wraps her hand around the back of my neck and pulls my mouth to hers, our lips moving together slowly. We stop, separate by millimeters, kiss again, deeper this time, her fingers on my spine now, pressing me toward her.

I'm rock hard, and she *has* to notice, but I don't care. I'm sure Hazel's figured out by now how much I want her.

Delicately, almost tentatively, she glides the tip of her tongue along my lower lip and I touch it with my own. Somehow, my hand got under her jacket and her shirt and my fingers are on her bare skin, my other hand still in her hair.

We move so slow I think I might explode, but exploring her

like this feels so *right* that I don't care if I do. I may as well be thirteen again, kissing a girl for the first time for how brand-new and wonderful everything feels, how much I don't want this to end.

There's a loud beep from the garage entrance.

We both freeze, the kiss ending suddenly. Then footsteps.

"Shit," Hazel whispers. "Are we even allowed in here?"

"*I'm* allowed everywhere," I whisper. "Remember?"

"So do we just walk out there and say hi, then?"

We're still holding each other tight, and I desperately want to pretend that nothing is wrong and keep making out with her.

But there are a couple of things that could put me in deep, deep shit with my father, and I've already done several of them tonight.

"Someone must have seen the garage door open," I say.

I should have gotten off the bike and walked it through a different door, but it wasn't the first thing on my mind.

Now I can see a flashlight moving over cars. God*damn* it.

"See that ugly box truck with the canvas over the bed?" I whisper, pointing.

Hazel looks around me, then nods.

"We're gonna get in the back of that, then sneak out after the guard walks past."

She nods. We tiptoe for the big, ugly, military-green truck, and I hold up the canvas flap. Hazel climbs in silently, and I follow her, letting the canvas close behind me.

The guard's footsteps echo toward us. There are a few holes in the canvas, and I can see the flashlight shine over walls and cars.

"Do you spend a lot of time hiding in ancient Soviet trucks?" Hazel whispers.

"It's not the first time I've hidden here," I say.

The footsteps are closer. Closer.

Then they *pause*. We stay perfectly silent, and even though it's almost perfectly dark, I can just see Hazel's eyes, looking at me.

The flashlight sweeps over the wall behind us, but she's close and it's dark and the only thought in my mind is *kiss her again* so I do. The footsteps move on, and after a long time, I pull away from Hazel again.

"Come on," I say, and hold open the canvas.

"Do we have to?" she whispers.

"We don't *have* to," I whisper back. "But it's a very good idea."

She hops out quietly, and I follow. I keep my hand on her back we creep along the wall toward the exit.

The guard's footsteps are starting to come back, more quickly than they were before, but then we're at the exit and Hazel reaches for the knob.

"Wait," I whisper, and dig through my pockets. I find a 25¢ Euro coin, wind up, and throw it as hard as I can across the garage, then hold my breath.

There's a faraway clink. The footsteps stop. The flashlight beams over the far wall, and I push the exit door open into the cool night. Hazel slips out and I follow her to the hedge, and we slip through it to a different part of the garden than the one we were in before, this one filled with some kind of flowering shrub.

I point toward the castle.

"Can you get back from here?" I ask.

"Do I just walk toward the palace?" she whispers.

I nod.

"Then yes," she says, but she turns and looks at me again, her eyes searching mine.

We're out in the open, and even though it's three in the morning, guards patrol the gardens all night.

"I mostly had a really good time," she whispers. "Thanks."

"I'm sorry it wasn't a completely good time," I whisper back.

I want to say *stay here, we'll duck behind the bushes and no one will find us*, but I don't. I've done enough dumb things tonight.

But I do one more anyway, pulling her in and kissing her one more time, long and slow, right out in the open like this. When we pull away I'm breathing hard and I can feel my self-control slipping away. Not that I ever had much around her.

"Go," I whisper.

She kisses me on the cheek, pulls away, and walks toward the castle. I watch her walk, half wishing that I wasn't watching her go, half watching her ass in her jeans, which does *nothing* for my raging erection.

Finally she disappears. I sit on a bench, the dew sinking through the fabric of my pants, but I barely even notice.

All I can think of is her mouth on mine, her skin under my hand. Her saying *you sure you're not the bad brother?*

Hazel *clocking* that guy with my motorcycle helmet.

I smile to myself, leaning back on the bench.

Barbarian, I think, grinning.

CHAPTER SEVENTEEN
HAZEL

The next morning, I'm drinking coffee in my chambers, wearing a bathrobe and pretending to read the news, when something slides under the heavy wooden door of my rooms.

That's new, I think, and go check it out.

It's an envelope.

No: it's an envelope with a wax seal on the back. I pick it up, raising my eyebrows as I hold it to the light.

I'm *pretty* sure it's the royal seal of Sveloria, which would make this official royal correspondence. I try not to smile as I turn it over and open it.

Inside is the *very* official-looking letterhead of His Majesty, Crown Prince Konstantin Grigorovich, Minister of Military Affairs, Lord of the Realm, on *nice* paper, so thick you could almost build furniture out of it.

Below that is messy, all-caps handwriting that *has* to be Kostya's.

Dear Hazel,

It would be an honor to give you a tour of the palace dungeons, if you're still interested in the darker aspects of Svelorian history.

Please reply with your availability for four-o-clock this afternoon, outside the first floor chapel.

Most sincerely,

Kostya

Stuck to the bottom of the formal correspondence is a sticky note.

Civilized people reply in writing, with a note given to any member of the palace staff. Don't worry, they know who I am.

I grin, then try not to grin, then grin again because who cares, no one's watching me. I stuff the letter into my backpack, somewhere I'm hoping no one will look. Then I take it out and leave it casually on the dresser, because it'll look *more* suspicious if someone finds it in the bottom of my backpack, right?

It's a very official, polite note. He's extending me a hospitable invitation, and I don't have to hide it.

The corner of my sitting room has a desk in it, and when I open a drawer looking for paper or something, I find nice stationary, a nice pen, and thick envelopes. I sit down, call on my vague memories of Miss Manners, and write back.

Dear Kostya,

I would be delighted to tour the dungeons this afternoon at 4 and learn more about your country's fascinating history.

Sincerely,

Hazel

For a minute I debate re-doing the whole thing and writing something besides *sincerely*. Is this a "best" situation? What about "yours truly," or "regards," or "truly best regarding yours" or some other nonsense?

Chill, I tell myself.

I read the letter over again, fold it, and stick it in the envelope. I hesitate for a moment, then write "Kostya" on it in Roman letters instead of Cyrillic, because I'm pretty sure I'd fuck up the

Cyrillic. Then I get dressed, brush my hair, and head down to breakfast, where the first palace staff member I see notices the envelope I'm carrying and asks if I have correspondence.

"I'll see that His Highness receives it promptly," she says, nodding at me.

"Thanks," I say.

That was easy, I think.

AT THREE-THIRTY, I'm standing in my massive closet, looking at dresses. I've got on a knee-length floral sundress that's nice-looking but not particularly sexy, but I'm debating whether I should change or not.

On one hand, this is cute and respectable.

On the other hand, I'm not sure *cute and respectable* is how I want to look for Kostya, because it's sure as hell not how he makes me feel.

You're still gonna be in the palace, dumbass, I think. *You can't exactly parade to the chapel in a miniskirt and thigh-high stockings. Not that the closet your mother stocked has either of those things in it.*

Plus, it could just be a tour of the dungeons.

I think yet again about last night, about Kostya's tongue in my mouth. His goddamn *massive* erection pressing against me, his fingers hot against my spine.

And then I'm wet again, for about the fiftieth time today.

I'm pretty fucking sure this isn't really a tour of the dungeons. I cross my arms and glare at the dresses in the closet, even as I know I'm overthinking it.

Then there's a knock on my door. I frown and pad to it barefoot, a knot tightening in my stomach.

Maybe his schedule changed and he just showed up here, I hope.

The knot pulses, and I open the door.

It's my mother, a stern-looking woman I don't know, and a garment rack. I stand there like an idiot for a moment.

"Hi," I say.

My mother raises her eyebrows.

"This is the palace seamstress, Irina," my mother says.

She waits, looking at me. Irina's face doesn't move.

"You have a gown fitting appointment right now?" my mom says.

I have absolutely no idea what the *fuck* she's talking about. I never made a gown fitting appointment, and it is *not* happening right now because my dungeon date is in half an hour.

"A gown fitting appointment?" I ask, trying to sound polite.

"For the masquerade ball two nights from now," my mother says, using her special *Hazel, you are testing my patience* tone of voice. "Can we come in?"

I finally remember my manners, and open the door for them.

"Yes, please," I say. Irina enters, rolling the garment rack behind her, and my mom follows.

Once we're in my sitting room area, Irina gives me a long, appraising, head-to-toe look. I can practically see her thinking *well, I'll do what I can.*

"Mom, could I speak with you privately for a moment?" I ask.

I don't wait for her to answer, just walk to my bedroom. She follows, and I shut the bedroom door behind us.

"Did you forget?" she asks.

"Mom, what the hell is this?" I hiss.

"The king and queen are holding a masquerade ball the day after tomorrow," she says, half-shrugging. "I think it's partly because we're here, and they're trying to royal it up for us."

"This is the first I've heard of this," I say.

"No, I told you about it before," she says. "You just forgot."

"You didn't."

"Yes, I did."

"I'm *one hundred percent certain* you didn't tell me anything," I say, already fuming.

Her lips thin.

"Do you have plans already?" she asks.

"No, but that's not the point," I lie.

"Hazel, I apologize that I didn't tell you about this," she says, in her diplomat's tone of voice that says, clear as day, *I still think I'm right and you're wrong, but I'm apologizing anyway.*

I'm so mad I want to scream, because she *does* this. We've had this fight before: she signs me up for something, doesn't bother telling me, and then acts like she's Saint Eileen for apologizing.

"You have to tell me things," I say through gritted teeth.

"I apologized," she says, and I want to say *but we both know you didn't mean it.*

Instead I take a deep breath and remind myself that I'm not a teenager any more, even though when she does this I instantly feel like my angry, overly dramatic sixteen-year-old self again.

"Mom," I say, forcing myself to approach this reasonably, "I'm happy to attend palace events, and I appreciate that I'm here on an incredible, *free* vacation, and I don't mind you making commitments on my behalf, but I would very much prefer it if you consulted me first."

I think it might be the most mature sentence I've ever uttered.

My mom's jaw flexes a little, and I can tell that she's still annoyed and still thinks I'm wrong, but instead she nods.

"I'll try to be more mindful in the future," she says.

"Thank you," I say, and open the bedroom door.

I think some diplomacy might have rubbed off on me after all, I think.

"You look nice, by the way," she says as we walk back into the living room. "Are you going somewhere?"

I panic and lie.

"No, I just thought I should look nicer if I'm going to be living in a palace," I say, smiling at her just a little too much.

She nods, and then I'm in front of Irina, whose facial expression hasn't changed this whole time.

What the hell did you lie for? I think. *You don't have anything to lie about. It's just a palace tour, and now if you go back and tell the truth, it's going to be weird.*

"You have strong shoulders," Irina says, and nods in approval. "But we'll need to take the bust in."

Inwardly, I sigh. Then I look at the clock and hope I can explain this to Kostya.

FORTY MINUTES LATER, I'm standing on a footstool wearing a floor-length dress. It's black lace over a flesh-colored lining, with a halter neck and a low back, pinned in a few places, and my mom and Irina are talking about it.

It turned out that my own input was limited to vetoing dresses that I absolutely, positively hated. Like the marigold-yellow one that was inexplicably tight through the hips and loose through the waist, and made me look like a lumpy, jaundiced banana.

I liked the green one with the half-cape, but it was deemed too "showy" for an American, and I learned years ago that I should pick my battles with my mom carefully. Besides, this one looks good too.

"She can't wear a bra with that," my mom says to Irina. "The back is pretty low, is that too immodest?"

"No," Irina says. "The women will be very..."

She moves her hands in front of her like she's grabbing two enormous bosoms.

Okay then.

I glance at the clock, my stomach clenching. 4:15.

He thinks I stood him up. I'm stuck here, my mom asking whether I look too slutty in the dress she chose, and he thinks I stood him up.

I take a deep breath, doing my best not to act like I want to tear this dress off and run through the palace halls looking for Kostya.

"I will give you the stick-on bra," Irina tells me. She walks over in front of me, and stands there, hands on hips, a measuring tape around her neck, staring directly at my boobs.

Then she reaches out with both hands and runs her fingers along the crease beneath both breasts, frowning. I pull back just a little, instinctively.

Jesus, buy a girl dinner first, I think, but I don't say anything

"It's very secure," she says. "The bra sticks here, and it will give you more volume, more lift. Don't worry."

I just nod, because I wasn't worried.

I've gotten this far in life with these boobs, I think.

"Thanks," I say.

"I think this will do nicely," my mom says.

"Take it off," Irina says. "I'll have it to you the morning of the ball."

"That sounds perfect," I say, and wait for her to leave.

After a moment, she sighs a little, walks over to my mom, and they both turn around at least. I quickly get out of the formal dress and into the cute sundress I was wearing earlier.

Ten minutes later, at almost 4:30, I finally get rid of my mom and Irina, but not before discussing shoes, makeup, hair, and what mask I'm going to wear. Apparently someone's taking this masquerade ball seriously enough that we all have to wear Batman-style eye masks, as if I won't recognize everyone *anyway*.

Irina tells me to drink lots of water and bathe in oatmeal "for my complexion." I wonder what the hell is wrong with my complexion.

When the door shuts after them, I give them a two-minute head start so I don't run past them in the palace halls. I brush my hair again, brush my teeth, and put on sandals.

Then I walk to the first floor chapel as fast as humanly possible, praying that maybe I'll run into Kostya as he leaves or something.

CHAPTER EIGHTEEN
KOSTYA

It's 4:03 when I finally extract myself from a meeting about declaring the official moss of Sveloria. It was surprisingly heated, even though I can't tell one type of moss from another. The proponents of one moss — I don't even remember which — felt that the *other* moss was too reminiscent of Sveloria's Soviet past. The proponents of *that* moss felt that the *first* moss presented too strong a monarchic image, and that choosing the *wrong* moss sent the wrong political message to the rest of the world.

My job, as the crown prince, was to sit there, take their concerns seriously, and pretend that I could see any difference at all in these two mosses.

The king has started sending me to meetings like this that he doesn't wish to attend. In a way, it's good practice. The official moss of Sveloria *is* state business, after all.

At least the United Svelorian Front attacks in the north seem to have stopped. Maybe my father *was* right. I'd rather be hearing about moss than about more burned farmhouses.

It's just that moss is state business I couldn't care less about, particularly when all I can think about is being alone with

Hazel again. Her letter is still folded into my pocket, delivered to me this morning as I listened gravely to the concerns of a business owner who felt he was being taxed too much.

I didn't hear a *word* that man said.

By the time I get to the door outside the chapel, it's 4:05 according to my watch, but I don't worry. I like to let it run a few minutes fast so that I get places on time.

There's no sign of Hazel, and I relax a little. I doubt she would come, see that I'm not here, and leave again in just a few minutes. Besides, this part of the palace doesn't get much traffic, so it's a nice respite from my day.

I walk to the end of the hall and look out the big, wrought-iron window there. Since I'm on the ground floor, this window also has thick iron bars across the outside, and the windowsill is a couple of feet deep. Even though my mom and I lived here when I was younger, the royal family didn't officially summer here until I was eight or nine, after the civil unrest had ended. I remember curling up in these thick windows and looking out at the beautiful scenery.

That was when I learned all about the castle's murder holes, the heads on spikes, and the deep dungeons with secret exits. As a kid, after watching the country nearly crumble, knowing that I was living somewhere designed to be defended made me feel safer than I'd felt in a long time.

I check my watch again.

4:15. I frown and look down the hallway, my other hand going to the letter in my pocket.

Did she change her mind? I wonder. *Did she get held up?*

It's not good manners to keep the Prince waiting, I think.

I'll tell her that when she gets here.

Minutes tick past. 4:20, and I'm starting to think that whatever happened, she's not coming. I tell myself that she was held up somehow, but there's a kernel of worry somewhere in the pit of my stomach.

What if she's changed her mind since last night? What if she was just being polite when she kissed me back because she's afraid of me?

I swallow hard and take a deep breath, remembering her hand on the back of my neck, pulling me toward her. The way she pressed herself against me, throbbing erection and all.

That was more than politeness, I tell myself.

I glance down at my knuckles, still bruised and purple. My lip is barely swollen anymore, but still split, and I don't know how many people believe that I got the injuries sparring with Niko. Most people here don't question what I tell them, but I haven't seen my father more than in passing for several days.

I *know* he wouldn't believe me for a second.

4:30. My heart sinks, but she's not coming. Something has happened, and as I walk I tell myself over and over again that it's something beyond Hazel's control and not that she changed her mind.

For all you know, there's a messenger somewhere in the palace looking for you, I tell myself as I push open the door to a stone staircase.

I only get one flight up before a door above me swings open. I can't see whoever it is, but they're clearly in a huge rush, thundering down the stairs. It sounds like a herd of elephants.

Elephants wearing heels.

I stop on a landing in front of a window, arms crossed in front of my chest, trying not to smile.

Svelorian women don't stomp down stairs.

A moment later there's a flash of blue as she whirls around the turn in the staircase, one landing above me.

Hazel glances down at me, stops suddenly, and clears her throat.

"Kostya," she says, a little out of breath.

"This is terribly rude," I say, and force myself not to smile at her.

Hazel makes a face and descends the last flight of stairs. She tucks her black hair behind one ear and then she's standing a couple feet away from me, a polite distance. Her dress is a patterned blue, perfectly tasteful and demure, but all I can think about is what's under it.

"I'm sorry," she says, still breathing a little faster than normal. "Did you know there's a *masquerade ball* the day after tomorrow?"

"Is it that soon?"

"You throw *masquerade balls* here?" she asks, like I've completely missed the point.

"I don't throw them," I say, looking down at her. There's a window behind me, and anyone at all could come into this staircase at any minute, but I still have to fight the urge to bend down and kiss her, unzip her dress and slip a hand inside.

Shit, my dick's already at half-mast and rising quickly.

"I don't mean *you*, Kostya, I mean the royal *you*," she says.

"I believe this one is hosted by my mother, the Queen, and Yelena Pavlovna," I say. "And I really did forget it was that soon."

Hazel's eyes narrow at *Yelena Pavlovna*.

"Miss Pavlovna hosts events at the palace?" she asks, cocking her head, her voice cooling just slightly.

I don't correct the wrong form of address, because I can tell that Hazel's driving at something, but I'm quickly starting to realize that she's moving one step ahead of me here, and I'm stuck trying to figure it out.

"She's hosting this one because it was her idea, and she talked my mother into it," I say carefully.

"Is she close with your family?" Hazel asks. That teasing look is gone from her eyes. Her voice is bordering on a whisper, and there's something I can't read on her face.

"Her father is one of the richest men in Sveloria," I say.

"He runs the state-owned oil company, and he and my father are... associates."

I wouldn't say my father has *friends*.

"Yelena tends to get what she asks for," I go on.

"And she asked for a masquerade ball," Hazel says. "With gowns and masks and dancing and shit."

"She thinks this is a fairy tale," I say. "Yelena's twenty-two. She doesn't remember the civil war or the bombings or the fighting in the streets, she just remembers growing up in a mansion with servants. Her whole life, her father has been rich and powerful and she's been his little princess. Now he's angling for his daughter to *actually* be royalty."

We stare at each other for a long moment, and I can tell from Hazel's face that there's a million things she's not saying right now.

"It's not working," I say. "I don't care what my father thinks, I'm not interested in Yelena no matter how much he tries to push her on me."

I pause again.

"I think I'm her date to the masquerade, though," I say reluctantly.

The corners of Hazel's eyes wrinkle, just a little.

"You think?" she says, softly. I can't tell if she's teasing me.

"I get told a lot of things," I admit. "I don't always pay attention to the unimportant ones."

"This ball seems pretty important," she says, the corners of her eyes just crinkling. "At least, it had better be. I just got felt up by a seamstress for half an hour."

That shouldn't be a sexy thought, but my cock twitches anyway.

"You'll be in attendance?" I ask.

"Of course," she says. "But you'll have to figure out who I am, since I'll be wearing a mask."

"I'll just look for the girl doing shots of vodka and waltzing wrong," I say.

Hazel laughs.

"I know better than to do vodka shots now," she says. "And I'll have you know I learned to waltz for my best friend's bat mitzvah, only eleven years ago."

"Do you remember how?" I ask.

"I'm hoping it'll come back to me," she says. "Otherwise, I'm about to embarrass all my dancing partners."

I hold out my left hand and bow slightly.

Hazel raises one eyebrow and looks at me.

"It's an invitation to dance," I say, still holding my hand there. "I thought you knew how."

"You know we're in a staircase, right?" she asks.

"Are you declining?" I ask, and let myself smile, just slightly. "It's very poor manners to decline a dance with a royal, you know."

"How many times are you going to use that line?" Hazel teases, taking my hand. "With you, it's always royal this, royal that."

I slide my other hand around her back, cupping her shoulder blade, and Hazel frowns, then rests her arm on top of mine, her hand just above my bicep. Our sides are touching lightly, and I swallow, reminding myself that there's a window just behind us, that we're essentially in public.

"See?" she says.

"We haven't done any dancing yet, *zloyushka*," I say.

"But this was better than you expected," she says.

"I'll count off," I say. "One-two-three, one-two-three..."

We both try to step forward and kick each other. Hazel bursts into laughter, and I grin down at her.

"Shit," she says.

"Aren't you glad I'm teaching you to do this now?" I ask. "You could have kicked an important official."

"I doubt they'll let me dance with anyone important," Hazel says, still laughing. "Everyone here knows I'm a walking disaster. I'm sure I'm only invited because they had no choice."

I count off again, and this time she gets it right. We waltz around the landing very slowly and I count to three in English, over and over again.

When we're back where we started, still in formation, I pause for a moment.

"You ready for something new?" I ask.

"Okay," Hazel says.

CHAPTER NINETEEN
HAZEL

Before I know what's happening, Kostya's pushing me backward, my head plummeting toward the floor. By some miracle, I manage not to scream, but I can hear my gasp echo off the stone walls.

Then he holds me there for a moment, my hair just brushing the floor. His face is inches from my stomach, his strong hand still under my back. He's holding up most of my body weight with one arm.

"Relax," he says. "I'm not going to drop you."

I take a deep breath as liquid fire surges through my body, and I pray that he can't somehow tell that I'm dripping wet from a damn *waltz*.

"Promise," he says.

I force my core muscles to relax, and my spine bends further, my head going back.

Just before he lifts me again, I feel something brush my stomach lightly, through my dress.

Did he just kiss me? I wonder, but then we're face-to-face again, closer now, and my hair is wild and I'm breathing hard.

"Are your father's advisors going to be doing that?" I ask, a little breathless.

"I hope not," he says, his voice low, a light in his gray eyes. "I wouldn't want some dirty old man dropping you on the dance floor."

He slides his hand down my spine until it's resting on my lower back. My hips press against him, almost on their own, his huge erection against my lower belly as a hollow ache opens up inside me.

I've never had this reaction to anyone, ever. I feel like I'm putty.

"What dance is this?" I ask, my eyes on his.

He doesn't answer, just looks at me for a long, long moment.

Then he kisses me again. I can't help myself, and I wrap my hand around the the back of his neck, holding him to me. I open my mouth under his and deepen the kiss as he walks me backward until I'm up against the cool stone wall, the granite pressing against my shoulder blades.

Now we're next to the window, so anyone outside can't see us, but anyone who comes downstairs could. I can't bring myself to care, though, because Kostya is pressing himself against me like he's drowning and I'm a life raft.

After a moment, he pulls away and rests his forehead against mine, looking down at me. He runs one thumb along my jaw and then down my throat to the hollow, and his touch sends shivers down my whole body.

"*Zloyushka*, I can't seem to make good decisions around you," he murmurs.

"Makes sense," I say, and take the front of his shirt in my hand, pulling him in. He lets me.

"It does?"

"Bad girl, bad decisions," I say.

He chuckles as he kisses me again, then moves his lips along my jaw and to *that spot* right under my ear.

A very quiet noise escapes me, and I swear to god Kostya *growls* in response.

"I've been wondering whether you'd make a noise if I did that," he says, his lips barely brushing me.

I force myself not to make another one, breathing hard. His lips trail down my neck, slow and hot, and my toes curl inside my shoes, my hand in his hair as he flattens his tongue into the hollow of my throat.

I swallow hard, and he chuckles again.

"Almost as good as the noise," he says, and it feels like his low, rough voice vibrates through my whole body.

"Should we be not in public?" I whisper. My whole body feels like jello.

He doesn't even answer me, but suddenly he crouches, puts one shoulder to my stomach, and lifts me over his shoulder.

This time I *do* yelp, but Kostya doesn't respond as he takes me down the last flight of stairs and pauses at the bottom.

"You can't just carry people off like this," I say into the middle of his back.

I don't know why I'm protesting. I've never been with someone who could just toss me around like this before, and *Jesus* is it hot.

Kostya doesn't respond, but he turns left, and then he's putting me back down in a black sliver of shadow beneath the stairs.

"This is my kingdom and my castle," he murmurs. "I *can* carry people off if I want."

"But I'm the barbarian," I tease.

He's stroking my hip with one hand, the other on my waist. I'm pulsing with desire, desperate for him to push my skirt up and my panties down.

I run one hand down his torso, over his respectable button-down shirt, and feel the rippling muscles underneath. My fingers come to rest on the top of his belt buckle, just above the world's most obvious hard-on.

Kostya kisses me hard again, his tongue snaking into my mouth, but God, I want *more*. I want more so bad I'm nearly shaking with it.

Hesitantly, I grab his hand and slide it up my torso until he's palming my breast. My nipple stiffens *instantly*, and even though I've wanted this almost since I got here, for a moment I'm nervous that I'm being too forward, that he's going to think proper girls don't ask men to feel them up in stairwells.

Then Kostya pinches my nipple through my dress and bra, and I moan quietly into his mouth.

"I told you already," he says, still pinching, "I like barbarians. I've had enough of princesses to last me a lifetime."

Now he's got both his hands on my breasts, and he pinches both my nipples at once. I gasp, doing my best not to make much noise and failing.

I can't help myself any longer, and I run the palm of my hand down his hard, thick cock, through his pants. He pinches both my nipples again and groans, loud enough to echo. My back arches off the wall.

"Shh," I whisper. "We're in a stairwell, you know."

"Only because I don't think I can make it to my rooms," he says. "I wanted to do this last night in the back of an old Soviet truck, but we nearly got caught."

"This has about the same ambience," I whisper.

He leaves one hand stroking my nipple and moves the other back to my hip, then hikes up my skirt until his fingers are on my bare thigh.

"No, someone probably died in the back of that truck," he murmurs.

My eyes pop open and I just *look* at him.

"Pretend I didn't say that," he says.

"Make me forget it," I say.

Kostya pushes his fingers under the side of my panties, stroking them toward the juncture of my thighs.

"Like this?" he whispers.

"Still remember," I say.

I grab his cock through his pants and squeeze. I swear he throbs in my hand.

"You can take it out," he says into my ear. "It doesn't bite."

He strokes his thumb over my panties, brushing my clit and lips, and I gasp and turn my head away, forcing myself not to make too much noise. I'm positive that my underwear is totally soaked, but given that I'm writhing up against a wall, it's not like it's a secret that I'm turned on as *fuck*.

Kostya strokes me again. I unzip his pants, and his cock *springs* out, thick and swollen and *huge*. I wrap my hand around it and stroke it from root to tip as he finally slides his fingers inside my panties, finding my clit and circling it slowly.

I exhale and try to melt into the wall behind me.

"Forget yet?" he asks.

"Forget what?" I say.

Kostya chuckles, and *then* I remember. He kisses me again, hard, as he rubs my clit and I stroke his cock. His hand moves deeper and then he's stroking my lips and slipping his fingers inside.

I gasp as he moves them inside me, the heel of his hand still on my clit. He's watching my face with a combination of fascination and lust that I've never seen on anyone's face before, and it's intoxicating.

"Your eyelids flutter when I do that," he says, his voice a low growl. He moves his fingers inside me again, the heel of his hand rubbing hard against my clit.

"That's because it feels fucking *good*," I whisper.

He does it again, and this time I bite my lip almost hard enough to draw blood.

Then he whispers in my ear.

"You know what I heard about American girls?"

I take a deep breath.

"It better not be that we're easy," I gasp.

For good measure, I stroke him from root to tip, hard, his cock pulsing in my hand.

"I heard your pussies taste like Coca-Cola," he says.

"I don't think that's true," I whisper.

"There's one way to find out," he says. "And I've been thinking about it since you tried to burn your shirt."

Kostya bites my earlobe for good measure.

He moves his hand again, and I suck in a breath. Kostya just laughs, and then he's on his knees, his fingers still inside me, his head under my skirt.

I have no idea how the hell this is going to work, since I'm still standing, but he's kissing my belly and then my hips and he hoists one thigh over his shoulder, while he trails kisses along the inside of it, his fingers still moving inside me the whole time.

I glance down. The hand that's not finger-fucking me is stroking his cock. I look around for a moment, just to take a reality check.

The crown prince is about to eat me out in a stairwell with his head up my skirt, I think.

Yes. Correct. Insane, but correct.

He flicks his tongue lightly over my clit, just enough to tickle me, and I gasp again. His fingers move again, and I realize that in a few minutes, I'm probably going to come as hard as I've ever come.

Then something *shrieks.*

It's an alarm, some electronic noise that's so loud and grating that it feels like it's making my teeth buzz. My eyes snap open and I nearly fall over, but Kostya somehow manages to catch me, despite being on his knees and having both his hands *occupied.* I clap my hands over my ears despite myself as Kostya stands and stuffs his cock back into his pants.

Is this a fire drill? And are you fucking kidding me? I think.

Then I look at Kostya's face, and my breath catches in my throat, because he's *worried.* He takes one of my hands gently in his and moves it away from my ear, and I try not to notice that he's still slick with my juices.

"We have to go, *now*," he shouts.

"Where? What's going on?" I shout back, but he's already pulling me by the hand, through the door and into the hallway, where I subtly try to rearrange my underwear.

"Something bad," he shouts back.

He's walking so fast that I'm nearly jogging to keep up, turning left and right through maze-like hallways until I'm more than lost, and the constant sirens aren't helping at all. My brain feels like it's being shaken, like my eyeballs are vibrating with the noise, and then finally Kostya drops my hand and we go around a corner, where he opens a big double door.

Is this the conservatory? I wonder, totally confused.

It's not the conservatory. This must be a different floor, because instead of the conservatory's high windows and polished floor, there's a small room with two armed guards and a metal vault door.

I stop short, because now I *really* don't know what the fuck is going on. Kostya strides to the door and puts his hand on some kind of scanner, but one of the guards comes over to him, points at me, and says something in Russian.

Kostya shakes his head and replies, and it sounds curt and commanding, but so do most things in Russian.

Now the *other* guard comes over, and he says something. I can hear the door unlock, and Kostya pulls his hand from the scanner, draws himself to his full height, and says something very *commanding* to the first guard.

The guard responds. The other guard responds. Both of them have huge machine guns and Kostya's got nothing at all, but even as it escalates into a Russian shouting match, he doesn't back down.

I stand in the first doorway, holding my breath. The tiny amount of Russian I know doesn't help at all when everyone is shouting and angry, so I have no *fucking* clue what's going on or what they're arguing about.

Finally Kostya *roars* something and slams his hand against the vault door.

Both the guards go quiet, and all I can hear is the alarm shrieking. Then Kostya says something again, and turns to me.

"Hazel, come on," he says, and opens the vault door. The guards glare as I walk toward it, and I still have no idea why.

I just nod at them and step through. Then the heavy door swings shut behind us, silencing the alarm, and Kostya leads us down a gray concrete hallway toward another, more regular-looking door.

CHAPTER TWENTY
KOSTYA

We're walking through the entryway to the bunker. I can finally hear myself think, now that the goddamn alarm is out of earshot. My stomach is twisted into a thick knot, because if there's something worse than something going wrong, it's not knowing what's gone wrong.

Plus, I cannot fucking *believe* the timing.

Halfway down the hall, I stop, glance at both doors, and take Hazel's shoulders in my hands.

"It's not a fire drill," she says.

Her eyes are wide as she looks around the concrete hallway, pipes and electric cords running along both sides.

"No," I say. "That alarm means there's a black-level threat."

Her eyes widen a little more.

"Meaning there's been a threat to a member of the royal family or the cabinet," I say. "The black level protocol is for all remaining members of the royal family and cabinet to secure refuge in a bunker. There are a couple around the palace."

"Okay," she says, and sucks in a breath, nodding like she's trying to take it all in.

It's a lot, especially considering what we were up to about two minutes ago.

"You're not supposed to be in here," I admit. "This bunker is for royals and high-level officials only, so if there's anyone inside already, there will be some questions."

She nods, then takes one of my hands in hers.

"The guard didn't tell you what happened?" she asks.

I just shake my head, and she kisses my hand.

"I hope it's nothing," she whispers.

"Me too," I say.

The thought of my father, mother, or little brother hurt or dead makes me nauseous. Even though the cabinet members aren't family, I still know them all. I know their families.

Please, God, let this be a false alarm, I think.

I let Hazel's hand go and open the second door. Beyond it is pure, inky blackness, so thick I feel like I could reach out and touch it. We're the first ones here, then, so I find the switch on the wall and turn on the overhead lights.

They flicker to life one by one, ugly and fluorescent, but the whole bunker is ugly so it's only fitting. The door we came through opens onto a landing, and an aluminum staircase leads down to the main area of the bunker, the size of a large living room with an arched ceiling overhead.

All concrete, of course. The place was built by the Soviets, who may not have realized there were other building materials.

We walk down the staircase and into the main room. Underneath the landing is a hallway that leads to a few rooms: a perfunctory kitchen, two dormitory-style bedrooms with rows of bunk beds, and a makeshift office. I head for the office and Hazel follows me.

I don't even sit down before I pick up the phone and hit the red button on it. After half a ring, someone picks up.

"Report," Chief Minister Arkady barks at me in Russian.

"Kostya in the basement dungeon bunker, along with Hazel Sung," I say. "Crystal sardine."

Quickly, I pray that I got this month's password right.

Chief Minister Arkady heaves a sigh of relief into his end of the line.

"Kostya, good," he says.

Then I hear him talking to someone else in the room, and all I can make out is *go tell the Queen*.

That means my mom is okay. The knot in my stomach loosens, just a little, and I look over at Hazel. She's sitting on an ugly wooden bench, elbows on knees, watching me.

"What's happened?" I ask.

"There's been an assassination attempt on the King," he says, gravely.

"An attempt," I say. My heart squeezes in my chest.

"The bullet only grazed his shoulder, thank God," Arkady says.

"My mother? Misha? The cabinet?"

"All well right now," Arkady says. "Everyone at the palace is fine."

I cover the mouthpiece of the phone and whisper, "Assassination attempt, but everyone is fine," to Hazel.

She nods.

Then Arkady pauses, and even over the phone, I know that's not everything.

"Tell me," I say.

It's a long, slow, halting story full of holes, but it's essentially this: my father was in Tobov, the capital city, for a meeting of the Council on Black Sea Fisheries. As he was leaving, a gunman leapt out of the crowd and got off one shot at him before my father's guards brought him down.

Then it gets complicated, partly because no one seems to have all the information. The gunman was screaming about a partner, or maybe many partners, hiding in wait around the city. There were strange reports from air traffic control of a squadron of unidentified planes flying south over the mountains — a blip on the radar for a moment, then gone.

The military has been intercepting something that *looks* like coded messages all day, sent via fax machine from service stations in remote areas to other service stations in other remote areas. And then there are the rumors: someone's seen a fighter jet, someone's learned that Russian hackers are planning to breach our national security and sabotage the state-run oil company, there are submarines in the Black Sea headed for Velinsk.

"It's probably all nothing, except for the assassination attempt," Arkady says. "You know how things spin out of control. But at this stage, we have to take it all seriously."

We talk a bit more. I speak with my mother, who's nearly beside herself, sobbing into the phone. My father is meeting with his military advisors, so I can't speak with him yet, but we agree to video conference in fifteen minutes and I hang up the phone.

Hazel looks at me.

"Someone tried to assassinate my father," I say.

I can barely believe it, but as soon as the words are out of my mouth, anger flares inside me. Suddenly, I'm seeing red.

How dare they? How *fucking* dare they, after everything my father's done for Sveloria?

No, he's not always the gentlest leader. He has some policies that I think are stupid, that I wish he'd do away with, but twenty-five years ago Sveloria was a war-torn wasteland that had been utterly wrecked by the Soviet Union, and now it's a peaceful country with a thriving economy.

I jump up and start pacing back and forth in front of the ugly, boxy steel desk.

Now someone wants to *murder* him?

"Is he okay?" Hazel asks.

"The bullet grazed him," I say. "He's fine."

"Is everyone else okay?" she asks.

I turn and pace the other direction, and as I do, I realize she still looks worried. It stops me in my tracks.

You didn't even ask about her parents, I think.

"He said everyone in the palace was fine," I say. "I'm sorry, I didn't ask about your parents."

Hazel half-smiles, and shakes her head, looking at the floor.

"I'm sure you'd have heard if they weren't," she says, but there's still a flicker of worry in her eyes.

"I told Arkady you were here," I say. "At least they won't worry."

"Thanks," she says.

There's a long pause as Hazel looks at the floor and I pace back and forth, trying to collect my angry, scattered thoughts.

"Did they catch the guy?" she asks.

"Yes, but they don't know if he's working with others," I say.

Pace, turn. Pace, turn.

"It's the USF," I say. "I fucking *know* it is."

"I thought they were defunct," Hazel says.

I stop pacing for a moment.

I shouldn't tell her that the United Svelorian Front is active again, that they've been wreaking havoc and my father has throttled the media. She's an American, and she's not even in Sveloria on official business. She's on vacation.

But she's also here, with me, in a goddamn *bunker*, and I think she deserves to know why.

"They're not exactly defunct," I say, slowly.

I tell her about the raids, about the burned farms, about the anti-government attacks.

I tell her about how my father is handling the situation, how I think it should be handled, how the USF isn't actually united at all, that some of its constituent groups are peaceful protestors who want reform and some are violent militias who just want to watch the world burn. That we think they might have Russian backing, but that we don't really know.

I sit next to her on the bench and tell her about the rumors, about the jet planes and hackers and submarines. Hazel just listens, nodding until I finish.

There's silence. She looks at her hands.

"I guess that's why my mom is here," she says. "I thought it was weird that she got sent somewhere without too many problems."

The phone on the desk rings. I touch her knee lightly, then stand and answer.

"Kostya."

"Where are you on the video call?" my father growls into the phone.

I glance at the state-of-the-art monitor on the desk. I haven't even turned it on.

"I'm glad to hear you're well," I say, my own voice sounding hollow. "I've had some technical difficulties. I'll be on in a few minutes."

"Hurry up," he says, and hangs up the phone. I bend down and boot up the computer, and it whirs to life. The technology down here gets updated at least every year, which is more than I can say for the canned food in the kitchen.

Hazel stands.

"Prince stuff?" she asks.

I nod.

"Hours of it, I'm afraid," I say. "In Russian."

She half-smiles.

"Don't worry, I'll find a way to entertain myself," she says, and walks out of the office.

It's incredible how quickly a situation can go from heart-stopping to tedious. Within thirty minutes of listening to my father and his military advisors argue, bicker, shout, and point fingers at everyone from the Russians to Turkey to "the young people," I've had enough of them.

We still don't know what's going on. Most of the rumored threats don't seem credible, but we're still untangling everything. I'm barely participating, and in another window on the computer, I've got Twitter open.

If there's a silver lining to the assassination attempt, it's that it's been too big to ignore. My father can muzzle the TV stations and newspapers, but he can't muzzle thousands of people with phones. *Now*, at least, the people know what's happening like they deserve to.

After two hours, I sneak out to use the bathroom. Unlike the rest of the bunker, this room is all stainless steel, with a toilet, sink, and shower big enough for exactly one person.

Hazel's sitting at a table in the main room, an ugly gray blanket wrapped around her, and she looks up when I come out.

"How's it going?" she asks.

I just shrug.

"No one knows anything, so this is useless, but they'll never admit it," I say, walking toward her.

The table is covered with a half-finished puzzle of an elaborate castle, the box off to one side.

"There are books, but everything is in Russian," she says. "I'm not a puzzle person, but it's this or stare at a wall."

"Interesting choice," I say.

"Because I'm in a castle, putting together a puzzle of a castle?" she asks, turning a piece around in her fingers. "The only other one is a basket of puppies, and I wasn't in the mood."

In the office, I can hear the shouting escalate, and I close my eyes briefly.

"Go," she says. "I'm fine out here."

I nod. I'd much rather be here, even helping Hazel put together this stupid puzzle, than arguing with men over video chat. I can still smell her faintly on my fingers, and even though it ought to be the last thing on my mind right now, I can't help but be distracted.

Stop it, I think. *There's a time for ruling and there's a time for fucking around.*

I walk back into the office, where men are still shouting in Russian.

ANOTHER FOUR HOURS LATER, we finally wrap things up. There's no reason that we didn't wrap it up already, because we haven't gotten more information in ages. Air traffic is still looking for those jets, and the military police are still trying to uncover a larger conspiracy behind the assassination attempt. That means we're all still in Soviet bunkers and there's nothing we can do besides sit on our hands and wait.

My father dismisses his advisors, then looks straight into the camera.

"Kostya, stay on the line," he growls, and then gets up from his chair. I'm left staring at the concrete wall of a different bunker.

I sigh and lean back in the chair. It's steel and leather, but it's old and the leather is dried and cracking, showering bits onto the concrete floor.

Everything about this bunker is harsh and ugly, a throwback to the way things used to be, a sharp contrast to the sunny, beautiful palace above us.

At least it's here, I think. *No matter how good things seems some-times, we'll always need these.*

On the computer screen, my father sits in his chair again. He's wearing a jacket, so I can't even see his bandaged arm. I sit up straight.

For one crazy second, I think he might be about to tell me that I was right about the USF all along, but then he opens his mouth.

"I had the military police raid several illegal gathering places in the gray district last night," he says. His voice may as well be made from concrete.

Shit, I think. The last thing I'm in the mood for right now is getting into yet another argument with my father.

"Several of the officers reported seeing someone who looked quite a bit like you at an illegal drinking establishment," he says.

"My face isn't that unusual," I say.

He glares so hard I'm surprised the monitor doesn't burst into flames.

"Don't play games with me, Kostya," he says. "I will *not* have you undermining my authority by going directly against my orders, and I don't care who you are. While I'm still drawing breath, *I* am the King and you are my subject. Is that clear?"

I clench my jaw and don't answer. He barely seems to notice as he leans forward, toward the camera.

"I know you think that because your brother is a spoiled teenager you're the only option I've got to succeed me," he says, his voice getting even lower and harsher. "You're not. I can choose whomever I wish."

I glare back. It's technically true, but it's not that easy. I'm popular with the people of Sveloria; if he named someone else to the throne, he'd launch Sveloria right back into civil war.

He knows that. He knows I know that. But here he is, trying to strong-arm me anyway.

"Of course, father," I say. My voice is ice. "Are we done?"

"One last thing," he says. "Watch yourself with that American hussy."

My blood *boils*, but I force myself to remain perfectly still and expressionless, even as my hand curls into a fist below the desk. I want to defend Hazel to him, but I know it's worse than useless.

For years, I obeyed his orders to the letter. The first time I really disobeyed him was when I joined the Royal Guard.

Since then I've broken the rules a little more, but never seriously. I've never done anything to bring harm to Sveloria. Unlike *him*.

I'm fucking tired of it. I'll do what he wants most of the time, but not here. He can't order me to take up with a wealthy man's simple daughter over the sharp, beautiful American in the next room.

"Goodbye, father," I say, and cut the connection.

For a long moment, I stare into the black screen, fuming. If I were anyone else, this wouldn't be an issue. There wouldn't be this ridiculous pressure not to be with an American, the pressure to produce as many heirs as possible with a nice Svelorian girl.

The computer chirps again, and I take a deep breath.

Niko pops up on the screen, and I exhale.

"Ambassador Towers and Mr. Sung would like to speak to Miss Sung, if she's available," he says.

I almost laugh. Of course she's available. What the hell is she going to be doing?

"One moment," I say, and stand.

CHAPTER TWENTY-ONE
HAZEL

I'm leaning my chin in one hand, staring at a puzzle piece of yellow fur. I finished the castle, though there are a couple of pieces missing, and moved onto the puppies.

This one is actually harder, because every puzzle piece of dog fur looks exactly the same. All I've really got to go on is gradations of light and color, plus the shape of the puzzle piece itself.

Not exactly thrilling, but there's nothing else to do. The only book in English is the Russian-to-English dictionary, and at least the puppies are cute.

It's a moment before I realize that the bunker's gone quiet. Kostya kept the office door slightly ajar, so for the past hours I've been listening to men talking, shouting, and arguing in Russian. Not the most soothing soundscape, but it was nice to know that at least I wasn't alone down here in this Cold War bunker.

Kostya opens the door and leans out.

"Hazel," he calls. I look up. "Your parents want to talk to you."

I jump up, leaving the blanket in the chair where I was sitting, and walk for the office in the tube socks I found when my shoes got too uncomfortable.

There they are, their faces on the screen.

"Sweetheart," my mom says.

"I'm okay," I say, sitting in the chair. Kostya's in the doorway. He nods once at me and then disappears.

"I'm so sorry about all this," she says.

"Mom, it's not—"

"I never should have suggested you come here," she says, and I think my iron-willed mother is close to tears. "I knew that the situation was worse than they were letting on, but I didn't think it was *this* dire, and — oh, God, I'm just so glad you're okay."

My dad's got an arm around her, holding her tight.

"You guys okay?" I ask, even though it's rhetorical.

"Perfectly fine," my dad says, rubbing my mom's shoulder. "We were relieved to hear you were with the prince."

"I ran into him after my fitting and he offered to give me a quick tour," I say, hoping that I'm better at lying over video than in real life. "I guess the closest bunker to us wasn't too popular."

I'm pretty sure I'm blushing.

"These things are very safe," he says. "Built to withstand nukes, so they're pretty serious."

"Any news?" I ask. "I've been listening in a little, but it's all Russian."

"Nothing concrete yet," my mother says. "But they're working on it. The King says we'll be out of here in a few more hours. I'm just glad you're all right," she says. "We have to go, official business. Stay safe, all right? I love you, Hazel."

"Love you, sweetheart," my dad says.

"Love you guys too," I say, and the screen goes black.

I rest my head in my hands, silently thankful that my parents are okay. I have no idea what I'd do here without them.

Then, despite myself, I think of Kostya with his face up my skirt, and I press my thighs together.

He reappears in the doorway, and I stand, walking around the desk. I lean back against it, the hard steel cutting into the backs of my legs.

"Your parents okay?" he asks.

I just nod.

"Shaken up, I think. Yours?"

Kostya shrugs, leaning against the door frame. His sleeves are rolled up and his shirt has the top two buttons undone.

Even here, now, in this bunker after hours of stress, I can't help but watch the way he moves, the calm self-assuredness he has.

"My mother is borderline hysterical and I'm not sure my father's noticed yet that he was shot," he says.

"They're a strange couple," I muse. My mind is half on this, half on the stairwell.

Then I look at Kostya again.

"Sorry," I say. "Opposites attract, I guess."

He shakes his head.

"My mother was two months pregnant with me when they got married," he says. "When my father became king, he changed the marriage license so it looks like they got married first. So they could be the perfect, ideal family."

"There's a lot of pressure on a ruler," I say. I think of Yelena, the wannabe-princess who throws masquerade balls, and for a split second I'm angry that *anyone* could think that Kostya could ever be with her.

"He found out where I was last night," Kostya says. "One of the military police recognized me."

He glances around the corners of the office, almost looking amused.

"He got shot today, the country might fall apart, and he's angry that I'm going to illegal bars," he says, half to himself. "You know what else he's angry about?"

"What?" I ask.

He gives me a long, long look, and I feel like it goes straight through me and lights my core on fire.

"Me?" I ask, softly.

"He's furious that I could have my pick of any Svelorian girl, and instead I'm spending my time with a trashy American," he says.

I swallow as heat pools inside me.

This is terrible timing, I think. *You cannot get horny the same day as an assassination attempt.*

I glance down. Judging by the lump in Kostya's gray pants, I'm not the only one.

"The trashy American probably shouldn't be spending her time with you, either," I say.

Kostya grins. Then he straightens up and walks over to where I'm standing and rests his hands against the desk on either side of me, our faces inches apart.

"Probably not," he says, his voice a low growl. "I always seem to get in trouble when she's around."

"You know what they say about American girls," I say. He's even closer now, and I'm panting for breath. "Trouble."

"I think it's just this one," he says. "I can't seem to behave myself when she's around. I gave her the shirt right off my back when she asked."

I slide one finger under the waistband of his pants and tug gently.

"She sounds dangerous," I say.

"She is," Kostya says. His hand moves to the small of my back and presses me against him. "When I'm with her I end up running from the police and getting into fights. I've still got a split lip."

"Are you sure that was her fault?" I tease.

I lift one hand to his face and touch his lip, the thin red line just visible.

"The last time I ran into her, I ended up eating her out in a public stairwell," he whispers. "And I can't stop thinking about it."

His erection *throbs* against me.

"There was a national crisis today and I was hard the *whole fucking time*," he whispers. "Someone would ask me a question and I'd be staring off into space, wishing my tongue was in her pussy."

I turn bright red, even as heat surges through me.

"That's not very princely," I say.

"Fuck princely," Kostya says, and kisses me. I open my mouth instantly and let him in.

This isn't like the kiss last night, slow and sensuous. This is hard and fast, an I-fucking-need-this-now kiss, a wound-so-tight-I-might-explode kiss.

Kostya pulls back and I bite his lip just hard enough that he growls, then moves his lips past my ear and down my neck, dragging a low groan out of me.

"Fuck, that's sexy," he says, his lips moving against my skin. He nips at the cords in my neck and I gasp.

"Please don't leave a mark," I say.

He laughs.

"I know better," he says.

He nips again and pushes my skirt over my hips and I gasp at the cold steel desk against my ass. He lifts me onto it and I instantly wrap my legs around him, squeezing his thick erection against me. We kiss again and his hands are scrabbling for something on my back.

We pause.

"Where the fuck is the zipper?" he says, panting for breath.

I reach over to my side and pull it down and then he's pulling the dress over my head and off. I unbutton one more button on his shirt and then pull the whole thing messily over his head, running my hands down the hard, broad muscles in his chest and abs.

Kostya pulls one bra strap down to my elbow. The second my nipple is visible it's between his teeth and I can hear myself make a guttural, *animal* noise.

"You even sound like a barbarian," he says, my nipple still in his teeth.

He pushes me backward onto the desk as he drags my other bra strap down and pinches my other nipple. I arch my back and groan, the sound echoing around the concrete office.

Suddenly, the computer chirps, and the screen flickers to life.

I gasp and put my hands over myself, as if I could possibly act like I'm not nearly-naked on this desk.

Kostya's totally unruffled. He reaches over and yanks the cables from the back of the monitor without missing a beat, and the screen goes mercifully dark.

"Camera's in the monitor," he says, and kisses the space between my breasts, sliding his fingers under the sides of my panties and pulling them off, his lips moving quickly down my stomach.

"Wait," I gasp. "Microphone? Can they hear us?"

Kostya ducks for a moment. My bra's tangled around my waist, and I get it off as I hear the sound of one thing after another being unplugged, and then he stands again and tosses a surge protector onto the desk next to me with a crash.

"No," he says, and plants a kiss on my stomach, dipping his tongue into my belly button.

It tickles a little. I laugh, and I can feel Kostya smile against me.

"Are there noises you don't make?" he asks.

"I don't quack," I say.

He pushes my thighs apart and my knees over his shoulders, then slides one finger slowly down my mound. My body jolts when he runs it over my clit, and then he slides it between my lips.

"You don't quack *yet*," he says. "You're wet enough to be a duck."

It shouldn't be sexy, but it is.

"I think I'm wet enough to be a shark," I say, which probably doesn't make sense but I don't care.

Kostya slides the underside of his tongue down over my clit, and my body jolts again with the sweet pressure. He starts licking me slowly and firmly, flattening his tongue as he licks up, curling it as he licks back down.

"Jesus fucking Christ," I gasp, because he is *really good* at this.

He keeps licking and licking, but already, I can tell I'm gonna come if he doesn't stop soon. It's like he found a light switch inside my body and flipped it and suddenly every nerve in my body is lit up.

Kostya runs his fingers along my lips, just barely nudging inside, and I groan. I'm grabbing the edges of the desk, both hands clenched, because the last thing I want to do is grab Kostya's head and ruin this.

Then he suddenly slows his tongue, pressing even harder as he slides his fingers inside me, all the way to the knuckle.

"Oh, *fuck* yes," I whisper, because words are hard.

He moves his fingers inside me once. My toes curl and I gasp, so he does it again, in time with his tongue, then again and again. It's so good that I feel like I'm floating somewhere above the desk, in danger of crashing down.

"Kostya, you're gonna make me come," I gasp.

His fingers move harder, and I nearly shout, the noise trailing off into a moan.

"*Really* hard," I say, my voice halfway to a whisper.

He keeps going and I'm millimeters from the edge, moaning my face off, lying on a Soviet desk while the crown prince eats me out.

Then his hand snakes up my torso and pinches one nipple.

"Holy fucking shit," I gasp, and then I come so hard I can't breathe.

All the muscles in my body clench at once. My vision goes white at the edges, and I squeeze my eyes shut. I can hear myself moaning *fuck yes* over and over, but I can't even feel myself saying it as I rock back and forth, my body wracked.

It feels like it takes a long time before it's over and I can open my eyes. I take a deep breath, and Kostya stops licking me and kisses the inside of my thigh, right next to his face.

I realize that I've got my hand on his, clutching it to my chest and squeezing, so I let it go, but he leaves it there for a moment.

I take another deep breath, just trying to collect myself. Kostya kisses the crease where my inner thigh meets my torso, and I giggle. He growls.

I sit up and he finally slides his fingers out of me and pulls me forward on the desk until his cock is right between my legs, so I wrap them around him and squeeze. He kisses me hard, and I can taste myself.

"Do I taste like Coca-Cola?" I ask.

"No," he says, grinning. "Better."

I unbuckle his pants and push them down, grabbing his cock in one fist.

"Is this from eating me out?" I murmur.

I think I turn slightly pink when I ask, but he talks dirty to me, so I figure it's fair.

"It's from eating you out," he says, thrusting into my hand and groaning into my ear.

"And it's from making you come so hard I thought your pussy was gonna break my fingers," he goes. "It's from your tongue in my mouth, and from your hand on my cock, and Jesus, *zloyushka*, it's from watching your ass as you walked away last night."

I rub my thumb over the head, slick with pre-cum, and he growls softly, going even harder in my hand. I bite my lip, almost breathless with desire, and then push him away from the desk.

He gets his pants off, kicks them away, and lets me push him back against the concrete wall of the ugly office. I kiss him slowly, stroking his cock with one hand, and trail my lips down his body until I'm on my knees in front of him.

I don't tease him. I slide my lips around the head of his cock and look up at him as I lick at the underside, and then push my mouth down the shaft as far as I can.

Kostya groans so loud I can feel his cock vibrate in my mouth. I pull back and look up again, and he's still watching me, so I keep going, stroke after stroke, taking as much of him in as I can.

My jaw starts to get sore, but I ignore it, listening to his breathing become irregular.

"Stop," he finally whispers.

I pull back until just the head of his cock is in my mouth, and look up at him. I take my lips off slowly, and I think he shudders, then pulls me to standing. He kisses me hard and slow, like he's trying to collect himself.

"I want to come fucking you," he murmurs.

My breathing hitches. I swallow and then just nod.

"Good," I whisper.

He slides his hand between my legs and along my lips, kisses me deeply again, and smiles.

"Shark," he says, then pulls me toward the desk. He sits on the chair and I straddle his lap and before I know it his cock's in my fist again and he's kissing me, my back up against the cold steel desk.

I swallow.

"Do you have—" I ask, but he opens a desk drawer and starts fishing through it.

I raise my eyebrows. He closes that drawer and opens another.

"One of these has a false bottom," he says, opening a third drawer.

He feels around for a moment, then grins and pulls out a condom.

"The bunker has condoms?"

"People get bored down here," he says, unwrapping it and rolling it onto his girth.

"Is that why we're doing this?" I tease. "We're bored?"

He runs his fingers down my body slowly, then moves them between my legs and starts rubbing my clit lightly.

"If it is, let's get bored together all the time," Kostya says.

He kisses me, fingers on my clit, spikes of pleasure already working their way through my body. I put my feet on the seat of the chair behind him, my elbows on the desk behind me, and arch myself up until he's right at my entrance.

Then I take a deep breath, because while Kostya definitely has the biggest cock I've ever seen in real life, I'm also ten times as wet and ready as I've ever been before. He stops rubbing my clit and moves both hands under my ass, the muscles in his arms bulging.

"I promise to fuck you slowly," he says, and kisses me right below the sternum, the strangest combination of filthy and sweet I've ever heard.

I relax a little, my elbows still on the desk, and ease the

head of his cock into me. It's bigger than anything I'm used to, but God it feels *good* and my eyelids flutter shut as I sigh.

He lifts me a little and then I sink another inch onto him, then another. I feel like lava is running down the inside of my skin, and then his lips are on my neck.

"You feel even better than I imagined," he whispers.

I arch and ease down a little more, and he growls into my ear.

"Going slow might be the hardest thing I've ever done," he says. "But now I can feel every inch of your pussy. And *zloyushka*, I can already tell I'm never going to get tired of watching you slide onto my cock."

I take the last inch of him staring straight into his eyes. Even sitting on him, he's a tiny bit taller than I am. I wrap my legs around him and then pull his face down toward mine and kiss him hard as I move my hips back and forth, still leaning against the desk.

Kostya moans into my mouth. I gasp and stop, because *Jesus* that felt good, almost dangerously good.

"You okay?" he murmurs.

I just nod, breathing hard.

"Better than okay," I whisper.

Kostya moves again, gently, his hands on my hips. I moan softly, holding my forehead to his.

"Still okay?" he asks, but now there's a teasing edge to his voice.

"You feel incredible," I say. Now I'm moving my hips in time with him, squeezing him with my legs, taking him as deep in as I possibly can and moaning every time he hilts himself. We're not moving fast, but every time he moves it hits every pleasure spot inside me.

Suddenly Kostya pulls me all the way down, as hard as he can, and stops.

"Don't stop," I say, but he holds me there.

"You're gonna make me come," he says, kissing me slowly. "Fuck, I'd come just watching you fuck me."

"That doesn't make sense," I say, and flex my hips, moving him inside me.

"Don't," he murmurs.

I move again, and he groans.

"Come on," I whisper.

He growls something in Russian into my ear and moves his hips against mine, sinking himself deep, the edge of the desk digging into my spine.

I gasp, sparkles flickering through my vision.

"Kostya, make me come again," I whisper.

He pulls me onto him hard, again and again. My legs are still wrapped around him, my toes curl, and I know I'm going to have a bruise tomorrow where I'm up against the desk but I don't give a damn. I feel like I'm disintegrating and being carried off by the wind.

Then Kostya puts his lips to my ear and says something in Russian, a long string of rough, guttural consonants that send prickles down my spine. He fucks me again and I squeeze my legs around his waist, right on the brink.

"Oh, *fuck*," I whisper, and then I come so hard I almost can't move.

I feel like I hit a brick wall but in a good way, stunned and gasping as my body takes over and it's all I can do to hang on and ride this out, jolt after jolt as Kostya groans into my ear. Just as I slow, I can feel him pulse and then explode inside me as he pushes me hard against the desk, his face in my neck, my arms wrapped around his shoulders.

Finally, we go still. We're both breathing hard and I can feel Kostya's heart beating against my chest.

"*Below never at no,*" he murmurs.

I stroke his hair.

"What?" I ask.

He squeezes my hip in his hand one more time and then sits up so we're face to face.

"Sorry," he says, a lazy smile lighting his gray eyes. "Fucking incredible."

He kisses me one more time, and then we untangle ourselves clumsily until we're both standing. The concrete floor isn't as cold as I was expecting, and I look down at my feet.

I've still got the ugly Soviet tube socks on.

I just start laughing.

CHAPTER TWENTY-TWO

KOSTYA

Hazel doesn't get dressed before she walks to the bathroom, still laughing at her socks, and I watch her walk away. I never want her to put clothes on again.

Once the bathroom door shuts, I take the condom off carefully, tie a knot, and drop it on the desk. There, at least, I won't forget to deal with it.

There's a surge protector on the desk, lying there like a dead eel. The monitor cables are splayed over the desk, and I think I bent one of them when I ripped it out. Not to mention when I unplugged everything that was below the desk.

This stuff is going to take forever to reboot. You're supposed to turn computers off, not rip the cords from their sockets, but it's not like I'm sorry.

I came so hard I *forgot English*. I've spoken it fluently since I was a kid. Hell no, I'm not sorry.

Hazel pads back in and then leans against the doorframe. Nothing but socks is a *good* look on her.

"I guess we should plug everything back in," she says, eyeing the computer.

"We should," I say, looking at myself reflected in the glossy black screen. "But for the record, I'd rather watch you walk around the bunker in nothing but socks."

"I'm improper enough fully dressed," she says, and walks to the other side of the desk, leaning over it on her hands.

I stand and lean in as well.

"I know," I say, and kiss her.

WE GET DRESSED, I flush the condom and pray that it doesn't clog the pipes, and then I spend the next fifteen minutes lying on the concrete floor as we figure out what plugs into where. If this were a regular computer, it wouldn't be so bad, but of course it's not. It's a super-secure, top-secret, ultra-powerful government computer, though all that really seems to mean is that the tangle of wires involved is nearly impossible.

I hear a thump on the desk above, and then Hazel sighs.

"Okay," she says. "Try plugging in the monitor now."

"Which cord is that?"

A thick black cord wiggles. I grab the end and push it into the surge protector, then wait.

And wait.

"Mother*fucker*," Hazel mutters.

There's a pause.

"Oh!" she says.

I hear duct tape unwind and tear, and I pull myself out from under the desk, peering over the top as she does something with the tape behind the monitor.

"You broke the hell out of this," she mutters.

"I had a good reason," I say.

"Tell me if it's on," she says, and wiggles something.

The screen flicks to life.

"Yes, there," I say.

She tapes something very carefully, then pulls her hand away.

"Still?" she asks.

"We're good," I say.

First, the computer has to scold me for improperly shutting down, then check that I didn't fuck it up too much, THEN recatalog a library or some bullshit. Finally, I'm logged into the video conference again, and the second I do, a screen pings and pops up with Niko's face on it.

"Oh, Kostya," he says, like he's surprised.

"We had technical difficulties," I say.

He just nods. I can't tell whether he believes me or not.

"We'll probably be cleared to leave in the morning," he says. "But not before then."

Hazel's still standing behind the monitor, watching me. I look at the clock and realize that it's two in the morning.

"Hold on a moment," I tell Niko, and mute the microphone, then walk around the desk.

"What's going on?"

"Still nothing," I say, and put my hands on her shoulders. "We're here overnight, though. Go to bed."

"You sure?" she asks, flattening one hand against my chest.

"Unless you want to listen to endless, boring details on air traffic control in Russian," I say.

"Not particularly," she says. "You'll be in?"

"Soon, I hope," I say.

I kiss her again and force myself to keep it short and nearly chaste, because Niko's waiting.

"Call me if you break the cable again," she says, and walks out.

I watch her go, disappearing into the pitch-dark dormitory room. Then I turn and look at the back of the monitor, which is half-covered with some sort of duct tape harness keeping the cable in place.

I'm probably going to be hearing about that soon, but right now, I still don't care.

I un-mute myself and sit. Niko sighs.

"Okay," he says. "Status report…"

After forty-five minutes, Niko's finally gone through everything important. He's got circles under his eyes, and I probably do too.

I sign off and walk back into the main room of the bunker, open a cabinet, grab a flashlight, and then hit the lights. Everything plunges into pure, inky blackness, the kind of darkness that only exists when you're fifty feet underground, so thick it feels like it's running through your fingers.

I turn the flashlight on for a moment, see where the furniture is, and turn it off again. Even as a kid I kind of liked the dark, because it made me feel invisible, and sometimes that was what I wanted.

Then, in the Guard, that comfort with the dark came in handy night after night when there were no fires, no lights, not even cigarettes for fear that the enemy could spot us. Some of the men I served with still sleep with a nightlight on, but I've never been able to do that.

At the door of the dormitory I flick the flashlight on again and point the beam at the floor. In the reflected light, in the last of the eight bunk beds, I can see Hazel curled up under an army-green blanket, her hair fanned out behind her.

I turn it off and run my hand over each bunk bed until I get to the one next to hers, where I strip and pull back the scratchy sheets, get in, and stare at the bottom of the bed above me even though I can't see it.

A few feet to my left, Hazel shifts in her sleep. Then she shifts again, and sighs.

"That's you, right?" she says.

"Reporting in," I say.

"I couldn't sleep," she says, her voice quiet and dreamy in the big space.

Her bed creaks, and I hear her shift again, and then her hand's on my shoulder.

"God, it's dark," she says. "I can't see my hand in front of my face."

I scoot over and she gets into bed next to me, gingerly feeling out where I am.

"Just for a minute," she says. "Then I'll get in my own bed."

"You're not afraid of the dark, are you?" I ask, rolling onto my side.

I put one hand on her belly, and she puts a hand over it. She's wearing a t-shirt from one of the dressers down here, underwear, and nothing else.

"Not anymore," she says. "When I was a kid, at my first-ever sleepover, my friend convinced me that all closets were portals to monster-world, and when it was dark, they'd slowly push the door open, come out, and eat me."

A sleepover? I think.

I've seen them in movies, but I never spent the night at a friend's house when I was a child.

"Not a very good friend," I say.

"I think we were six," she says. "And I got over it."

"Americans really have sleepovers?" I ask.

Hazel laughs.

"What do you mean?" she says.

"You go to someone else's house, eat pizza and watch movies, and then sleep there?"

"Yeah," she says, sounding confused. "Well, not as adults, but we do it all the time as kids."

She pauses.

"Why?"

"I always thought they were made up for movies, like pie-eating contests, or beer pong," I admit. "I never attended a sleepover. I don't think they happen here."

Now she's laughing even harder, her stomach shaking under my hand.

"You laugh at me too much," I say, nuzzling my forehead into her hair.

It's not true. Even though I'm always puzzled, I'm getting attached to the sound of her laugh, the way her eyes crinkle at the corners, and I'm always surprised at what she finds funny.

"I thought you'd been to the U.S. a couple of times," she says.

"I have," I say. "Everyone is too friendly, but the burgers are delicious and you're very orderly drivers."

"Pie-eating contests and beer pong are also both real," she says.

I exhale into her hair.

"Really?"

"Really."

"People make pies only to see who can eat them the fastest?" I ask.

I've never made a pie, but I understand it to be a time-intensive process.

"Yup," says Hazel.

"And people also toss balls into cups full of beer and then drink them," I say.

"Also yes," says Hazel.

"Why not just drink the beer?"

She pauses for a long time.

"Because there's an added element of fun, I guess," she says. "It's sort of competitive, and silly, but it also gets you drunk?"

"But you could just get drunk," I point out.

"Sure, we could all sit around drinking vodka alone, stoically looking at pictures of our dead ancestors," she says. "Or we could enjoy ourselves."

"Now you're making fun of me," I say.

"You can be very serious sometimes," she says.

I stroke her stomach with my thumb and think for a moment. I *should* be trying to get some sleep, but I'd rather lie here, talking to Hazel.

"Are cowboys real?" I ask.

She drums her fingers against mine.

"They used to be," she says. "It's a job that doesn't really exist any more."

"Prom?" I ask.

"Yes," she says. "Think of it as a masquerade ball, without masks, for teenagers."

She's teasing me again.

"*I'm* not throwing the ball," I say. "I didn't even remember it was soon."

"I didn't think masquerade balls were real," Hazel admits. "Especially the part where I have to actually wear a mask."

"This is only the second that's been held," I say. "The first was last year. Before that, the last was probably more than a hundred years ago."

"Why'd they start again?"

I sigh.

"Yelena," I say. "She wanted it, so her father convinced mine that it would be symbolic of the return of the monarchy, remind the people of old times, inspire national pride, that sort of thing."

"And you disagree."

"I think the people would rather have their roads kept free of potholes," I say into her hair.

Hazel wiggles, turning onto her side so that I'm spooning her, my arm tight around her chest.

"It'll at least be something to tell people about," she says. "I went to a real castle, met a real prince, went to a real masquerade ball. God, it sounds like Cinderella or something."

"I don't remember the Soviet bunker in Cinderella," I say.

"She didn't smoke pot on the roof either," Hazel says. She sounds like she's starting to drift to sleep, and I can feel my body finally giving up.

As small as this bed is, it's warm and cozy with her against me, her body fitted perfectly to mine.

"In the original version, her stepsisters cut off their toes to fit the slipper and it filled with blood," I say.

Hazel squeezes my hand in hers.

"Kostya, you say the weirdest shit," she says.

"It didn't work," I say. "The prince still knew the right girl."

There's a long, long pause.

"Was it because she still had toes?" Hazel finally asks.

"You need toes to be a queen," I say. I can feel sleep tugging at me, and I'm not sure I'm making much sense.

"I should get in the other bed so you can sleep," Hazel says.

"Two more minutes," I say, and pull her tighter against me.

I JERK awake when the phone rings. We're still in the same position, and half my joints are creaky. My left arm is completely asleep, and Hazel kicks my shin as she wakes up.

It rings again.

"Is that the phone?" she asks.

I sit on the edge of the bed and find the flashlight on the floor, turn it on, and shine it at the ceiling so the light reflects.

"I'll get it," I say, and walk for the office, wearing

nothing but my boxers. Hazel pads along behind me and slumps tiredly onto a wooden bench when I answer the phone.

"You can come out," Chief Minister Arkady says. "It was just one crazy person. Everything else was smoke with no fire. Security council meeting in thirty minutes, and your father wants to see you first."

We hang up. Hazel leans against the concrete wall, yawning.

"All clear," I say, offering her my hand. "They're waiting for us."

She takes it, and I pull her up. Hazel slides her arms around my waist.

"I'm sorry your dad got shot at, but I'm glad we got to be in a bunker together," she says.

I kiss her, long and slow, ignoring my erection.

"I'll think differently about desks forever," I say.

"And desk chairs," she says.

"I don't know if I'll see you before the ball," I say. "I have a feeling I'll be kept busy."

"It's okay," she says. "There's a country to run and everything."

"Save me a dance," I say. "Royal orders."

Hazel rolls her eyes, but she's smiling.

THE AIR outside the bunker smells incredible, like roses and lilacs and baking pies and sunshine. When we come out, Hazel and I walk together to the wing of the palace where the living quarters are, and then give each other a polite, cordial good-bye. I force myself not to watch her walk away.

In the rest of the palace, everything seems oddly normal. Anna's at her desk outside my father's office.

"Good to see you're well, Konstantin Grigorovich," she says, nodding once.

"You as well, Anna," I say.

"He's expecting you," she says.

I steel myself, because I have a feeling that this isn't going to be pleasant, and push his door open.

"Father," I say.

"Konstantin," he says, still writing something at his desk.

Shit. It's never good when either of my parents uses my full name.

"Sit," he orders me.

My father finishes writing something, folds it into an envelope, seals it, puts it aside, and reaches into a desk drawer.

A moment later, my leather jacket is flying at me, and I snatch it out of the air by reflex. I'd completely forgotten about it.

"A mechanic found that yesterday on that piece of shit you insist on keeping in the garage," he says.

"I went for a ride," I say.

"To where?" he asks. His hands are on the desk and his back is perfectly straight. Even though he's almost seventy, my father's always had an imposing, commanding presence.

We don't always get along, but I've always respected *that.* It's a good thing to cultivate if you're going to rule.

"I rode to the sea cliffs and back," I lie.

He leans forward slightly.

"You must think I'm stupid," he says, his voice very soft. "So I'll let you try that again."

"I'm not a prisoner here," I say, even though I know avoiding an answer is the same as admitting guilt. "There's no law against taking a ride at night."

He stands, thrusting his chair back, and begins pacing behind his massive, ornately carved desk.

"You were in the gray district," he says, barely-controlled

fury in his voice. "You were seen at an illegal drinking establishment. You, the heir to the throne, were *flagrantly disobeying* your own laws."

I nearly say *they're your laws*, but it sounds childish, so I bite it back.

"I disagree with those laws," I say, simply.

"I don't care," my father says. He's still pacing. "They're the laws, and until I'm dead and you're on the throne, Konstantin, they are your laws."

"Are you going to threaten my claim to the throne again?" I ask.

He laughs, hollowly.

"I don't make threats for show, Konstantin," he says.

"You would throw the country into civil war over me getting a drink with my friends?" I ask, and I stand as well, my jacket clenched tightly in my fist.

"Once the people know you're a degenerate with a taste for American pussy, how many do you think will side with you?" he snarls.

"I've been perfectly polite to Miss Sung," I say through my teeth.

"You stare at her like you're a dog and she's a bitch in heat," he says, disdain dripping from his voice. "And you don't know the first thing about her."

I know way fucking more than you think.

"She's a foreigner in a strange country, and I've helped her get settled here," I say. I'm trying to control myself, but my voice is shaking with fury.

A bitch in heat. If he were anyone but my father, I'd have punched him already.

My father puts both hands on the desk and leans over it.

"You can have anyone you want except the diplomat's daughter," he says. "And what do you do?"

"Would you rather I get someone pregnant so I'm forced to marry them?" I ask.

"Careful," he says.

"It worked for you," I say. "Now you've got a docile queen, an heir, and a spare."

"That's right," he says, his voice getting dangerous. "I took back what was mine and I made you so you could rule it when I'm gone. And it's your job to do the same. A Svelorian heir. With a Svelorian girl, not this idiot who thinks she can drink like a man. Lust after someone who won't cause an international crisis, Konstantin. You're dismissed."

I turn and walk out, too furious for my brain to form words. I nod curtly at Anna, who must have been able to hear the shouting, but who says nothing to me.

I've got fifteen minutes until a full day of endless meetings, briefings, people buzzing on about one thing or another until my brain turns to mush, but I go to my rooms and stand on the balcony, elbows on the railing, overlooking the Black Sea.

I don't understand my father. At this point, I don't think I ever will. He got shot yesterday, but now all he wants to talk about is whether I'm sleeping with Hazel. There are problems in the country, real, terrible problems, and he's concerning himself with my love life.

I take a deep breath of the salty air. I flex my hands against the railing. I need to have a good shooting session. I need to go for a run somewhere and just be alone in stillness.

I need to stop thinking about last night, about Hazel saying *I'm a shark*, about her getting into bed next to me in the pitch black darkness. I rub both hands over my face, like that will help.

Then I take a fast shower, put on fresh clothes, and go do a full day of prince shit.

CHAPTER TWENTY-THREE
HAZEL

My parents hug me for about half an hour. They seem slightly unhappy that it was just Kostya and I in the bunker, but I go on and on about how *boring* it was, how all there was to do were puzzles and the dictionary, and how he was busy the whole time and didn't have any time to even talk to me.

I'm not totally sure whether they buy it or not, but I give it my best shot.

As I'm leaving their quarters, my mother calls out to me.

"Your afternoon activities are still scheduled, by the way," she says.

I take a deep, calming breath before I turn around.

"And what are those?" I ask.

"Dancing lessons and a mani-pedi," she says. "They're on the schedule I slipped under your door yesterday afternoon."

"I've been in a bunker," I say.

"Me too," she says.

She has a point.

"Okay," I say. "Thanks."

Needless to say, the dancing lessons aren't as fun as the one Kostya gave me, but they're probably more useful. Best of all, the dancing instructor, a tiny old man with enormous glasses, promises me that the modern, young people aren't very strict at all about their dancing.

Sounds perfect.

The woman who does my nails clicks her tongue disapprovingly at my short, unimpressive nails. She tries to shape them the best she can, then paints them bright, stop-sign red without even asking. By the time I realize what she's doing, it's too late to stop her, so I just let it happen.

I know I'm going to chip half of them by the time the masquerade happens anyway, so it isn't like it matters that much.

When I get back to my room, schooled and polished, I'm a little disappointed that there's no note from Kostya under my door. I know he's busy, and I know he has things to do besides flirt with me, but I was still secretly hoping.

Then it's late, and I'm exhausted, so I fall into bed.

At 7:30 the next morning, there's a knock on my door. I'm awake, but still lying in bed, staring at the ceiling, so I roll out of bed.

The knock sounds again.

"Coming!" I shout.

Maybe it's Kostya, I think as I grab the black silk robe that came with the room.

It's not. It's Irina, the palace seamstress, and she's got a rack of clothes behind her.

"Good morning," she says.

"I already picked a gown," I say, my brain not fully firing yet.

"Yes," she says. "Alterations are ready and you need to try it on again."

"Right," I say. "Uh, please, come in."

Five minutes later, I'm standing in nothing but my underwear as Irina applies double-sided tape to something that looks a little like a dead jellyfish, but firmer. I'm not awake enough to protest any of this, and besides, she seems like this is a normal thing for her to do before eight in the morning.

"Arms up," she commands, and I lift my arms over my head. She plonks both jellyfish onto my boobs and then squeezes them.

It's the least sexy I've ever felt while rounding second base, that's for sure.

After a moment, she steps back and examines her work.

"Much better," she says, nodding.

Irina orders me into the dress, and then spends several moments examining parts of my body up close, including the way a seam wrinkles directly over the curve of my ass. After a bit, she seems to decide it's okay, and I look over my shoulder into the mirror.

Oh shit, I think.

The dress looked fine before alterations, but *hello*, bootylicious.

Irina sees me looking and almost smiles.

"This dress is a husband-finder," she says, and gives my butt a friendly pat.

I GET a break for a couple of hours, but still no correspondence from Kostya.

It's not like he's some guy who didn't text you, I think. *You're fucking in secret while he runs a country. He probably couldn't send a note without getting busted.*

Starting in the early afternoon, my mom's lined up a whole beauty *regimen*, even though I begged her not to, pointing out that I've got eyeliner already. She just told me to relax and enjoy being pampered, so that's what I try to do as a very friendly woman wearing a leopard-print bustier puts curlers in my hair and applies layer after layer of makeup.

On layer two, I'm nervous. By layer four, even though she won't show me yet, I'm certain that I look like a cartoon panda, and I'm panicking. There are false eyelashes. There is a worrying color of eyeshadow, but every time I try to stop her, she just tells me to trust her.

It's the same thing for my hair. I try to tell her that when I wear it up, I prefer to wear it lower and not piled on top of my head, but does she listen? Fuck no.

Finally, she spins my chair toward the mirror, and I hold my breath in horror.

Staring back at me is a hooker from an 80's movie. She used the wrong shade of foundation, and since she wanted to cover my freckles, she used a *lot* of it and I look like a garish clown. I've got the wrong shade of blush on, along with blue eyeshadow that's nowhere near the actual contours of my eyes.

And my hair. Jesus, my hair. It's a pile of awful curls on top of my head. I hate every single thing about this.

"What do you *think*?" she asks, grinning.

I force myself to smile back, because I can't change this now.

"Great!" I say.

The moment I'm out of her sight, I *run* to my room. I'm still getting the foundation off when there's a knock on my door.

"Hazel?" my mom calls.

"Come in!" I shout.

I hear her walking through the rooms.

"We should go in a few—"

She stops short, and I can see her over my shoulder in the bathroom mirror.

"Oh, dear," she says.

"Help," I say, desperately.

She steps up behind me and surveys my hair as I wipe blush off myself.

"You do your face. I think I can give you a passable chignon with this mess," she says.

"Okay," I say.

Sometimes it's useful to have a mom who plans. Ten minutes later, my hair is in a not-fancy-but-perfectly-nice knot at the base of my neck, my face is clean of foundation, and I'm leaning toward the mirror, swiping on eyeliner. I kept the fake eyelashes, but ditched pretty much everything else.

Finally I step back and look at myself.

"*Much* better," my mom says. "I'm so sorry. She was highly recommended."

She points at the bed.

"Dress, stick-on-bra, underwear, shoes, necklace, earrings, mask," she says. "We'll meet you in five. I gotta go put my own mask on."

"I can't believe there's masks," I mutter.

"They can be very traditional," she says, giving me a light hug. "By the way, the Queen says that a few pieces of double-sided tape under the mask works wonders."

I make a face, and my mom laughs as she leaves. I get dressed like lightning, and check myself out in the mirror.

From prostitute to class act in fifteen minutes, I think. *Thank god for teamwork.*

Then I stick the mask on my face and fly out the door.

WHEN WE WALK into the ballroom, I think two things right away.

One, it's enormous and beautiful, crystal chandeliers hanging from the ceiling, tall windows looking out over the ocean, a string quartet playing on stage. The woodwork is all beautifully carved, obviously something else they managed to save from the Soviets.

Two, with everyone wearing these lace masks over their eyes, I feel like I'm walking into a weird sex club with my parents. It's not a feeling I really enjoy, and I wonder if I'm the only one thinking it.

I hope I'm the only one thinking it.

We run the gauntlet of officials and high-ranking people, and of course my parents have to stop and have a quick chat with everyone. More than one mostly-drunk old man gives me an up-and-down look and then tells me to save a dance for him, and it makes me feel slimy, but I smile and agree while hoping he'll forget.

The whole time I'm smiling, saying niceties in Russian, and scanning the room. I have no idea if Kostya's here yet, but I feel like a pre-teen with a crush at a middle school dance, my heart beating fast and my palms sweaty.

I thought I'd feel half naked with my low-backed dress, but looking around, I feel like a nun. All the women here are wearing brightly-colored dresses, hair piled high, cleavage on full display.

Yet again I feel like an alien who's just come to Earth to observe human behavior, because Svelorians are confusing as hell. On one hand, women aren't supposed to curse, they don't drink vodka, they're demure and polite and always dressed to the nines.

But on the other hand, my backless, bootylicious dress may as well be a paper bag here. At least *now* I understand why Irina was so concerned about my bust.

I sneak a glance down. They're not winning any prizes, but they... exist.

Better too conservative than too slutty, I tell myself.

Can you imagine if you showed up with your tits half out and everyone else was wearing high-necked Elizabethan gowns?

Another old man shakes my hand, kisses my cheek, and touches my shoulder a little too long, but then I finally spy Kostya, taking a glass of champagne from a tray. My heart does a little flip in my chest, and I stare a little too long, because he's wearing his military dress uniform and *damn*.

God *damn*.

Then he hands the glass of champagne to Yelena, standing right next to him, and I force myself not to make a face.

"Everything all right, Miss Sung?" the man says.

I look at him, smile, and nod.

"Good," he says, and grins lecherously to me.

I walk away, following my parents, but I sneak a look back at Kostya. Now he's drinking his own champagne. His mask is solid black, more *Zorro* than sex club.

Just as I'm about to turn my head, he looks right at me. I swallow hard and look away, forcing myself not to smile.

CHAPTER TWENTY-FOUR
KOSTYA

"Kostya," says Yelena's soft voice.

"Yes?" I ask.

After one more moment I tear my eyes away from Hazel's back. Her dress ends right above those two dimples, and just thinking about them makes my mouth go a little dry.

"Is something wrong?" she asks, her big blue eyes looking up at me.

For at least the twentieth time in the past week, I feel guilty for how I treat Yelena. Just because I don't find her attractive or interesting doesn't mean I should be openly gawking at someone else while I'm escorting her at the masquerade ball *she* organized.

"I haven't been sleeping well," I say, which is at least true. Last night I wasn't in bed until nearly four in the morning, and I wake up by six at the latest, no matter what.

She pats my arm.

"I've arranged for Turkish coffee in the gallery at ten," she says. "Though I'm afraid it will smell too strongly, and then the drapes in there will never let go of the scent."

"I'm sure it will dissipate after a few days," I say, and Yelena heaves a sigh.

She's dressed like most of the women here: a bright red dress, hair piled elaborately on her head. The neckline on her dress isn't as drastic as most, but there's more than a hint of cleavage visible, and it pushes upward every time she breathes.

I dart my eyes at the spot where Hazel was again, but she's gone.

"There's Vika and Sasha," Yelena says, suddenly perking up. "Let's go say hello."

I'M STARTING to feel like I'm playing hide-and-seek with Hazel. Yelena is still talking to her friends, the other daughters of rich men, and even though I've had two more glasses of champagne they're still not interesting.

I keep catching glimpses of black lace swishing through the crowd, and it's starting to drive me mad. To make matters worse, my father is here, my mother on his arm, striding back and forth and watching everything with his unpleasant hawk's gaze.

If I had any goddamn sense at all, I'd slip Hazel a note and show up in her bedroom later.

If I had *good* sense, I'd stop this completely.

"Excuse me," I say to Yelena.

I bow my head slightly and then walk away before she can protest that she wants to come with me. I don't know who told her it was attractive to act like a barnacle — probably her father — but someone did.

In one corner, my father is speaking with a few old men in one circle, their wives clustered together next to them. I keep scanning the crowd, hoping that I haven't escaped just as Hazel accepted a dance with someone else.

Since I have to look like I'm going somewhere, I head toward the bar, where a server in a tuxedo is standing in front of an enormous fountain pumping pink champagne punch. The thing is hundreds of years old and so gaudy it must have embarrassed even *my* ancestors, but it's present at every formal event in this palace.

By the time I walk up, he's already poured a champagne glass full of the punch, and he hands it to me, dipping his head.

"Your highness," he says.

I nod back.

"Is *that* who you are?" says a familiar voice behind me, and I turn.

"Miss Sung," I say, as formally as I can.

"Konstantin Grigorovich," she says. "I assume, anyway, with the mask and everything."

I hold out my right hand, and she takes it like we're about to shake hands on a business deal, but I bring it to my lips and kiss her knuckles longer than I should, her skin cool and soft under my hand.

Her eyes flick to my knuckles. They're almost healed, just ugly shades of yellow and blue now.

"Can I offer you a glass of punch?" I ask. "It's an ancient family recipe."

"Thank you," she says.

I take the glass of pink liquid from the server. Hazel thanks him, and we step away to stand beside a cocktail table. We're surrounded by people on all sides, and I know for a fact that anywhere I go in this ball people are looking at me, watching what the prince does.

Maybe that's why I like the dark so much. I can do what I want.

"Is it appropriate to toast with pink punch?" she asks, looking into her glass.

"Vodka is preferable, of course," I say. "Though this is mostly vodka."

"I thought this was champagne punch," she says, twirling the glass in her hand.

"We rarely pass up a chance to add vodka to something," I say.

She looks down at her drink, and even though the mask makes it hard to tell, I think she's smiling a little.

"Thanks for the warning," she says. "I'll try not to make another spectacle of myself."

I hold the glass up, just slightly.

"To my father, may he live to be an old man," I say. It's a very correct first toast.

"*Nah zdrovya*," says Hazel. We both take a sip.

"And to bunkers," I say, lowering my voice.

Hazel swallows, and her bottom lip twitches, like she's trying not to smile.

"To bunkers and desks and office chairs," she says, and we both drink.

"Are you enjoying the masquerade?" I ask. I feel like an idiot, trying to make pointless small talk with Hazel, but I have to act like we're friendly acquaintances at best.

"It's quite a spectacle," she says. "I feel a little like a pigeon in a flock of peacocks, to be honest."

I look at her, then let my eyes travel slowly down her body, making sure she sees me do it.

"You're a lovely pigeon," I say, already desperately fighting an erection. God, I should have taped my dick down or something.

She laughs, but under her mask she's turning pink.

"Thank you," she says. "Maybe pigeon was the wrong bird. Maybe I'm more of a duck."

Her eyes are sparkling behind her lace mask.

So this is how we're going to do it, I think.

"Or a shark," I say.

"Why would I compare a shark to a peacock?" she asks, tilting her head like it's an innocent question. "Sharks aren't even birds."

"Peacocks are barely birds," I say. "The pretty ones can't even fly. Better to be a duck. Then it doesn't matter if you get a little wet."

I swear I feel a prickle on the side of my neck, and I try to ignore it.

Hazel laughs and looks away briefly, like she's trying not to be embarrassed.

"I shouldn't have started talking about birds in the middle of the ball," she says, and takes a sip of champagne. "How dull."

"I disagree," I say, trying not to smile. "I find ducks *fascinating*."

"Now you're making fun of me," she says.

"Only because it's my turn at last," I say.

There's a pause. We both take a deep breath and look down, because this has gone quickly from small talk between acquaintances to something *much* more familiar.

"Are you enjoying the ball?" she asks.

I want to say *I am now that you're here*, but I don't.

"Of course," I say. "I always enjoy hosting formal events."

My neck prickles again, and this time I can't help but look.

My father's glaring at me from clear across the room. I turn my head back to Hazel, tamping down my anger.

"You do seem suited to it," she says, and I know she's making fun of me again, but I can't say anything.

"Thank you," I say, and drain my glass of pink punch, setting it on the table. "I should return to my date, I'm afraid I've left her alone for too long."

"Of course," she says, her tone suddenly stiff and formal.

"Give me your hand," I say, my voice as quiet as I can make it.

She does, and I kiss it again, only letting my lips brush her knuckles.

"You'd better save me a dance," I say to her hand, then straighten.

"You'd better behave yourself," she says, fighting a smile again.

Then I walk back to Yelena's side, my father's eyes tracking me the entire time.

ONCE THE DANCING starts in earnest, I'm in hell. Since Hazel doesn't have a date to the masquerade, every dirty old man in the whole place asks the American girl to dance.

I dance with Yelena, I dance with her friends, I dance with a whole slew of pretty, unmemorable girls with rich fathers, and I watch other men get to put their hands on Hazel's bare back while I have to pretend like I can't even see her.

We switch partners. Hazel dances with Niko and I dance with his girlfriend Marina.

"I heard you got caught the other night," she says. "Niko told me."

"Someone recognized me," I say.

"It's a real drag, being the prince," she says, totally deadpan.

"Tell Niko to go back to his dirt farm and abandon his dreams," I say.

We keep chatting. The dance ends, and I start leading Marina over to Niko and Hazel. I can propose we swap partners and not set off any alarms.

She gives me a look that makes my toes tingle. Then

someone touches her shoulder and she turns toward him, accepting the next dance.

I almost growl.

Marina dances with someone else, and I'm about to stand on the sidelines and simply watch when my mother comes over and looks at me.

Then she clears her throat.

"Mother, would you like to dance?" I ask, humoring her.

"As long as you're asking," she says.

I hold out my hand, she takes it, and we start moving around the floor again.

"Your father's not going to change his mind, you know," she says suddenly.

"About what?" I ask.

"About anything," she says. "He's a strong willed bastard, Kostya, and you know it."

I just look at her, taken aback. I've never heard my mother say *bastard* before, but she just gives me an *oh, please* look.

"He's not the only one," I say.

"You don't have to win," she says. "You just have to ride it out. Trust me."

I nod.

"He's not going to disown you," she says, her voice getting softer. "He's stubborn, not stupid."

"Those two things seem very similar sometimes," I say.

"They are," she says. "And don't let him bully you into marrying the wrong person. That won't work out for you any better than it did for me."

I look at her, surprised. She's never spoken to me this frankly before, and even though I knew she and my father hadn't been happy for years, I'm amazed she's saying this out loud.

"I love you and Misha, but if I could go back, I'd turn down the handsome solider and stay a seamstress," she says quietly. "I know you think you're keeping a secret, but you light up like a lantern around her, Kostya."

I swallow.

"It's that obvious?" I ask.

"Only because I'm your mother," she says.

The dance ends. I kiss her hand.

"Thank you," I say.

Then I look around for Hazel, because fuck it.

CHAPTER TWENTY-FIVE
HAZEL

The king's aide I was dancing with — Viktor, maybe — kisses my hand solemnly, does not smile, and thanks me for a lovely dance. I thank him for the same.

Then I walk off the dance floor. Apparently Svelorian women have cyborg feet, because they've been standing for hours in heels twice as high as mine, and none of them even seem to notice.

I, on the other hand, think I might die. I snag another glass of champagne, my third of the night, from a server with a tray and drink half of it quickly, hoping it helps the pain a little. At least, maybe it'll help me *notice* the pain less.

Then, when I'm nearly clear of the throng of people, someone touches my shoulder.

"Miss Sung," Kostya says.

I turn around. He's holding out his hand, and I put mine in it. He kisses my knuckles.

I swear he's enjoying this whole prince-at-a-ball thing a little too much.

"May I have this dance?" he asks.

It's all I can do not to laugh.

"I'd be honored," I say.

I finish the last sip of champagne and walk back to the dance floor, hand in Kostya's elbow. My whole body feels like it's filled with bees, and I tell myself over and over again that two people are allowed to dance at a masquerade ball. That's what people *do* here.

We get into position. My feet still hurt, but now at least I'm distracted as I look into his gray eyes. He strokes my shoulder blade with his thumb.

The music starts and we dance. He pulls me closer, a little too close, his mouth a few inches from my ear.

"That dress makes me want to bend you over the dessert table and bury my cock in you until you come screaming my name," he murmurs.

I trip over my own foot.

Kostya steadies me with his hand on my back, even as heat slides through me like a lava flow. I glance around nervously, but no one is showing a sign that they heard him.

"God *dammit*," I whisper.

He doesn't say anything, but his eyes are smiling as he looks at me.

"I guess you're really Prince Kostya behind that mask and not an imposter," I say a moment later when I've regained my composure.

"That's not proof," he says, totally straight faced. "I'm sure I'm not the only man here who's had that thought."

I scrunch my nose a little, and I see a smile flicker around his mouth.

"If I wanted to prove it, I'd tell you what you looked like in nothing but tube socks," he says.

"Lucky for you I'm the real Hazel," I say. "What if I were some official's wife?"

"Then you would be *very* scandalized," he says.

"I *am* scandalized," I say. "I nearly fell over."

"You were just surprised," he says. "It's different. If you were scandalized, you wouldn't be thinking about it right now."

I swallow, squeeze his hand slightly, and glance at the loaded dessert tables. I imagine myself pressing my face into the white tablecloth, clutching it in one hand as I moan, Kostya fucking me hard and deep from behind.

"And they say chivalry is dead," I manage to say.

"I'd make sure you come first," he says. "Chivalrous enough?"

His fingers curl slightly against my back, and I glance around the floor full of dancing couples, desperately wishing that they would all disappear.

"Which dessert table?" I ask.

"The sturdiest one," he says.

"Not the closest?"

"I'd walk an extra twenty feet to make sure I fucked you right," he says.

"I do appreciate a job well done," I say, my pulse racing.

We dance for a moment without speaking, and I just savor being close to him, even in public. I can feel eyes on us from the sidelines, or should I say: eyes on Kostya. There's Yelena, and there are her friends, the other girls the king's tried to push on Kostya.

My parents. My mom meets my eyes and gives me one of those *mom knows everything* looks, and I try to ignore it.

There's the King, looking unhappy.

He'd look *considerably* unhappier if he knew what his son had just said to me. I look away and pretend I can't see him.

The music begins to slow, and Kostya presses his fingers into my back a little harder, like he doesn't want to let go.

"Thank you for the dance," he says.

"You're welcome," I say. "I only tripped once, and it was your fault."

"I could make you trip again," he says, his voice low.

"Not now that I'm expecting it," I say, forcing myself to keep a straight face, because smiling at the prince has to look suspicious as hell.

"I knew you weren't scandalized, *zloyushka*," he says.

The music stops. We wait a beat too long, then separate. He kisses my hand again and then someone's there, talking to him, and he gets pulled away for another dance. I melt back into the crowd and finally find a place to sit down.

FIFTEEN MINUTES LATER, the doors to the gallery open and the smell of coffee wafts in. The ballroom begins to empty slightly, so I take a deep breath, heave myself to my feet, and make my way out there.

The gallery is hot, steamy, and I don't want coffee this late at night, so I go back to the ballroom. Before I know it I'm at the dessert table, and my toes curl as I wonder which one is the sturdiest.

Stop it, I think. *You're in public.*

I grab a few morsels and open the door onto the patio by the garden. It's cool outside but not cold, and I wander a bit until I find a bench hidden away in a nook and collapse onto it, slumping and leaning my head against the stone wall of the castle. I breathe in the rose-scented air from the garden, then lean down, take both my shoes off, and wiggle my toes freely for the first time in hours.

It feels so good I don't hear the footsteps. I don't even know anyone else is there until I hear him chuckling.

"Americans," Kostya says, and I open my eyes.

"Don't you have official prince business?" I tease. "Or something better to do than come find me in my moment of weakness?"

"I didn't have to find you," he says, and sits down next to me. "My eyes have been glued to your ass for *hours*."

"It does look pretty good in this dress," I admit.

Kostya just grins.

"And you said you were a pigeon," he says, and I laugh.

"It's true," I say. "Everyone seems so uptight, but then I get to a formal event and the women *all* have their tits out."

I sigh.

"I don't get it," I say.

He leans back against the wall, tilting his head against mine.

"Still not stranger than pie-eating contests," he says, taking my hand in his and lacing our fingers together. I laugh and squeeze his fingers.

"Pie is delicious," I say. "It's not that strange."

"But if you're eating as part of a contest, you're not enjoying the pie," he says. "It may as well be sawdust."

"I can't really defend pie-eating contests," I admit. "I'm barely American."

"Why?" he asks. "You seem very American."

"Because I'm loud, friendly, and don't know my manners?" I ask.

"You wore spandex pants to meet the royal family," he says.

I sigh.

"I barely lived there until I was a teenager because of my mom," I say. "We lived in Croatia for a while, then Poland. Ireland. Brazil. Then they sent me to boarding school."

"Your parents did?" he asks, sounding puzzled.

I nod.

"They wanted me to have at least a couple years of stability," I say. "Where I could make friends and keep them for a while. Stay in one place for a couple years, at least."

I swallow and look ahead, remembering that first day.

Getting off the plane in Boston, my parents helping me set up a room, and then driving away. Me feeling like an alien with all the other American teenagers.

"I think it was pretty hard for them," I say.

"What about you?" he asks.

"It was hard at first," I say. "But I got used to it. Then I got kicked out when I got caught smoking pot on school grounds."

"I knew it," he says. "Bad from the beginning."

"It turned out you needed richer parents than I had to get away with that kind of thing," I say. "So I went to another one and didn't get caught."

He chuckles.

"Of course," he says.

"You went to boarding school too, right?" I ask.

"Only one, in Switzerland," he says. "I didn't get kicked out."

"You were probably quarterback of the football team, valedictorian, and class president," I tease.

"Rugby," he says. "I don't think I broke a rule until I was twenty-three."

"And now you've broken at *least* a couple," I say. "Better stop now or you'll develop a taste for it."

He brings my hand to his mouth and kisses it.

"Too late," he says. "You're a very bad influence, *zloyushka.*"

"Good," I say. "You needed one."

He kisses me briefly, both of us still leaning against the wall.

"I'm coming over tonight," he says, lowering his voice.

I can't help but smile.

"You don't have to escort Yelena home or something?" I ask.

A tiny twinge of jealousy worms its way through my chest, but I ignore it.

"I might," he says. "But I'm coming all the same."

We kiss again, longer this time, his lips moving against mine before we pull back.

"Keep your dress on," he says, his voice dropping. "I want to take it off you with my teeth."

My whole body flushes with heat.

"Then don't take too long," I say. "I've waited enough already."

We kiss, longer and slower. He puts his hand to my face and runs his thumb slowly along my cheekbone, just underneath my mask.

"I should go before someone comes looking for me," he says when he pulls back.

"We could go to my room now and you could make excuses later," I say. "It's better to apologize than ask permission, you know."

Kostya just chuckles, his voice low and gravelly, and kisses me again.

"Keep the dress on," he whispers, and stands, straightening his uniform. I stay on the bench, kicking my feet.

As he turns to leave, his back suddenly straightens and his face goes stony. A bad feeling gathers in the pit of my stomach, and I sit up straight and slide my feet into my shoes.

Please not his father, I think.

"Yelena," Kostya says.

That's better, but not by much.

She answers him in Russian, her sweet voice soft and confused. Then she walks forward, sees me, and freezes.

"Good evening, Miss Sung," she says, still very formal with me.

She reaches out and takes Kostya's arm, her eyes flicking from me to him and back, like she's trying to add something together and can't quite manage it.

"Good evening, Yelena Pavlovna," I say, and stand in my

unfastened shoes. I hope I don't need to take a step, because I'll fall over.

She looks up at him.

"Your father asked me to find you. He's giving a toast before the final dance."

Kostya nods once.

"Of course," he says. "It was a pleasure talking to you, Hazel."

"You as well, Kostya," I say.

Yelena gives me one last glance, and they walk away. I sit heavily on the bench and stare at the stonework path for a moment, trying not to think *what if she'd come thirty seconds earlier*.

I refasten my shoes, take a deep breath, and delicately scratch my face underneath my mask.

We're not keeping this secret, I think. *Just because I haven't actually told anyone doesn't mean they haven't found out.*

Hell, Yelena, his *actual* date to this event, came about ten seconds too late to catch us making out. This secret thing isn't *working*.

I walk back toward the ball, just as Kostya escorts Yelena back into the ballroom through the open glass doors. I don't want to be jealous, but right in that instant, I *am*.

I'm stupidly, childishly, petulantly jealous that she gets to have him escort her around, that she can come find him if she wants. That she gets him in public and I get him in garages and bunkers, after midnight, in the dark.

Put on your big girl panties, Hazel, I think.

Then I walk into the ballroom and listen to toasts.

I WALK with my parents back to the guest wing of the palace. The moment we're out of sight of Svelorians, I make my parents wait for me to take off my shoes, then stretch my toes against the wooden floor.

"I don't know how those women do it," I say. "They're robots, Mom. Robots with robot feet."

She laughs.

"They're just used to wearing heels," she says.

"I gotta say, being a man is pretty great," my dad teases. "No heels, no childbirth..."

"Shut *up*," my mom and I say in unison.

Then we laugh again. We're both slightly tipsy. I think she's still relieved that the assassination attempt turned out to be nothing, and I've got my own reasons for being in a great mood.

We reach the junction of the hallway where they go left and I go right, and my mom gives me a hug.

"We'll see you Tuesday," she says.

"Tuesday?" I say.

"The King set up some meetings while he's at the economic summit over the weekend and asked me to join him," she says.

"I just wanted to go to Kiev," my father adds.

It sounds vaguely familiar, so I just nod.

She hugs me again, a little tighter this time.

"Hazel, be safe," she says. "And *behave yourself*."

She emphasizes the last part just a little too much.

"Don't I always?" I ask.

My mom just sighs, then relinquishes me to my dad.

"Stay out of trouble, freckles," he says. "At least try."

We head to our respective rooms. I shut the door and lock it behind me, then toss my shoes under the bed, and get the mask off my face and toss it on the dresser.

I hesitate for a moment, then reach into my dress, unstick the jellyfish bra, and throw it into a drawer. It's not exactly a sexy look.

Then I wonder what I'm supposed to do while I wait.

After a while I settle for reading in a big leather armchair, but I can't focus. I'm reading the same paragraph of *Alice in Wonderland*, the only English book I could find in the Kiev train station before I left, over and over again, listening for a knock on the door.

I read it again. Think about the dessert table. Squirm. Read the paragraph.

I want to take it off you with my teeth.

Read the paragraph again.

There's a noise on the balcony, and I freeze. Even though I'm on the second floor of a literal fortress, I reach up and turn off the light, then turn off all the lights as I move through my rooms, still in my formal gown.

Quietly, I walk to the French doors and stand behind the curtains. Part of me thinks I'm being crazy, and part of me is remembering that *someone* wanted the king dead. Maybe they're trying again and they have the wrong room.

In the corner of the balcony, a hand grips the railing of the balcony, then another. I realize there's a third option and I'm an idiot.

I swing the French doors open and lean in the doorway just as Kostya pulls himself up and over the stonework railing, then stands on the balcony.

His formal jacket is open to his white undershirt and he's breathing hard from the climb, his chest expanding against the thin fabric. Slowly, he reaches up and takes a rose from between his teeth.

If this were in a movie, I'd roll my eyes, but as it is I'm breathless with desire, totally captivated as we stare at each other.

"I told you I was coming," he says, just a hint of a smile on his face.

"I believed you," I say.

Kostya walks toward me across the balcony and holds out the rose. It's ragged at one end where he ripped it from the bush, and I take it from his fingers, my heart beating so hard I can feel it in the soles of my feet.

"You should have told me you were going to climb the balcony," I say, holding the rose up to smell it.

"Why's that?" he asks, but he's smiling.

"I'd have let my hair down so you could climb it," I say.

Kostya puts one fingertip in the hollow of my throat and then slides it down my sternum, still smiling, his eyes lit up like he's laughing at some joke.

I shiver as his finger moves between my breasts, my nipples hardening instantly.

"*Zloyushka*, you're impossible," he says, his voice low and gravelly.

I want to lean back against the doorframe and *beg* him to put his hands on me. I feel like I've been waiting forever for this, and now he's torturing me with one fingertip.

"Why?" I whisper.

"I climbed up a stone wall in my dress uniform, and now you're making fun of me," he teases, moving forward. He's still warm from the climb and I can feel his body heat radiating off of him, making every inch of me feel warm and feverish.

"Don't you think climbing a tower with a rose in your teeth is a little too fairy tale?" I tease back.

He just chuckles, then wraps his hand around my back and pulls me to him.

"If you think I'm here to *rescue* you, you've got the wrong idea," he whispers into my ear.

CHAPTER TWENTY-SIX
KOSTYA

I don't know what's gotten into me. Maybe it's that I've had just enough drinks at the ball to do something crazy and questionable, like climb up a stone wall to a balcony when I could just use the door.

Maybe it's how crazy hot Hazel is, and how I've been wound like a spring for two days now. Maybe I needed to let off some steam before I saw her so I could take my time.

But maybe it's the way she laughs sometimes and I don't know why, but I laugh anyway because she makes me happy. Maybe it's how she swears like a sailor and doesn't bat an eye. Maybe it's how despite all her missteps, the spandex pants and the vodka shots and smoking on the roof, she's more than capable and poised when it matters.

I could have any girl I want, but I want to *win* Hazel.

"Then what are you here to do?" she asks.

I kiss her on *that spot* right below her ear, and she gasps softly.

"I already told you," I say. "I'm here to take your dress off with my teeth, like I promised I would."

I kiss her neck, and I can feel her pulse racing beneath my lips.

"And I'm going to take it off you slow and lick every single inch of your body until you're wound tight enough to snap," I say.

I nip at her collarbone with my teeth, and she makes a soft noise, her fingers clutching at my side. I can't help but chuckle again.

"So you're going to torture me?" she asks, her voice vibrating against my mouth.

"Only for a little while," I say, and put my face to hers, our foreheads touching. "Then I'm going to make you come so hard you forget your own name."

I kiss her and she opens her mouth under mine, like she's desperate to have me inside her *somehow*. Even though my dick is already hard enough to cut glass I go slow, sliding my tongue along her bottom lip and into her mouth before I pull back, both of us breathing hard.

Hazel gives me a long, burning look. Then she takes my hand in hers and leads me from the balcony through her living quarters and to the bedroom, her long dress swishing along the floor, her ass swaying from side to side in her dress.

She doesn't usually walk like that, not even in heels. My mouth goes dry.

The second we're in the bedroom I shut the door and pull her against me. She's still facing away, her back against my front.

I run my hands up her torso slowly, reveling in every inch, over the bottom curve of her breasts until I reach the hard peaks of her nipples. I brush my fingers over them lightly, one by one, and Hazel gasps.

I do it again.

She reaches one hand up and puts it around the back of

my neck, then arches against me. Her breasts press forward into my hands, and her ass is against my erection.

"Not bending you over and fucking you right now might be the hardest thing I've ever done," I murmur.

As I say it, I pinch both her nipples between my fingers and she sighs.

"There's nothing stopping you," she says, her voice low. "For the rest of the night, every time I looked at that dessert table I got a little wetter. Now I'm always going to associate petit-fours with wanting you to fuck me."

Dear *god*, I like hearing her say she wants to fuck me.

"I already told you what I'm going to do," I say.

"You told me you'd take my dress off," she says.

"Impatient," I say.

"Torturer," she says.

Her dress has an eye hook at her neck and then a zipper at her lower back, so I unhook the first with my hands and then hold it there as I get on my knees, take the zipper pull between my teeth, and slide it down, pressing my other thumb into the dimple in her back.

I plant kisses all the way up Hazel's spine, and she arches it slowly as I work my way back to standing and finally let her dress fall to the floor. Now all she's wearing is a thong, and she leans her head against my shoulder, then slides the flat of her hand against my aching erection.

I *growl*, the sound coming from somewhere deep inside my chest, and Hazel laughs softly. She does it again, her palm traveling from root to tip and this time her whole body moves in one slow, sensuous roll, my hands digging into the points of her hips.

I'm starting to wonder if I over-promised, because I don't know how long *I* can last, my cock practically ready to explode. She does it again, her head against my shoulder, her eyes closed, and she bites her lip.

I lean over and kiss her while I slide one hand between her legs. She moans into my mouth, and her panties are so soaked that her thighs are damp. Her body jolts when I run my fingers over the fabric between her legs.

"Is this because of the dessert table?" I ask.

"You make it sound like tiramisu turns me on," she says, sliding her hand down my cock again, her voice low. "It's from looking at the dessert table and thinking about you fucking me."

I rub her lightly through the soaked fabric, and a noise comes out of her throat. I rub harder, then slide my fingers underneath the side of the fabric and touch her skin-to-skin, pushing my fingers back and forth slowly over clit.

Now she's stopped rubbing my cock through my pants and she's just leaning back against my chest, breathing hard, like she's surrendering. I rub her again and she makes a soft moan, her head turned to one side, and I withdraw my hand.

Before Hazel can move I spin her around and kiss her hard, then walk her backwards toward her bed, my mouth still on hers. I toss my jacket behind me without looking and she tugs at my shirt so I take that off too.

I push her further onto the bed and she squeals, then laughs as I bend over and kiss her fiercely on her stomach, expanding and tightening as she breathes, her hands on my head. As I work my way down, past her bellybutton, I can *smell* how aroused she is.

It's intoxicating. Beyond maddening. I nearly lose control and bury my face in her, because what I *want* to do is lick her until she comes again and again. I want to hear her scream as I suck on her clit and I want to put my tongue in her pussy as she clenches around me, because Hazel losing control is the single most beautiful thing I've ever seen, and I'd watch it all day if I could.

I take the band on her thong between my teeth and pull it

off her to the sound of her soft laughter, then push her thighs apart with my hands and kiss the inside of one knee, then the other.

Hazel moans softly and I work my way up, my fingers digging into the soft flesh as I try to slow down and tease her, but I don't know that it's working. I don't even know who I'm torturing any more, me or her, as I finally reach the juncture of her thighs and lick her slowly, the tip of my tongue just barely touching her lips before I roll it over her clit.

A tremor runs through her whole body when I do it, and I hear her breathing hitch.

"Fuck, Kostya," she whispers.

I do it again and again until she groans, and then I force myself to pull back. I trace a circle around her clit with my tongue as she sucks in a breath. After a moment I repeat the cycle, lick-circle-lick-circle, and then I repeat it again and again.

Each time she gets louder, her breathing rougher, I can feel her body tensing. Finally she grabs my head with one hand and when I stop licking her, her fist closes around my hair.

"Fuck!" she shouts, and I can't help but laugh, kissing the soft inside of one thigh as I watch her chest heave.

"I told you what I was going to do," I say. "*Zloyushka*, I could tease you all day and never get tired of watching you come undone."

I'm still wearing pants, and I'm so hard I think my dick might just fall off, but I can't help myself. Watching Hazel like this does something to me I can't explain, lights some fire so far buried inside me that I didn't know it existed.

I lick her again and this time she just says, "Oh..." so softly I can barely hear it, but she lifts her hips toward me like she's pleading with me. This time I take her right to the brink before I stop. Her toes are curled and she's crushing her pillow in one fist, the other still in my hair.

I get my pants and boxers off in half a second and toss the condom from my pocket onto a pillow. She's flushed, her hair wild, and her eyes are half-closed.

"You're a sadist," she whispers as I crawl over her.

"I warned you," I murmur, guiding her hand to my cock. I groan as she wraps her hand around it, and then she strokes me as I kiss her deeply, kneeling between her thighs. I can't keep myself from thrusting into her hand, and she wraps her legs around my hips.

I want to be inside her so bad I can barely breathe, but somehow, I resist.

I break the kiss and reach between her legs again, sliding two fingers into her wet, swollen pussy. I just barely bend them and her eyelids flutter the way they did in the stairwell, so I do it again. This time she grabs the back of my neck and pushes back against my hand, looking at me through half-closed eyes.

My cock throbs, but I force myself to ignore it. I move my fingers again and again, and Hazel's hand drifts from my neck to my shoulder as her hips move faster and harder against my hand. She puts one leg over my shoulder and pushes back hard, like she wants me deeper.

I add a third finger and she groans, eyes closed and her head to one side. Now I'm barely moving my hand at all, because she's doing all the work, moving her hips and fucking herself with my fingers, biting her lip, sighing and moaning.

It's *incredible* to watch, so hot I'm a little afraid I'll come without even getting to fuck her, but I can't stop, like I'm hypnotized by how sexy she is as she moves more and more insistently. I can't believe I'm lucky enough to be here, to be the one watching her fuck my fingers, and flexing her hips hard against my hand half-buried in her tight, warm pussy.

She moves like she *needs* this, like she's barely in control of herself any more.

I bend over to kiss her and she opens her eyes in surprise, going motionless.

"Jesus, don't stop," I whisper. "I could watch you fuck my hand all day."

She swallows, then moves her hips again slowly until my fingers are in her to the third knuckle and I flex them, just barely. Hazel bites her lip and arches like she needs *more*, giving me a look that's so raw and needy it takes my breath away.

"Stop torturing me, Kostya," she whispers.

I finally grab the condom from the pillow, tear the wrapper off with my teeth and unroll it one-handed onto my desperately-hard cock. Hazel watches me, hips working against my hand until the condom is on, and then she reaches down and takes the hand that's in her by the wrist.

She keeps my fingers in her as she rolls over onto her hands and knees. I move my fingers inside her one more time, harder than before, and she rocks back into me for a long moment before I pull my fingers out and slide them over to take her by the hip.

I push Hazel forward until she's on her knees, both hands around the post of the four-poster bed, hips back, and I'm right behind her. She reaches back and grabs the back of my head so I lean forward and kiss the corner of her mouth, the only part I can reach, and Hazel half-laughs and then bites my lip.

"Fuck me, Kostya," she says.

I growl at her and the tip of my cock is at her entrance. She's so wet and slick that I just slide along her lips, like it's my first time or something.

I bite her earlobe and she reaches down, grabs my cock, and pushes the tip inside her.

I exhale and grab the bedpost myself, because I want to *bury* myself inside her right then. But I'm still afraid of hurting her, so I stroke her hip and pull back a fraction of an inch so I can slide in further, little by little.

But then Hazel pushes herself back and before I know it, I'm balls-deep inside her and I hear myself *grunt* into her hair, a primal, animal noise I didn't even know I could make.

"Oh, *fuck*," Hazel gasps. I open my eyes to see that her knuckles are white on the bedpost. Her pussy flexes around me so hard I can barely think straight.

"You okay?" I whisper into her hair, desperately trying to keep it together, just *hoping* I'm speaking English and praying I'm not hurting her.

"I'm fine," she whispers, and clenches around me so hard I have to take a deep breath. "Fuck, I'm fine. *Jesus*, Kostya."

She moves her hips forward an inch and then pushes back again.

"Oh, my *god*, I'm fine," she breathes. She moves again, rocking her hips forward and then pushing back and each time she does she lets out a breathless little moan.

I lean my forehead against the back of her head and just watch my cock disappear into her, my thumb in the dimple on her back as I let her fuck me, trying as hard I as I can to stay in control.

It's hard. It's almost impossible, and it's almost all I can do to close my eyes and press my face into her hair.

Suddenly she slides back and then stops, wrapping her arm backward around me. It's a little awkward but I lean into her.

"This?" I growl, pushing against her.

Hazel just moans and moves her hips so I just barely move inside her.

"*Fuck* yes that," she says, and then her hand is on the side of my face and she's twisting toward me.

"Kiss me while you're inside me," she whispers.

I lean forward and she leans backward, and the angle's not quite right but we kiss anyway as we move against each other. I can tell I'm nearly at the end of my rope, nearly out of whatever self-control I had left, and when I pull away from her I kiss her shoulder and pinch one nipple.

"I don't have much longer," I murmur into her ear, rocking against her. "I can only be inside you for so long before I explode, *zloyushka*."

She moves her hips again, harder, and we both groan at the same time. Hazel leans her head forward until it's resting on the bed post. We move together, and we start out slow and deliberate but it builds and builds until I'm driving hard into her with every stroke, pulling her hips back against me as if I can somehow get deeper.

"Oh that's good," she whispers, and I do it again and again until suddenly she pushes back and grabs my shoulder. I'm sunk completely inside her as her hips flex, her pussy muscles fluttering and squeezing.

"Kostya, I'm gonna come so fucking hard," she gasps.

I move my hand to her clit and rub.

"Good. I love feeling you come," I whisper.

She explodes, moaning, her pussy clamping down as she rocks back and forth and in seconds I'm coming too, growling in her ear as I come harder and longer than I ever have in my entire life as she keeps moving.

At last we both slow, and then finally stop. I've got an arm locked around her waist now and I don't remember doing that, but I hold her close and her chest expands and falls against my arm.

All of a sudden, in that afterglow, I feel wildly, almost insanely protective of her, like she's *mine* and I'd fight a tiger bare-handed if it came into the room right now. I don't know what to do so I kiss her on the top of her head and hold her tight. After a moment she lets go of the bedpost and slides her hand over mine, lacing our fingers together.

I squeeze, she squeezes back, and maybe for the first time in my life everything feels quiet and still and *right*.

CHAPTER TWENTY-SEVEN
HAZEL

Kostya kisses me on the top of my head, and then clumsily on my ear. I squeeze his hand, let him go, and we finally untangle ourselves from each other. He grabs tissues from the bedside table, wraps the condom in them and tosses the whole gross bundle back onto the table, but I couldn't care less.

I sit up against the headboard, the pillows behind my back, and he lets me pull him in until he's leaning against me, his head on my chest, my right arm slung over him. I run my hand through his hair and he makes a barely-audible grunt, somewhere low in his chest.

"You purring?" I murmur.

"I'm contented," he says. "Like a house cat in a sunbeam. Meow."

I laugh and he smiles, then plants a kiss on the inside of my elbow.

The bedroom is mostly dark, but the curtains are translucent enough to let some moonlight through. We sit there, like that, for a long time. I stroke Kostya's hair, my other arm across his chest, and he strokes my arm with his fingertips, back and forth.

I've never seen him like this before, perfectly relaxed and totally unguarded, sprawled across the bed like he doesn't have a care in the world. I get the feeling that not many people have seen Kostya like this. Maybe none.

"I'm getting better at that," he says, his voice low and slow and sleepy.

"At what?" I say, still twisting my fingers in his hair.

"At making you laugh," he says. "That time I even meant to do it."

I laugh again, leaning against the headboard.

"Thanks," I say.

"This is why we're not a secret," he says. "My mother told me tonight that I light up like a lantern when I'm around you."

"I thought it was because I act like a shy teenager when we're together," I murmur.

He looks at me, eyebrows raised.

"Shy?" he asks.

"I mean in public," I say.

"Good," he says. "Don't be shy around me."

"We're naked right now because you just fucked my brains out," I say. "If that's shy, I'd almost hate to see not shy."

I'm sliding downward slowly, the pillows shifting under me, so now I'm at a forty-five degree angle and Kostya's head is on my stomach. He turns his head and kisses it, and I think both of us are slowly falling asleep, tangled together in a mass of limbs and bed sheets and pillows.

"Do you have to leave?" I finally ask.

"No," he says.

"You sure?" I ask.

"Are you trying to get rid of me?" Kostya asks.

"I just don't want you disowned, exiled, and penniless," I tease.

I meant to make him laugh, but instead his face goes serious and he looks at me.

"I'm just going to tell him," he says, his gray eyes steady. "He can't do anything. He won't disown me. He can't force me to marry anyone. All he can do is be angry, and I don't care any more."

I hold my breath and bite my lip.

"Are you sure?" I ask.

Kostya just nods.

I'm not sure how to phrase this next thing, so I take a deep breath and just let some words fly out of my mouth.

"We've only known each other for what, a week and a half?" I ask. "I don't want you to ruin your relationship with your father over something that might not..."

I swallow, and Kostya's just staring at me.

"I mean, it's just, you know, what if I go home at the end of the month and, like, you come to your senses or something and realize that you fucked up your relationship with your dad because of some American girl?" I say, all in one breath.

"*Zloyushka*, what the hell are you *talking* about?" he asks. "I'm *at* my senses. However you say that."

"What if it turns out I'm a serial killer?" I say.

For some reason it's the first thing that pops into my head.

"Then we'll deport you back to the U.S. to stand trial, and I'll still have made it clear to my father that he doesn't control who I'm with," Kostya says.

It sounds so *sensible* when he says it out loud.

"I'm not a serial killer," I say.

"I didn't think so," he says.

Then he lifts himself off my stomach and puts his head next to mine. He takes my hand in his and locks our fingers together.

"I know relationships don't work out sometimes," he says. "But I climbed up two stories of stone wall with a plant in my mouth because I thought it might make you smile. And it did. And it was worth it, because I feel like I'm the moon when you smile at me, and I would be an idiot if I didn't at least try."

He kisses my hand, and I don't answer, because there's suddenly a lump in my throat.

"Tell me now if I'm wrong about this and I shouldn't try," he says, his voice barely a whisper.

"No," I whisper, swallowing hard. "I mean, no, you're not wrong. You should try. We should try."

Stop talking, I think.

"Good," he says, simply. "I'll talk to him when he's back from Kiev."

He pushes my hair out of my face with his other hand, and then kisses my forehead.

"Do all Americans make everything seem so complicated?" he asks.

"That was *nothing*," I say.

After a few more minutes we both get out of the bed. I find him an extra toothbrush and he brushes his teeth as I get the rest of my makeup off, totally naked the whole time. As he leaves the bathroom, he puts one hand on my ass and squeezes just a little, kissing me on the cheek.

"I like seeing you naked," he says. "I'll be in your bed."

He leaves the bathroom and I blink at myself in the mirror, then smile. When I get in bed he's half asleep, and he rolls over and puts one arm over my stomach.

"*Spokushki,*" he says.

"Don't let the bedbugs bite," I say, and I'm asleep almost instantly.

It feels like thirty minutes later that there's a knock on my door, but the sun is already streaming through the windows.

I'm lying on my stomach and Kostya has one arm and one leg half-slung over me, his face buried in the fluffy white pillow.

I hear the knock again, and this time he wakes up, too.

"Who is it?" he asks me.

"I don't know yet," I whisper, getting out of bed. "Stay out of sight," I say, and put on the black bathrobe that came with the room.

"You want me to hide in the closet or something?" he asks, his voice extra raspy and gravelly.

"Just don't walk out naked," I whisper, and close the door slightly behind me.

You can't see the bedroom door from the front door, and it's probably just someone who wants to know if I have any laundry, so I'm not that worried about it.

It's not.

It's my mother, and she's in a bit of a state.

"Hazel, can I borrow your deodorant?" she asks. sweeping past me and into my rooms.

"Sure, just stay there, I can—"

She sweeps past me, into my living room, toward the bathroom.

"I know we both get the nervous sweats, so yours will probably work pretty well," she says.

"Yes, it's fine, let me go find it though the bathroom's kind of a mess so—"

She's not listening. She's looking past me in the direction of the bedroom.

All my insides wrap themselves around my windpipe, and I follow her gaze, praying that I don't see Kostya standing there, totally naked with morning wood.

I don't. The bedroom door opened itself, like doors in old houses do, and lying in full view on an ottoman in the bedroom is his formal military jacket. Even from here, it's perfectly obvious what it is.

"Deodorant's in the bathroom!" I say, and grab her arm, trying to haul her away, like I can magically make her unsee the jacket.

"*Hazel*," she says, and gives me her cut-the-bullshit look.

It's a strong one.

"Please tell me that jacket belongs to one of the many pudgy, middle-aged generals who were in attendance last night, and not *the crown prince of Sveloria*," she whispers.

I swallow.

"It belongs to a general?" I whisper back, heat flooding my face.

She gives me the look again.

"Just leave and pretend you never saw it," I whisper. "It's fine."

My mother glares at the jacket.

"At least tell me it was just the once," she says.

I open my mouth, then shut it. My face has gone nuclear.

"You're the diplomat," I whisper. "*I'm* on vacation!"

"It's still bad form!" she whispers. "Now this has to be disclosed to the state department, there's paperwork, you have to give a statement to the embassy. It's a whole mess now."

"There's paperwork about who I, uh..."

"Unless you just snuggled all night, yes, there's paperwork," she whispers. "And, actually, yes, even then, so never mind."

She glances at the door again, and I hear a slight rustle inside the room. I'm *sure* Kostya can hear all this.

"At least tell me you were careful," she says, her voice dropping to an actual whisper. "You've still got that IUD, right?"

"Yes, and we were careful and I'm not an *idiot*, mom," I say.

She looks like she might disagree, but there's another rustle in the bedroom and we both look over.

Kostya steps into the doorway, bedsheets wrapped around him several times, *very* securely.

"Good morning, Ambassador Towers," he says, nodding his head slightly, one hand holding the sheets firmly in place.

"Good morning, Konstantin Grigorovich," she says, her tone very, *very* formal.

I pinch the bridge of my nose between my finger and thumb.

"Could you please call each other Eileen and Kostya and not make this any weirder than it already is, for fuck's sake?" I say.

My mother takes a deep breath.

"Hello, Kostya," she says. "I wasn't expecting to see you here."

"Hello, Eileen," he says. "I didn't know Hazel would have a visitor this morning," he says, his tone exactly as formal as hers.

"I didn't know either," I point out, my eyes still squeezed shut.

"You're accompanying my father to the economic summit in Kiev, correct?" he goes on.

"I am," she says.

Kostya and I look at each other.

"*Please* don't tell him," I say. "Please, Mom."

"I would prefer to talk to my father about this myself, when he returns," Kostya says. "He should hear it from me."

My mother sighs and crosses her arms in front of herself.

"Of course," she says, her voice softening a little.

"My deepest thanks," Kostya says, sounding very formal for someone who's wearing my bed sheets.

We all look at each other in silence for a moment.

"I should be leaving," my mother says.

"A pleasure to see you," Kostya says, and I nearly roll my eyes.

"You as well," my mom says, then looks at me. "Deodorant?"

I grab it from the bathroom, then escort her back to my front door. Kostya goes back into the bedroom and closes the door, firmly this time.

Inside the front door, my mom crosses her arms in front of her.

"He's telling his father and I had to find out this way?" she asks.

"You weren't *supposed* to," I say.

She glances at the closed bedroom door again and thinks for a moment.

"I had some suspicions," she admits. "We were hoping you were just flirting."

I make an *oops* face.

"Everyone says he's much more reasonable than his father, at least," she says. Her voice softens a little. "And he's got a cuter butt."

I go scarlet again.

"*Mom*," I hiss, but she just laughs.

Then she puts one hand on my shoulder.

"You like him for more than his cute butt?" she asks, softly.

I just nod.

"Okay," she says. "I'll do the paperwork."

"Thank you," I say. "And sorry."

She hugs me.

"I can't even tell your father," she says. "The man couldn't keep a secret if his life depended on it."

"I know," I say. "Thanks."

Then she leaves. I take a couple deep breaths, standing in the living room, and then walk to the bedroom and open the door.

CHAPTER TWENTY-EIGHT
KOSTYA

I shut the door behind myself and stare at the bedroom. Our clothes are scattered everywhere. Hazel's thong is on the back of a chair, my pants are half under the bed, and the used condom wrapped in a ball of tissues is still on the night-stand, even though I meant to throw it away.

We got lucky that Hazel's mom just saw the jacket, I think, smiling to myself.

I toss Hazel's thong from the chair to the bed and then sit by the window, opening the curtains enough to look out onto the Black Sea. It's a gorgeous Saturday morning, and in the distance, I can see sailboats moving away from the harbor in Velinsk.

After a few minutes, the door opens and Hazel comes back in. She sits in the armchair opposite me, and curls her legs under her. The black silk robe settles against the curves of her body, and I can't help but think about running my hands down her body through the soft fabric and wondering what noises she makes when she's still a little sleepy.

"That could have gone worse," she says.

I force myself to stop thinking about the filthy things I could do to her.

"She didn't seem angry," I say.

Hazel looks out the window at the sailboats and drums one finger on the arm of the chair.

"I think she'd prefer it if I didn't take up with a foreign head of state while she's serving as that country's ambassador," she says, slowly. "It complicates her job. But she's not mad about *you*, just your title."

She pauses again.

"I think she kind of likes you, actually," Hazel says. "She doesn't really share her personal opinions on the people she works with, but I *think* she likes you."

It's strange to hear that someone *likes* me. For most of the women I've been with, I was politically expedient for their parents or something to brag to their friends about. I'm useful and have an impressive title. Whether people like me rarely enters into the equation.

"I like her," I say. "She's good at her job and she respects your decisions."

"*That's* not always true," Hazel says. "I've made plenty that she didn't respect. She plans things for me without telling me first *all the time*. Every time we go somewhere here, she tells me not to wear leggings, like I didn't learn *that* lesson."

"My father's threatening to disown me and name my brother crown prince if I don't produce the right kind of heir with the right kind of docile, well-born, Svelorian woman," I say. "I was fourteen when he started lecturing me about the importance of having an heir. Like I'm just breeding stock."

"You win," Hazel says, and makes a face. "I can't imagine either of my parents telling me to *produce an heir*. Especially not when I was fourteen."

"He didn't mean for me to do it then," I say. "Though he certainly meant for me to do it by now."

She looks at me for a long moment, thinking.

"He's really gonna flip his shit, huh?" she says.

"Yes," I say, and shrug.

"What happens if he *does* disown you?" she asks.

"Then I become a royal in exile and find my fortune out in the world, like a commoner," I say. "And come back here when he dies."

"A commoner?" she says, totally straight-faced. "They don't even live in castles. You'd have to pay rent instead of living somewhere that your family has owned for hundreds of years."

"You're making fun of me again," I say.

"You used the word *commoner*," Hazel says, her eyes dancing, but she leans forward, her voice going soft. "*I'm* a commoner. Of course I'm making fun of you."

I lean forward in my chair and hold out my hand.

"You know what I mean," I say. "I'd have to go make myself useful instead of look important and do nothing."

Hazel takes my hand, and I pull her forward until she's straddling my lap, her robe just starting to come open.

"Kostya, if you think that's going to happen, you don't have to—"

I put a few fingers on her mouth, and she hushes.

"I'm telling him," I say. "And in case I get kicked out and never set foot in this palace again, I think we should stay here all day. Specifically, in your bed."

She laughs, and I pull the sash on her robe until it falls open, then pull her forward until we're face to face.

"Do you have any royal blood in you?" I ask.

She frowns.

"I don't think so?" she says.

"Would you like some?" I ask, and squeeze her ass.

Hazel makes a face somewhere between grossed out and amused, then finally laughs.

"That's not quite how that line goes," she says.

WE DON'T LEAVE her rooms. We barely leave her bed. I call down to the kitchen, request that food be brought to Hazel's rooms for two people, and don't explain why. Rumors spread like fire through the palace, so by nightfall, I'm sure that everyone's heard that the prince has been with the American girl, in her room, all day, and I don't give a damn.

All we do is fuck, talk, and nap. I've never been lazier in my entire life, and it feels wonderful to spend a whole day without anything I have to do, nowhere to go, and for once, nothing to worry about. I fall asleep with her on her side, curled around me, and I wake up spooning her tightly, my nose in her hair.

"We should get out of bed today," she murmurs.

"We got out of bed yesterday," I say, lazily stroking her hip. "I even took a shower."

"You never put on pants."

"I don't remember any complaints."

She rolls over onto her back and kisses me good morning.

"Maybe even out of my rooms," she says.

"Ambitious," I say.

It's noon by the time we leave. I have to ask someone to bring me regular clothes from my own rooms, and as we walk through the halls of the palace, I can feel everyone watching us while pretending not to.

He must know by now, I think. *Surely, someone's told him already that I spent the day in her room.*

The silence from him worries me more than if he called and screamed at me. I half expect that when he gets back I'll simply be given an official document and told that I'm no longer his son, but right now, it's impossible to worry about that.

We walk through the gardens. Hazel smells a rose, and I pick it for her, because I *can*. A gardener stares, so I pick another one and hand it to her.

"Okay, stop picking roses," she says.

"No," I say.

"How many do you think I need?" she asks.

I pick her another one, and she laughs.

"What if I don't take it?" she asks.

"An even number of flowers is bad luck," I say.

"You're making that up."

"I'm not. We put even numbers of flowers on graves."

I hold out the rose.

"Is that the last one?" she asks.

"You're impossible," I say. "I've got a castle with an entire rose garden and you won't take three flowers."

"Here we go again," she says, her eyes crinkling around the corners like she's about to laugh. "More 'I'm a prince' stuff."

"It's impolite to tease a royal," I say.

We walk to the massive garage. There are people everywhere on the palace grounds, and they're all watching us while pretending that they're not, so I ignore them.

"There are beautiful sea cliffs about twenty miles from here," I say as we walk between the rows of shining cars, perfectly parked. "You can almost see Turkey from them, and at low tide, there are caves below."

"Won't it be crowded on a Sunday afternoon?" she asks.

I pause for a moment as we walk.

"No," I say.

She sighs.

"Kostya, what's wrong with the sea cliffs?" she asks.

"Why do you think there's something wrong with them?" I say.

"Because of how you said it," she says. "That was your *I'm not telling you the whole story and it's because something is fucked up* voice."

I frown.

"I don't have that voice," I say.

"Then the caves are lovely and no one is there because they were all busy today?" Hazel asks.

"The caves *are* lovely," I say.

Hazel waits.

"And haunted," I finally admit.

"That keeps people away?" she asks.

"We're very superstitious," I say. "A hundred and fifty years ago, there was a lot of piracy on the Black Sea, and pirates would hide out in the caves."

"And an enterprising Svelorian king somehow killed them all while they slept?" she asks softly.

"It was an admiral," I say. "His name was Dubroshkov. The pirates slept in hammocks during high tide, so he sent in canoes rigged with gunpowder, then shot one from a war ship out on the sea."

Hazel squeezes her eyes shut.

"It triggered a chain explosion, seventy pirates burned to death, and there's a statue of Dubroshkov in the center of Velinsk," I finish. "I'm sure you've seen it."

"Did it stop piracy?" she asks.

"For a year or two," I say, and put my hand on her back, rubbing in slow circles. From the far corner of the garage, a mechanic looks at us and then looks away.

"The cliffs are still beautiful. I ride out there sometimes at night."

"Have you ever seen a ghost?" she asks.

"No," I say. "I don't believe in ghosts."

We stop in front of a low-slung, black Maserati that looks fast even when it's parked.

"Come on," I say. "We'll go for a ride in style this time."

Hazel looks unsure.

"Would you *rather* take the bike?" I ask.

"Maybe," she says, looking up at me. "No one will notice if I accidentally scratch it."

"Hazel, there's no damn point to being a prince if I can't give you flowers from my garden and I can't take you for a drive in my sports car," I say.

"That thing probably costs more than the house I grew up in," she says.

"It's only a Maserati," I say. "It's not a *fancy* car."

She gives me a slightly alarmed look.

"Joke," I say, and sigh. "Someday, you're going to laugh at one."

"Someday, one's going to be funny," she says, and stands on her tiptoes to kiss me quickly.

The mechanic looks over and away again, and I fight the urge to squeeze Hazel's ass. Instead I get the key from a finger-print-protected lockbox, walk to the passenger side, and open the door for her.

Just as she's getting in, I hear shouting. I turn my head and Hazel stands, both hands on the door frame.

We frown and look at each other. The shouting gets louder, and Hazel steps back, shutting the door.

Coming down the center aisle of the garage is Niko, running even with his limp, trailed by two much older cabinet chiefs of my father's.

"Kostya!" Niko shouts, a note of desperation in his voice I haven't heard in years. Not since the Guard.

He's calling me by my informal nickname in front of government officials. I feel like I've swallowed lead, like there's an enormous fist squeezing my lungs as I walk toward him, then break into a run.

Behind me, Hazel says something but I don't catch it.

Niko and I stop a few feet from each other. He's breathing hard and favoring his bad leg, standing slightly off balance, and I wonder how far he's run.

"Kostya," he gasps.

"Tell me," I say, speaking Russian.

Hazel comes to a stop a few feet away, keeping her distance, like she also instinctually knows something is very, very wrong.

"Your father's been murdered," Niko says.

I stare.

"There was an explosion," he says, still trying to catch his breath. "A car bomb. In Tobov. He didn't suffer."

My body's gone numb. I'm frozen. I couldn't move if I wanted to.

"I'm sorry, Kostya, I'm sorry," Niko says, the words spilling out of him. "We didn't know, there were no rumors, no whispers, nothing at all to suggest..."

He trails off. I'm barely listening. The last time I spoke to my father we fought and I stormed out, too angry to even say goodbye. I don't even know why he was *in* Tobov. I thought he was in Kiev.

The other men have caught up to Niko now, huffing and puffing and gasping like they're having heart attacks. Niko is still looking at me, jaw set, face rigid.

He takes a deep breath.

"Long live the king," he says.

CHAPTER TWENTY-NINE
HAZEL

I don't know what's happening, but I know it's bad. I don't need to speak Russian at all to see Kostya's face change when Niko tells him something, settling into a hard, stony mask. I want to shout *what the hell is going on?* but I know my manners for once, so I just stand there like an idiot.

More and more people keep trickling in, and I recognize some of them from the ball two nights ago, some of them from briefings. Some I don't recognize, but then Niko steps back and says something loudly, his voice raised, and everyone else echoes him.

I catch the word *korol*, king.

Suddenly I think I know what happened.

My stomach twists and I cover my mouth with both hands as everyone else in the garage goes down on one knee and Kostya just *stares* at them, beyond them, like he can't see anything.

The king was with my parents in Kiev, I think.

I feel nauseous. I'm shaking. I force myself to take deep breaths so I don't hyperventilate.

Everything is still for a long time. It's probably a few

seconds but it feels like hours, and then Kostya barks something and everyone stands, swarming around him as he gives orders in a flat, hard-edged voice.

People start rushing back out of the garage. One older man says something to him and Kostya nearly shouts at him, and I just stand there, watching because I have no fucking idea what to do. I still don't even know what's going *on*, not really.

Finally, when there are only a few people left in the garage, I walk over to one middle-aged man. I think we danced once at the masquerade, though I can't remember his name right now so I don't bother addressing him.

"What's going on?" I ask. It's impolite and informal but I do *not* fucking care right now.

He looks at me with his serious, lined face, and he's about to say something when footsteps come toward us and we both turn.

"A moment," Kostya tells the man. The man nods his head and leaves, and Kostya turns his hard gray eyes on me.

"My father was murdered twenty minutes ago by a car bomb in Tobov," he says, his voice flat and strange.

"I'm sorry," I whisper. "Kostya, I'm sorry, I'm so sorry."

He just nods.

"Your parents weren't with him," he says.

"Thank you," I whisper.

I want to reach out and grab him, hold him and stroke his hair but we stand there, locked in place like we're statues. I can feel tears running down my face, but I don't reach up to wipe them away.

"You'll have to excuse me," he says, his voice stiff and formal again. "There's a lot to do."

"Of course," I say. "I'll help however I can."

He starts to step away, then hesitates. He looks at me, and for a moment he gives me a long, wistful look.

"I'm sorry about the sea cliffs," he says.

Then he walks away.

WE'RE all herded back into bunkers. There's an enormous one below the garage, it turns out, and that's where we are as we slowly find out that it's worse than we thought, that the elements of the United Svelorian Front that everyone thought were small, fringe elements were larger than anyone in the government suspected.

Kostya's father is dead. The train stations are shut down, occupied by insurgent forces. The two airports are shut down, also occupied. The border crossings. The USF is making demands. At least, I think that's what's happening. Once in a while, someone comes over and updates the idiot American.

Everyone is constantly shouting in Russian, and I feel beyond powerless. I can't even understand what they're saying, let alone do anything at all, so I sit in a folding chair in the corner with my head in my hands as my mind spins.

I don't know how long I've been like that when there's a hand on my shoulder, and I jerk my head up.

"Hazel," Yelena says, smiling down at me sadly.

I blink.

"What are you doing here?" I ask, formalities and politeness a distant memory.

"The queen and I were talking about putting a pond in the gardens," she says, her soft voice sad. "She wanted my opinion."

A pang of guilt stabs through me. Not only are my parents okay and Kostya's father is dead, but now I'm talking to the perfectly nice girl I stole him from.

"Oh," I say. "How is the queen?"

Yelena's brow knits together slightly, then relaxes.

"She'll be okay," she finally says.

She grabs another folding chair and settles in next to me, her dainty hands in her lap. I have no idea why, because it seems like she should probably hate me or at least not really like me or something.

"I think you might need a translator," she says.

We sit together for a long time. She translates random snippets of conversation, tells me where cities and towns are, fills me in on the background story to all of this.

Yelena tells me that the USF started as a political group in Sveloria, not terrorists. They were populists, for the most part, and they wanted western-style reforms: a free press, free assembly. Some kind of representation in the government, even if it was only ornamental, but Kostya's father refused everything, sometimes even tightening restrictions.

So the USF radicalized, becoming violent, and when they did, Kostya's father crushed them mercilessly. The remnants fled to the mountains, where Kostya himself fought them years later.

Just as Yelena finishes, there's another wave of shouting. Before Yelena can translate, Kostya storms out of the room, past us, and up the stairs. There's the sound of a heavy door slamming shut, and then a moment of total silence before people stream after him.

I look at Yelena.

"Something like, 'If they want to fucking kill me I won't wait for death like a fox in a hole,'" she says, frowning. "Do foxes have holes? Is that the right animal?"

"They do," I say.

Then we look at each other. I shrug. Yelena kind of shrugs.

"Let's get out of this stupid bunker," she says.

YELENA and I work side-by-side through the afternoon, into the night and just past sunrise. The palace was full of people who don't live here, so we find beds and food for everyone. Communications are still up, so I work with one ear listening to the BBC. After a long time, my text to my parents that I'm alive finally gets through, and minutes later, CNN is reporting that there's an American citizen among those holed up in Velinsk.

I'm on my back, underneath a desk, trying to troubleshoot an ancient desktop computer as Yelena translates the error messages for me when someone comes into the room and nearly kicks my head.

I look up. It's some kid, maybe fifteen.

"Are you Hazel Sung?" he asks in English.

"Yes," I say.

"America's calling," he says.

He doesn't get more specific. I follow him through the noisy halls of the palace to the cabinet offices, then into a large meeting room. It's nearly empty: two officials and Kostya, all looking at a blurry projection on the wall. They look tired, totally exhausted.

"Miss Sung?" a voice says from a speaker.

"Yes," I say.

One of the officials points at a chair and I sit.

"I'm Marcia Bloom, the Secretary of State," the projection says, and I blink at it.

"Pleased to meet you," I say automatically.

"I wish these were better circumstances," she says. "I've known your mother for many years."

I just nod.

Our meeting only lasts five, maybe ten minutes. I think she just wants to make sure that I'm all right and not under duress, and she seems relieved that I'm acting relatively normal. She asks me to keep her updated on the situation, but also makes a vague comment about working for the state department on an informal basis.

I'm too tired to parse that, but when the call ends, I'm relieved that they made contact and I'm not all alone out here. It makes me feel better to think that someone's watching me.

As I leave the room, Kostya rises, and then the two other men rise. Kostya waves them down, but then escorts me out and shuts the door behind him. We're in a hallway that's not exactly private, but there's no one immediately around us.

"Thank you," he says.

I look around. There's no one. I take one of his hands in both of mine. I squeeze it, but he doesn't squeeze back.

"I'm sorry," I say again, uselessly.

"I don't know what's going to happen," he says. "I don't know how this is going to go, but we would very much like to have the U.S. on our side."

There's no one here, I think. *Say something real.*

I feel awful immediately. This is probably the worst day of his life, and I'm upset about *me*?

His hand is still in mine. I just nod. I've been awake for almost twenty-four hours, most of those hours have been bad, and I'm trying not to cry.

"Of course," I say. "Anything I can do to help."

I squeeze his hand again. He holds on, but he doesn't squeeze back.

I let his hand go.

He swallows, looking at me for a long time.

"I'm sorry," he says, and then goes back into the meeting room.

CHAPTER THIRTY
KOSTYA

Four days later, I'm staring at the iPad that Niko just handed me, and Hazel's face stares back. It's an old picture, badly lit, a little blurry.

But it's unmistakably her. And she's unmistakably wearing a lacy bra, lacy panties, a garter belt, hose, and sky-high heels. She's got a big red cup in her hand, and she and another girl dressed the same way are leaning on some guy as he reaches around and grabs both girls' breasts.

I'm *furious*. I've slept maybe eight hours in the last four nights, ever since my father was assassinated, and my temper is on a hair trigger. I want to murder this fucking asshole in the photo for touching Hazel. I want to murder the shithead who published this trash, and I want to murder the small-dicked douchebag who found the photo in the first place.

"If this is what I get for removing censorship from the press put it the fuck back in place," I growl at Niko. "Fucking behead them all. Drown them in the Black Sea. I don't care."

He doesn't move. He knows better than to actually do any of that.

"Read the article," he says, arms crossed.

I scan it. Fucking salacious trash, obviously. The *Tobov Post* isn't even a newspaper, it's a rumormongering website that normally limits itself to movie stars and pop singers. Now that there are no consequences for reporting on whatever they want, they've instantly latched onto the rumors about the brand-new king and his American girlfriend.

Then I pause. I re-read a sentence.

My heart stops for a moment.

Sources also say that Sung, 25, dropped out of medical school after carrying on a sexual affair with her married professor.

Niko and I stare at each other. We're alone in a tiny office.

"Is it true?" he asks, his voice low.

I clench my jaw. My stomach plummets, because I want to say *no, of course not.* I want to say *she's awkward, not despicable,* but I can't. I never did find out why she dropped out of medical school.

"I don't know," I say.

I've barely seen her in four days, and I haven't been alone with her for more than two minutes. The last time was yesterday when I was taking a breather in a nook off a staircase, looking out the window, and she charged through the door with an armful of ethernet cables, heading somewhere else.

Neither of us said a word. We just looked at each other for a few seconds, and briefly, I felt like my capsizing world was righting itself again, like maybe there was this one small spark of light.

Then one of the cabinet aides burst through the door, asking her what kind of cables they were looking for, and they were gone again.

All I thought about for *hours* was the look on her face.

My father's dead, my country's falling apart, and I'm thinking about the way a girl looked at me.

That's why it's probably better that I don't see her.

I LAST THREE HOURS. It's driving me crazy, the incessant, gnawing worry that Hazel isn't who I thought she was. That she would do *that*, sleep with a married man. Be a home wrecker.

I don't even know why it matters right now. I'm deliberately trying to see her as little as possible, and I have no idea what she thinks about that, but everything has gone to shit and I'm doing the best I can. The second I can get the airport re-opened I'm sending her home, and God only knows if she'll ever want to come back to this hellhole.

I send someone to go find her. When she walks in her hair is in a high, messy bun, her eyes are puffy and purple with lack of sleep, she's wearing ill-fitting jeans and a t-shirt, and she's still more beautiful than I remembered and I hate it.

Neither of us say anything. The aide leaves and shuts the door behind him. My heart feels like it's pumping sandpaper through my veins.

"Did the State Department call again?" she asks.

"No," I say, and hand her the iPad with the article on it.

"Fuck," she says, looking at the picture. "What is this? What's it say?"

I'd forgotten the article was in Russian, but there's a link to an English translation at the bottom. I take it back and click it.

"That picture is from college," she says, pinching the bridge of her nose between her finger and thumb. "It's six years old, I was dumb and drunk and I went to a lingerie-themed party at this frat house because I was hoping—"

"Read the article," I say, handing it back.

She scans it. Halfway through she puts one hand to her mouth. When she finishes, she squeezes her eyes shut for a long moment, like she's trying to collect herself.

"You never told me why you dropped out of med school," I say.

"I didn't know he was married," she says, still not looking at me.

I want to believe her. I want desperately to believe her, but how could she not *know*?

"How?" I ask, my arms folded across my chest.

Hazel pulls out a chair, thumps the iPad onto the desk, puts her head in her hands, and takes a deep breath.

"My last year of med school, I was miserable," she says quietly. "I'd realized I didn't want to be there anymore, I didn't have any friends, I didn't like what I was doing, but I was too much of a pussy to drop out and admit that I'd fucked up and wasted a couple of years."

She thumps a fingertip on the table.

"So when my young, cute professor asked me to drinks to 'talk about my work,' I said yes, because I was flattered that he asked *me*, and because I felt like I couldn't make things any worse," she says, swallowing. "He told me he'd just gotten divorced, and when we went back to his place it was this ugly one-bedroom apartment full of boxes and crappy furniture, and he didn't have a ring on, so I just believed him."

Even though this is all in the past, jealousy tightens in my chest at the thought of Hazel with someone else.

She's staring at the table, her eyes vacant and empty, leaning her head against one hand, and she swallows again and sighs.

"We weren't supposed to be fucking in the first place, so I didn't tell anyone, so there wasn't anyone to say, 'Hey, watch out, Evan's actually just separated and he told me that they're still trying to make things work,' and it wasn't like I was going to look up divorce records," she says, her finger slowly tracing circles on the table.

"And then one day I came over late at night, and his wife

was there, and he sat on the couch while she screamed at me and called me a stupid slut. He wouldn't even look at me."

Hazel clears her throat, and I frown in disbelief.

"He let her do that?" I ask.

"Yup."

"He did this to you and then let another woman call you names?" I ask, my voice getting hard.

Hazel just looks up at me.

"Spineless coward," I say. "Are all American men sniveling worms?"

She smiles, looks at me, and stops.

"No, I just got lucky," she says. "And he didn't *do* this to me. I knew better than to sleep with him in the first place, but I did it anyway. I just thought it was a bad decision for a different reason. Anyway, I dropped out of school, sublet my apartment, and sold a bunch of my stuff, and traveled for a few months because I figured if I was going to be a fuckup I should at least be a fuckup doing something I really wanted to do, and now I'm here."

"Why didn't you tell me?" I ask.

She looks at her hands and flexes her fingers, like maybe she's holding the answer there.

"I didn't know how," she said. "At what point was I supposed to say, hey, here's the worst thing I've ever done?"

"At any point," I say, and I'm tired and irritable as fuck. I miss her even though she's right here, and I feel like I can't have her any more, so I'm picking a fight. "Anything would be better than finding this out from the fucking *Tobov Post*."

"Right, because now everyone knows that the American girl dresses slutty and fucks peoples' husbands," she says, and she sounds angry but also sad and tired. "I'm sorry, Kostya. I fucked up then, and I keep fucking up, and I'm sorry."

"What else?" I ask.

"What else *what*?" she says, leaning back and crossing her arms.

"What else don't I know?" I ask. "What else is the fucking *Tobov Post* going to smear you with?"

"It's not a smear if it's true," she says bitterly. "He was definitely married, definitely my professor, and I definitely fucked him."

Jealousy rolls through me again, and I try to shut it down, pacing back and forth through the tiny office.

"Just tell me what else so I'm not surprised," I say.

"Kostya, I don't even know what you want me to say," she says, eyes closed, her forehead in one hand. "That's the worst. That's the worst by a mile."

"You got kicked out of boarding school," I say. "You told me that."

She looks at me, with a long, slow look.

"Okay," she finally says. "I stole twenty bucks out of my mom's purse when I was thirteen and bought cigarettes. I lost my virginity at sixteen to a senator's son in the back of his Range Rover. I got a fake ID when I was seventeen and used to sneak out and go to bars in Boston. One time, I hit a parking sign with my mom's car, got a ding, and when she asked about it I lied. I tried cocaine once my freshman year of college, which was the same year I got so drunk I threw up on Boston Common. I went skinny dipping on Cape Cod."

She flings up her hands, slumps in the chair, and stares at me.

"It's normal stuff, Kostya," she says. "It was dumb, but I never hurt anyone besides myself. I never did cocaine again and a month ago in Amsterdam was the first time I'd smoked pot in a year and a half. I finally confessed to my mom about the car and it turns out she knew the whole damn time, because she's not stupid."

Her eyes are glittering with tears. She looks back down at the table, and I feel shittier than I even thought possible.

"Did you want anything else?" she asks, her voice hushed and strangled. "Maybe the time I killed my goldfish when I was ten because I forgot to feed it?"

"That's everything," I say, quietly.

She stands, her arms crossed in front of her, jaw clenched against the angry tears filling her eyes.

"Am I dismissed?" she asks.

I just want to fucking rewind. To five minutes ago, before I picked this stupid fight with the person who matters most to me. To yesterday, in the stairwell, when maybe I could have said *I miss you, I'm sorry, I want it to be different.*

To the day my father was murdered, when maybe we could have left twenty minutes earlier and driven away and just never come back.

"Things are starting to turn around," I say, swallowing. "We're gaining ground. The staff is going back home. We'll have the airport within a week."

"And then I go home?" she asks.

"Yes," I say.

She nods once, dodges around me, and leaves the office.

I sit in the folding chair, my elbows on my knees and my face in my hands, because right now, I hate this. I hate being King, I hate being in charge, I hate being watched every second, and I hate that I couldn't even stop that conversation from going down the drain.

I'm still sitting there when Niko finds me a few minutes later.

"Good news," he says.

"Please," I say.

CHAPTER THIRTY-ONE
HAZEL

I don't cry until I'm power walking down the hall, head down, trying to hide my face with my hair because I absolutely fucking hate it when I cry and I hate it worse when I cry in public.

I flee to the laundry room, in the basement, because it's warm and noisy and there's no one in there. For a moment I consider burying myself in the huge basket of clean sheets, but I settle for sitting on the floor in the corner, my back against an industrial dryer.

Then I just fucking sob. I'm angry at the *Post* for telling everyone why I dropped out of med school and for running that picture, but I'm mad at myself all over again for doing it in the first place. I'm angry at Kostya for being a dick about it, and I'm angry at him for not even *saying* something and just cutting contact without even saying goodbye.

"I'm sorry?" What the fuck is that?

Then I feel awful for being mad at him, because he has way bigger shit to worry about than my feelings, and I should give him the benefit of the doubt. I fucking *know* that, but I still feel like he's taken sandpaper to my heart. And now I'm going home, and even though I know it's obviously the best decision, I don't *want* to.

I want to stay here. I want things to be normal again. I want to go back to Kostya trying to make jokes in the rose garden.

After a while, I stop finding reasons that I'm crying and just cry until I've got the hiccups.

I'm in the laundry room for a long, long time.

KOSTYA WAS RIGHT, and things start to turn around. He figured out pretty fast that the United Svelorian Front wasn't united at all: the group responsible for his father's death was a tiny, fringe segment, and a much larger part of the Front would be happy with governmental reform instead of overthrow.

Plus, the peaceful factions resent the fringe elements for dragging them into this. It doesn't take much for the USF to start fighting itself while the Svelorian army nips at its heels.

Once Velinsk is safe, the palace workers all go home. Yelena goes back to her family's villa on the Black Sea, and suddenly, the palace feels oddly empty without her around to chat with me about the best time to go sailing on the sea, or her favorite shampoo, or home remedies for colds.

She's not smart, but she's a genuinely nice, good-hearted person. Especially after the week we've had, I think maybe that's better. Being smart hasn't gotten me much of anywhere.

The only upside is I'm alone in my rooms again, which I'd been sharing with Yelena, two of the women who do the laundry, and the chef. Not that I spend much time there; I spend half the day in briefings and meetings as the unofficial American presence in the palace, and the other half taking care of odds and ends that someone has to do.

I see Kostya constantly. He's in nearly every meeting, every briefing, every meal. We pass each other in the halls, exchange looks, and don't talk. He's always surrounded by people and I don't know what the fuck to say, or where to start, or whether I even should. I know he's got more things to worry about than me.

At least I sleep like the dead. Two nights in a row I fall asleep with a laptop next to me, trying to finish one last thing or go through one last briefing. Despite growing up with a diplomat, I don't know shit about any of this, and I'm desperately trying to learn.

The third night, I jolt awake and don't know why. The room is perfectly quiet and still, mostly dark, but I know *something* woke me up and got my adrenaline pumping.

Then I hear it: a soft but insistent knock on the door.

Something happened, I think. Anxiety squeezes my chest and my mind starts racing as I grab the black robe and pull it on.

There was another bombing. The USF is pushing back and coming for Velinsk, and we have to leave right now.

Kostya's dead.

That last thought makes my fingers and toes go cold. The knock sounds again, and I knot the robe around my waist, half-run to the door through the dark, and pull it open.

It's Kostya. He looks like hell.

He's still in the clothes he was wearing that day, dress pants and a button-down shirt with the sleeves rolled up, and it's rumpled and creased, like he fell asleep in it at some point. His eyes have dark circles around them, they're bloodshot, and he hasn't shaved in a day or two.

I'm sure I don't look much better.

"What happened?" I ask, the only question I can think of. Something has to be wrong.

"Can I come in?" he asks.

I step back and he enters, closing the door behind him.

We're in the living room in my little apartment. I'm very aware that I'm naked except this flimsy robe and he's still dressed like he's going to an office, and my arms are crossed over my chest like that will somehow make me more clothed.

I try not to think about the last time he was in this apartment. That was a week and a world ago.

"We should have the airport again within two days," he says.

I just nod.

"So you can go back to the U.S.," he goes on.

I almost say *yes, I understood the implication there* but I don't.

"But what *happened?*" I ask.

"I got a report from the seventh division that they're making good progress," he says.

"Is that it?" I ask.

His eyes flick to the windows behind me, the bedroom door, taking everything in.

"Yes," he says.

We pause for a long moment and look at each other, and then he looks away and runs one hand through his hair, the cords in his neck popping.

"It's two-thirty in the morning," I say. "And you came to tell me something might happen in two days?"

"I thought you'd want to know," he says.

I swallow hard and look at the floor. He didn't come to tell me that, and he's not still standing there because he came here to tell me that, but I don't know what to do. I don't know what he wants and I don't know what I want and I don't know how any of this should be working, right now, in the middle of all this shit.

He's here because it's your room, not to tell you that, I think.

I take a deep breath, then hold out my hand.

He looks at it, then at me. He takes it, his fingers warm and rough just like always.

I lead him to the couch. I sit and then pull him down until we're half-sitting, half-lying, propped up on one arm, his head on my chest. My robe's come partly open, and after a minute he puts both arms around me, his rough stubble on my bare skin.

I drape one arm across his shoulders and stroke his hair with the other hand, and he lets me. For the first time in days I feel like I'm doing the right thing at last, even though I couldn't put it into words.

I just know, deep down, that this is why he's here. This is what he needs. Gradually, he relaxes into me, his shoulders losing tension, his breathing getting slower and evening out.

"I met my father for the first time in this palace," he suddenly says, and I jump.

"I thought you were asleep," I say.

"Not quite," he says.

"You remember meeting your father?" I ask.

"I do," he says. "I didn't know that was strange until years later, when I was a teenager. I guess for most people, their fathers are always... there."

"I don't remember meeting mine," I say.

"It wasn't really the first time," Kostya says, shifting a little. "He was around when I was very young, but I don't remember that at all. I didn't recognize him when I met him here."

I can't imagine *meeting* my father. He's just there, a fixture in my earliest memories.

"I was two when the Soviet Union fell, and my father left to lead the monarchist forces against the communists," he goes on, his voice half dreamy. "He sent my mother and me to safety. The last few years of the civil war, we were here, back before it was restored, and it was filthy and dilapidated, but it was beautiful in the way old, dilapidated things can be."

I keep stroking his hair and let him talk.

"I used to find things," he says. "Cufflinks, a hair comb, an old iron wedding ring. A silver spoon. A carving of a bear. All these little treasures that would be nothing to anyone but a five-year-old, but I used to keep them safe in a box I found and I never told anyone."

"Do you still have them?" I ask.

"I do," he says. "It's so strange, sometimes, to walk around this place like it is now and think about what it looked like the first time I saw it. That's what it looked like when I met my father. We were in that ballroom where the masquerade was, and it was morning, so the sun was coming in through those big windows."

His hand moves against my back, stroking me absentmindedly. I fight to keep my eyes from filling with tears, because for a moment, this feels normal.

"Actually, most of the windows were broken and there was a breeze," he says. "My father was up on the dais, and he was wearing his military uniform, surrounded by other men in military uniforms. I entered with my mother, through those big doors, and I remember her saying, 'Kostya, go say hello to your father,' and I wasn't quite sure which one he was."

I can't even imagine that.

"How old were you?" I ask.

"Six," Kostya says. "I'm not sure he ever quite forgave me."

"Of course he did," I say.

"I shouldn't speak ill of the dead," Kostya says. "It's bad luck."

"I won't tell," I say.

"I owe everything to him," Kostya says. "I'm here and not herding cows in the mountains because of what he did. He used to tell me all the time, 'blood isn't enough,' that just having a lineage didn't mean shit unless you could back it up. And he could back it up."

He pauses and swallows, his fingers still moving against my back.

"I don't know if I can back it up, Hazel," he whispers. "I'm afraid everything he fought for is slipping through my fingers, and if I don't stop it, we'll have five more years of civil war. He brought Sveloria from a backwater to a first world country, and I don't know if I can keep it that way."

I have no idea what to say. Anything I can think of sounds like a kindergarten teacher's encouragement, so we're quiet for a long time.

"I don't think I ever loved my father," Kostya finally says, his voice low and quiet. "He'd lecture me about continuing the bloodline and having children, and I'd think, *I'd rather not be a father than be a father like you.*"

He's silent a moment.

"I didn't want him to die like this, Hazel," Kostya finally says.

"I know," I say, and kiss the top of his head.

We're quiet again.

"Can I sleep here?" he asks, his fingers on my back. "I don't dream when I sleep with you."

I push both of us up, and he looks at me like he's still waiting for an answer. His eyes are even more bloodshot now. I stand and hold out one hand again, and he takes it.

"Come on," I say.

In the bedroom I move the laptop off the bed and Kostya just looks around tiredly, like he doesn't understand what a bed is any more. I walk to him and start undoing the buttons on his shirt, and as I do he takes both my hands in his and leans his forehead down to touch mine.

For long moment he just rubs his thumbs over my knuckles, like he's trying to think of how to say something.

"I'm sorry," he says, his voice close to a whisper.

"Kostya, don't be," I say.

He laces his fingers through mine, his palms against the backs of my hands.

"*Zloyushka*, I don't know what I'm doing," he says. "I don't know how to be the king, and I don't know how to keep my country from disintegrating, and I thought if I could ignore you I'd stop thinking about you all the time and I'd get better at what I'm supposed to be doing, but I couldn't. And I didn't."

This time I can't stop my eyes from filling with tears.

"I wanted to protect you, and I couldn't," he says. "Not even from the *Tobov Post*."

"Kostya, you have bigger things to worry about than me," I say. "I'm fine. The *Post* can go fuck itself."

He half-smiles and squeezes my hands in his. A very, very distant bell tolls three times.

"I'm glad you slept with your married professor," he says.

"I'm not," I say.

"You wouldn't have come here otherwise," he says.

I sigh and let my eyes close, our foreheads still together.

"I don't know," I say. "Maybe."

"You're the American and I'm finding the silver lining," he says. "Something must have gone wrong."

He wobbles a little on his feet, and I tug at his shirt.

"Come on," I say, softly. "Go to bed."

I get the last button undone, push it over his shoulders, and ignore the heat pooling inside me. Once his shirt is off, he slides one hand down my back, along my still-open robe, and then pulls me toward him, swaying on his feet as he does.

He kisses me and I kiss him back briefly, my hand on his neck, and then pull away. I stroke his stubble with one thumb.

"Come on, *zloyushka*," he says, sounding half-drunk.

"No," I say firmly. "You're falling asleep on your feet."

"I'll make it fast," he murmurs.

"Not sexy," I murmur back.

Kostya sighs, his fingers circling on my back.

"You're right," he finally says. "You're naked and I'm so tired I'm barely hard."

"Your dirty talk is also pretty lacking," I tease, shrugging my robe the rest of the way off, and climb into bed.

He gets in after me, and his eyes are shut before his head's on the pillow.

"Let me get six hours of sleep, and then we'll fuck slow and hard until you come so hard your hair curls," he says.

My insides twist around themselves. Kostya barely opens one eye and looks at me.

"Was that better?" he says, his voice slurring.

"You're *filthy* for a king," I say.

He smiles, sleepily.

"I'm just honest," he says, and rolls over until his face is in my neck. "Sometimes in important meetings the only thing I can think about is what it feels like when you come with me inside you."

"Kostya, go the *fuck* to sleep," I whisper, wrapping my arms around him.

He sighs, but he doesn't say anything else. I stay awake for a few more minutes and listen to him breathe, then fall asleep myself.

CHAPTER THIRTY-TWO
KOSTYA

When I wake up, there's a moment when I forget everything that's happened. Hazel's curled into me, her back against my chest, my arms around her, and my father's murder, the insurgency, the fighting, everything seems like a long bad dream.

Then I wake up a little more and remember that it wasn't, that it *did* happen and I'm probably late for something.

Two more minutes, I think, and bury my nose in Hazel's hair.

"You awake?" she says, softly.

"Yes," I say. "What time is it?"

"Eight-thirty," she says.

"I should go," I murmur in her ear, but I run one hand down her side from her ribcage to her hip, her skin perfect and soft beneath my hand.

My cock is working again. I was already hard when I woke up, but as I stroke her side Hazel just barely arches her back, pressing herself against me, and my erection *throbs*.

I *need* her, so much it's visceral, like there's a raging tornado twisting deep inside me and this is the only thing I can do to keep it from destroying me.

I close my fingers around her hip and pull back. She arches again, harder now, and reaches her hand around to pull my head to hers, twisting her torso. I raise myself on my other elbow and we kiss hard, tongues in each others' mouths, as she rocks against me.

I groan into her mouth and she tightens her hand in my hair. I'm nearly dizzy with lust and want and the pure, primal sensation of *need*, and I touch the backs of her thighs and then push my hands between them until my fingers are on her slit, already slippery and wet.

She wraps a fist around my cock and I slide my fingers past her clit and relish the way her body gives a tiny jolt, like my touch is electric. Hazel moans as I rub her, and before I know it, she's guided the tip of my cock to her entrance.

"Condom," I gasp. "Nightstand."

"Are you clean?" she whispers.

"Yes," I say. She's warm and practically throbbing against me, and my mind is slowly blinking out.

"Then it's fine," she says. "I have an IUD."

I'm not exactly sure what that is. If I were smarter I'd find out, but right now, all I know is that it means I'm about to fuck Hazel skin to skin. I kiss the back of her neck slowly and she sighs.

There's a goddamn knock on the goddamn door.

We both stop, holding our breaths, as if the knock could have possibly been an accident.

The knock sounds again, louder this time. I roll onto my back.

"*Otvali mudak blyad*," I growl.

"Fucking mother*fucker*," Hazel fumes, and rolls off the bed. She finds the robe and pulls it on as I get up, putting on pants and at least getting my arms through my shirt.

There's yet another knock as Hazel heads for the door, and I stay back, just out of sight as she pulls it open.

"Niko," she says, sounding surprised.

"Good morning," he says. "Sorry to bother you, but we can't seem to find the King."

She pushes one hand through her hair.

"Come in," she says, sounding like she's admitting to stealing candy.

I'm buttoning the last button on my shirt as Niko comes in, but if he's surprised to find me getting dressed in Hazel's room, he doesn't show it.

"There's a problem," he says, crossing his arms.

I stand. Hazel perches on the arm of a chair, holding her robe closed tightly.

"The populist faction of the USF has taken Yelena Pavlovnova hostage," Niko says quietly.

Hazel gasps. I stop, one cuff half-buttoned.

"Yelena?" I ask.

"What happened?" asks Hazel at the same time.

Niko looks from me to her and back.

"Yes, Yelena," he says. "She disappeared from her father's villa sometime yesterday. No one is exactly sure when, but we received a photo of her with today's paper about thirty minutes ago."

"Is she okay?" says Hazel.

"Relatively speaking," Niko says carefully. "She didn't look visibly harmed."

"*Why* did they take her?" I ask.

Now I'm pacing the floor. I had just let myself think that things were starting to look up for us, and now a canyon has cracked open beneath my feet, threatening to swallow my whole country.

What the hell could they possibly want with Yelena? She can't tell them anything, and she certainly doesn't *know* anything.

"They're willing to release her in exchange for a meeting,"

Niko says. "They set the terms, but they want to do it on neutral ground."

Neutral ground is a fucking joke. Right now, there's no such thing, because *everywhere* within reach of the USF is dangerous.

I shouldn't even be considering this. If this is their negotiation strategy, their next step will be worse.

But they've got Yelena. Of all people, *she* doesn't deserve this.

"I'd be a sitting duck," I say.

"They don't want to talk to you," Niko says, and pauses.

I turn and look at him, and he looks at Hazel.

"They want to talk to you," he tells her.

"No," I say.

"Me?" Hazel says.

"*No,*" I say again, getting closer to Niko.

Like *fuck* is Hazel going out there, risking capture and possibly her life. Yelena's a nice girl, but the hell I'm trading Hazel for her.

"Why me?" Hazel asks Niko quietly.

"It doesn't matter, because you're not going," I say.

"Kostya, shut the hell up and let Niko tell me what's going on," she says, shooting me a glare.

"I'm not risking your life for hers," I say.

"You don't even know what's going on yet," she says.

"I don't need to know," I say. "You're not meeting with anyone. You're going home to the U.S., where it's safe, the second I can get you out of here, and that is *all* you're doing."

I'm terrified. The thought of Hazel putting herself in danger like this, with people who've already kidnapped one woman, makes me sick to my stomach.

"They want to meet with her because she's American," Niko says loudly over our arguing.

We both look at him.

"That's what we think, anyway," he says, his voice quieting. "It's a show of good faith on their part."

Hazel chews a thumbnail. A black hole opens in the pit of my stomach, because this is quickly becoming about much more than tiny Sveloria.

All three of us know what the show of good faith is: the USF can kidnap Svelorian citizens with impunity, but the moment they take an American, the United States military will drop the hammer. Fighter jets from the U.S. base in Turkey could be here in twenty minutes.

They would have to be *insane* to risk hurting an American citizen.

"The idea might be worth entertaining," Niko says.

"No," I say. "I'm not sending her to do my dirty work with people who've already proven they're willing to hurt innocent women."

"How many innocent people are gonna get hurt if this drags out?" Hazel says, her eyes flashing. "You've gotten lucky with casualties so far, Kostya, but if you dig in your heels, they're going to think they've got no choice."

"If we deal with them now, this ends with governmental reform," Niko says. "If we ignore this, we might risk a coup."

"I'm getting dressed," Hazel says, and walks to her bedroom, closing the door behind her. I stalk to the French doors that lead to the balcony and stare out at the sea. Niko follows, and we stand in silence together for a long moment.

"We used to talk about this when we were drinking in the gray district," he says softly, in Russian.

"We talked about what we'd change, not *this*," I say.

"If we allied with the populists, this could be over in a week," Niko says.

"They killed my father in the street like a dog," I say. "We should crush them. Annihilate them. Wipe them from the face of the earth."

"That's what he would have done," Niko says.

He doesn't have to say *and that's why he's dead* for me to understand it.

"Do you know what they want?" I ask.

"They want a Parliament, mostly," he says, and we look at each other. Then I look back at the Black Sea.

We've always talked about this. It's the twenty-first century, and as small as Sveloria is, a hereditary monarchy as the sole form of government seems quaint at best and dangerous at worst. I could never breathe a word of it to my iron-fisted father, but it's been in the back of my mind for a long, long time.

"I'm willing to talk," I say.

"They want Hazel," he says.

"That's out of the question," I say.

The bedroom door opens.

"Get me a meeting with Captain Ovechkin," I say quietly, still speaking Russian. "Keep it quiet. Bring Dmitri and Sergei."

Niko nods, and Hazel walks toward us, looking professional in black pants and a button-down shirt.

"Let's go at least hear what they've got to say," she says. She sounds less angry, but there's steel in her voice. "I'm willing to go if it means an end to this."

I just nod, and we leave Hazel's room.

THE DAY FEELS ENDLESS. Hazel, Niko, and I are in a windowless meeting room for hours with old men who advised my father and various people from the State Department on the screen in front of us.

We argue. We hash out plan after plan, then go back to

arguing. We imagine every possible scenario, change a detail, and argue about it all over again.

Intelligence comes in: the group who has Yelena now isn't the group who kidnapped her. That was the *volki*, the wolves, the same people who murdered my father.

"Not even the populists support the *volki*," Minister Arkady points out. "No one does. They're fighting an extremist, losing battle."

The USF is fracturing *fast*, but there's a delicate balance: if we do the right thing, we repair the country and make it strong. The wrong thing, and we rend it in two.

The half of the room that wants to send Hazel out — the half that includes Hazel — slowly wins. They're convinced that it's the safest for everyone, the best way to open negotiations.

Across the table, I catch Niko's eye. I can tell we're thinking the exact same thing: we spent years in the mountains fighting people like the *volki*. They're fanatics who won't give up, American military or no American military.

Everyone else in this room is lulling themselves into a false sense of security, telling themselves over and over again that this is safe, this is fine, this is an acceptable risk to take. These are men who fought with my father twenty years ago, but since then they've sat in comfortable chairs, getting fat on caviar and vodka.

I nod along with what they say, acting agreeable. Let them think their arguments are swaying me.

At four in the afternoon, after more than six hours, I stand.

"We'll take a break," I say, and look around at the blinking faces. "Come back here in two hours and we'll work on the details."

I leave the room first. Someone calls after me, but I ignore them, quickly going around a corner and down a staircase, taking the stairs two at a time, until I'm nearly in the basement, where I stop.

No one is following me. Good.

I walk into another hall. I turn a corner, and then the wooden doors of the chapel are in front of me and I swing them open.

Three men are standing inside, bathed in the light of the stained glass. They turn toward me as I enter.

"Captain Ovechkin, thank you for coming on such short notice," I say, and shake his hand.

"Of course, Your Majesty," he says.

"Sergei, Dmitri," I say.

The door opens again. Niko walks in, and Sergei crosses his arms in front of his chest, a pleased look in his eyes.

"All right, *your highness*," he says. "What shit are you getting us into now?"

"It's top secret and probably dangerous," I say.

Sergei and Dmitri both grin. Captain Ovechkin looks like he doesn't mind.

"We'll do it," says Dmitri.

CHAPTER THIRTY-THREE
HAZEL

When we reconvene at six, Kostya and Niko aren't there. The generals, the Americans on the teleconference, and I all look around at each other.

I wonder where the hell they are. They're both normally punctual to a fault, the first to get annoyed if someone else is three minutes late.

After five minutes of silence, Chief Minister Arkady clears his throat.

"We'll just begin," he says, and begins laying out his thoughts on the plan for tomorrow.

It's another ten minutes before Kostya and Niko come in together and silently take their seats. They don't offer an explanation, and no one's going to demand one of them, so we just carry on as though nothing strange just happened.

Slowly, we hammer out the plan. I'll be driven to the meeting place, an empty lot in the gray district, in a squadron of bulletproof cars, escorted by members of the Royal Guard. There will be snipers on the surrounding rooftops, the whole nine yards.

The leader of the USF Populists, Pavel Vasilovich, will

meet me there. We get Yelena first, and once she's safe, Pavel and I talk. I've got a list of what Kostya's willing to do and a matching list of demands, and it's safe to assume that Pavel has the same.

We exchange our lists. We shake hands. We both leave, and I come back here, safe and sound.

Sitting in this meeting room in the middle of a fortified castle, it all sounds so reasonable. Just another political discussion, nothing to get worried about. We meet, we exchange, we leave.

I know better. Right now, someone is going through the armory, looking for a kevlar vest that will fit me, but my real protection is believing that the other side isn't dumb enough to shoot an American.

That's what we're banking on. Everyone seems convinced, but even though I try to act like I'm not bothered, I'm nervous.

It doesn't help that Kostya's said about two words since he got back, almost like he's not paying attention. He just nods and agrees to everything everyone says, a total one-eighty from this morning.

Around nine, he excuses himself again, along with Niko, while I run through my script for the thousandth time. I'll leave at eight in the morning. Arrive eight-thirty. Perimeter cleared, snipers in place, everything checked and double checked.

I'll get out, talk to Pavel. Niceties, then real discussion, and I'll be out of there by nine-thirty. By ten in the morning, I'll be taking a bubble bath back in the palace.

I DON'T GET out of the meeting until late that night, and Kostya and Niko are still God knows where. Something is going on with the two of them. I don't know what it is, but it's making me uneasy, especially right now.

So instead of going to bed I wander around the palace aimlessly, trying to get lost, trying my best not to think about all the things that could go wrong in the next ten hours.

I'm not exactly afraid. I've seen my mother defuse a lot of tense situations. Growing up a diplomat's kid, in half a dozen different countries, I've walked into more than one situation where I didn't belong. I know that words have real power, and that people would almost always rather talk than shoot.

It doesn't mean I'm not nervous.

I end up by the drawing room where Kostya told me about murder holes and heads on spikes, and I wander in. I keep the lights off, because I'm not sure I want to be found, and I sit on a high-backed, ornately carved couch with the most uncomfortable upholstery I've ever encountered. It's facing the crazy-eyed portrait of Maksim the Second, and we stare at each other in the dark.

I've learned more about him in the past week. He's remembered as a fierce defender of the homeland, a man who fought off invaders and put their heads on spikes. Turns out that's just the tip of the Maksim iceberg.

Deranged is probably the right word. When there were no barbarians to decapitate and display, he ordered hands cut off thieves. Army deserters were drawn and quartered, usually while he himself stood there, watching. He suspected his wife of adultery and had her locked in the dungeons of another palace for three years, and she finally died of neglect when he forgot about her.

He wasn't even sixty when he died suddenly, vomiting blood. Historians agree that he was probably poisoned, but there were so many suspects that we'll never know who did it.

Now I'm sitting where he sat. Looking out at gardens that were once festooned with heads, and tomorrow I'm going to have a good, peaceful, by-the-book exchange with the people threatening Sveloria. At least I hope it's peaceful.

Footsteps echo through the hallway. Someone walks to the open door of the drawing room and stops, leaning in the door-way. I can tell it's Kostya from the way he moves.

"There you are," I say.

"You're just sitting here in the dark?" he asks, his voice low and quiet, and it sends an electric shiver through me. Despite everything that's happened today, I keep thinking about this morning, about his hand on my hip, about how he turns my mind to mush with need. About how *right* everything feels when we're together.

I look back at the crazy-eyed portrait on the wall.

"Maksim and I were having a moment," I say. "He doesn't really approve of me, but he's a painting, so he can go fuck himself."

Kostya closes the door behind him with a long, loud creak.

"My father wanted him there," he says, glancing at the portrait. "Probably to make sure people knew that heads on spikes were never too far from his mind."

"You disappeared," I say. "I was looking for you."

"I had to take care of some things," he says.

I wait for him to elaborate, but he doesn't.

"What's going on?" I ask.

"Nothing," he says, walking over to me.

"You know I don't believe you, right?" I ask.

He holds out one hand, his face nearly expressionless, his eyes burning.

I stare back, and I feel like a pinned bug again for the first time in weeks. There's something suddenly different about his mannerisms, a total one-eighty from last night.

Kostya's not asking me to take his hand. He's *telling* me. I take it.

He pulls me to standing, then takes my face in his hands, our bodies pressed together.

"Hazel, nothing's gonna happen to you," he says, his voice low and gravelly, those eyes boring into me.

I swallow.

"You mean tomorrow?" I ask.

"I promise you'll be okay," he says, not exactly answering my question. "I swear."

"Kostya," I say, because I don't actually know what he's talking about.

"There's no fucking point to being king if I can't protect you," he says, putting the pad of one thumb on my lips. "It's nothing but castles and cars and bureaucracy and bullshit if I can't keep the people I love safe."

My heart does a tiny flip in my chest, but I take a deep breath.

"What are you *talking* about?" I ask through his thumb.

"I'm talking about you," he says, like it's the most obvious thing in the world, but I feel like I missed a couple sentences of this conversation or something.

"Start over," I say. "What's *happening*?"

His eyes just barely crinkle around the corners.

"I'm being the fucking King," he says, nearly smiling.

"But—"

He shuts me up by kissing me hard and despite myself, I kiss him back, my hands around the back of his neck as he presses the small of my back so my hips lean into him, pressing along his delicious, hard length.

Then I put both hands on his chest and push, just hard enough that he stops kissing me.

"Wait," I say, a little breathless. "No. You have to tell me what's going on, Kostya. Pull your 'I'm the King' shit with other people."

His eyes crinkle again in his almost-smile.

"You know the English poem, 'You carry my heart in both hands,' or something?" he asks.

"Maybe?" I say.

He puts his hand over mine and presses it to his chest. There it is, the steady *thump-thump* of his heart.

"I may as well tear it out of my ribcage and hand it to you," he says. "I already feel like I have, like it's raw and beating and at any second you could squeeze it or drop it and I'd be finished."

Thump-thump.

"I won't," I whisper.

"I need you to trust me this once," he says. "You can have *this*—" he squeezes my hand over his heart— "as collateral, and if I'm lying to you, step on it or throw it in a fire. Do whatever you want. Just trust me."

Now I'm afraid, because that's not what someone says when they're going to follow the plan you've laid out together.

"No," I say. "I don't want collateral, I want—"

"Please," he murmurs.

I close my eyes, feeling the *thump-thump* under my palm. I take a deep breath and remind myself that there's a good chance he knows what he's doing.

Not that it changes how afraid for him I am, or how desperately I want him to be okay.

"I trust you," I whisper.

"Thank you," he says, and kisses me again.

My mind's a maelstrom. I wish he'd tell me what's going on, and I have a bone-deep bad feeling that it's dangerous. I wish tomorrow were over already. I wish we were waking up in my bed again, tangled up together, sunlight streaming in through the window.

But then Kostya deepens the kiss, and he presses his rough fingers to my spine, under my shirt, and slides them up notch by notch, and I force myself to let all that go. I focus on his tongue winding around mine, his heartbeat under my hand.

Suddenly, there are voices speaking Russian right outside the door, and I freeze. Kostya pulls his head back but his hands are still on me as the door opens and the lights flip on.

Two young men step inside and stop mid-sentence, staring.

Kostya growls in Russian, glaring hard enough to melt steel.

The men duck their heads, muttering apologies in Russian, and flee, the door closing behind them. He kisses me once more, briefly, and then strides to the window and yanks the shades shut with one quick, forceful motion.

He looks around for a moment, like he's trying to find something in the dark, then goes to one corner, bends, and comes up carrying a long, thick wooden beam. His forearms bulge as he fits it to the notches in the back of the door, barring it completely.

"There," he says, and pulls me to him again. "Anyone who wants to interrupt now had better have siege equipment, because they can knock until their knuckles bleed."

We kiss again, hard, his lips nearly crushing mine. I bite his lip as he pulls away, his hands already unbuttoning my shirt, and he growls at me.

I tear my half-unbuttoned shirt off, and before it even hits the floor Kostya's already shoved my bra over my breasts, then over my head. He pushes me against the wall next to the door, the plaster cool against my back as he kisses my neck, his teeth just barely brushing my skin as he works his way down.

I make a noise through my teeth, and then he *does* bite me.

"*Yahoo sea's tibia,*" it sounds like he says, chuckling softly.

My fingers are fumbling at the top button of his shirt, and it finally pops open.

"What?" I ask, moving on to the next one.

"I want to *devour* you," he says. His mouth is on my collarbone and he's unbuttoning my professional black pants, pushing them over my hips, and I kick them off as he pinches one nipple between his fingers and flicks his tongue over the other.

I moan, my eyes sliding shut. He bites my nipple, and I gasp, then hold my breath as he bites just a little harder, teasing it between his teeth.

Holy *fuck* it feels good, like light exploding through my body, just hard enough to set every nerve blissfully on edge.

I grab a handful of his hair and he sucks slowly, then finally pulls away.

"That good?" he asks.

"Yes," I gasp.

He bites my other nipple and I think I growl but then he's standing, kissing me on the mouth again and I'm finally pulling his shirt over his head. I put the palm of my hand on the base of his cock, through his pants, and drag it up his length slowly as he throbs beneath me.

"God, you do things to me," he whispers in my ear.

I get his pants off and kiss him again as he lifts me into the air and I wrap my legs around him, pressing the length of his cock against myself as he pushes me back against the wall. I'm pinned but I move my hips slowly, just barely rubbing him against myself, the delicious friction making me sigh.

"Fuck, I like that," he says, and moves me again. I reach down and wrap my hand around the head of his cock, surprised to find it already slick as I rub it.

"You still haven't made my hair curl," I say. "And you promised."

"I was so tired I don't remember exactly what I said," he murmurs. "You're gonna have to remind me, *zloyushka*."

He fucking remembers, he just wants me to say it.

"You said you'd fuck me slow until my hair curled," I whisper, squeezing the tip of his cock.

He kisses me, then pulls me away from the wall and carries me to the couch. It creaks when I hit it, and for a second I wonder if we're about to break a piece of furniture that's a hundred years old.

Then he's kneeling between my legs, and he grabs the back of my head and pulls my face to his.

"I think I said slow and hard," he says, his hand drifting up my thigh until his fingers brush my lips, sending a tingle through my whole body. I lean back on the couch and grab the carved wooden headrest behind me so hard that the couch creaks again, and he slides one fingertip up my slit, in a loop around my clit, and then back down.

"Don't tease me," I gasp. "Come on, Kostya."

"Why not?" he asks, doing it again.

I swallow hard.

"Because it's already been too long and I fucking *want* you," I gasp. "I nearly murdered Niko this morning."

He slides his fingers inside me and I arch my back and groan, hanging onto the back of the couch like it's keeping me afloat. Kostya hoists my legs onto his shoulders and then he's licking me, hard and fast, in time with his fingers moving inside me.

I think I whimper, it feels so good and I'm so tightly wound. It's taking all my self control not to grab Kostya's hair in my hands or clamp his head between my thighs, and as it is I'm panting for breath and slowly sliding off this couch, but he just keeps going.

It doesn't take much to get me to the edge, a sudden shiver slicing down my body.

"Stop," I gasp.

He gives me one more long, slow lick that makes my body jolt.

"What for?" he asks.

"I'm gonna come," I say, trying to sit up.

"And?" he says, his eyes crinkling. "I like making you come."

I let go of the headrest, but I slide off the ugly velvet couch and tumble to the floor, practically on top of Kostya instead.

"Sorry," I say, but his mouth is already on mine, and it tastes like me and it's dirty and sexy and just makes me want him more.

He pulls back and licks my wetness off one finger. Then he kisses me again.

"You're fucking filthy," I whisper, reaching down to take his cock in my hand.

"I told you, I'm just honest," he says, and licks another finger. "I like licking you until you come. I like the way you taste. I like you being naked in front of me. I like being inside you."

We kiss again, and I stroke his cock slowly so he groans into my mouth. He throbs in my hand, and I swallow hard, suddenly nervous about what I'm about to ask.

"Can I still fuck you bare?" I whisper. "It's safe."

Kostya just chuckles.

"Please?" I ask, my voice sounding husky to my own ears. "I want to feel *you*, not something else."

"It's not *safe*," he says as he runs a hand down my body.

"I've got an——"

He grabs my hips and flips me around, and I yelp. Suddenly I'm facing away from him, my forearms braced against the ugly couch.

"Not *that*," he says, his voice growling in my ear. "I don't *feel* safe about you. I feel like I'd walk through a burning building to be inside you, and that's hardly *safe*."

I reach behind myself, blindly, and rest my hand on the back of his neck. He slides the thick head of his cock along me and I arch my back until he's at the right spot and he sinks inside me, just barely.

Then he stops and runs his hands up my back, like he's hesitant, and I don't need him to fucking *hesitate*, I need him *now*.

"You're not gonna hurt me," I say, pushing back against him.

"Let me be careful with you," he whispers into my hair.

I reach back further behind me and try to grab onto his shoulder, *something* that will push him further into me, because I need this so bad it *hurts*.

"Kostya, for fuck's sake," I whisper, and he sucks air through his teeth. I dig my fingers into him and then he finally slides all the way inside me, his cock hitting every damn pleasure spot I've got.

"Oh, *fuck*," I whisper, one fist tight on the ugly couch. I press myself against him because Jesus Christ, it feels *good* to have him buried inside me again at last.

"I promised you slow," he says, kissing my shoulder.

"You promised me hard," I whisper.

We start fucking, and he goes slow and hard just like he promised, and it makes me feel like every inch of my body is also getting fucked, like I'm lost in a haze of pleasure and there's nearly no way out. I think I'm melting into this terrible couch, both fists probably ripping the ugly fabric, my face buried in it, and with every thrust I moan a little louder as he pushes me closer to the edge.

Then he stops. He drives himself into me so hard I *shout* and my fingers finally rip through the fabric, and then he stops.

"Don't stop," I gasp.

We're both panting for breath, and I know I'm close to coming, pleasure already whispering through my body like ripples in a pond. He doesn't move.

I look over my shoulder at him, leaning my head on one arm, and I reach the other hand back and stroke his hip, then flex my hips against him so his cock moves inside me, and *god* that feels good.

He pulls me up by the shoulder, then reaches in front of me and drags the couch forward until it's right in front of me and we're both kneeling upright, still on the floor.

"Do that again," he growls, so I flex my hips against him and this time he moves too, fucking me shallow but hard, grinding our hips together.

"This feels so fucking good," I whisper. I've got one hand clutching the couch and the other on his neck again, the only part I can really grab.

"There's a spot inside you that makes your fingers curl," he says, and thrusts, just a little.

My fingers curl on the couch and his neck, and Kostya growls, then does it again and again until I'm writhing and bucking against him. We're still going slow and he's got one arm across my chest, his hand on my shoulder as he buries his cock in me over and over and I feel like I'm a keg of gunpowder about to explode.

"Kostya, I'm gonna come," I gasp. "*Jesus*, I'm gonna come."

"Good," he whispers. "You're so fucking sexy when you do."

I think I'm unraveling, and I turn my head into his shoulder and he grips me even tighter and he thrusts again, hard and *deep*.

"Fuck, Kostya," I whisper, and then I think my body flies apart.

He holds me and we rock together and I'm exploding in slow motion and it feels so good I swear I'm floating. I can hear myself saying *god fucking yes Kostya Jesus yes oh fuck Kostya* even as my body floats away.

"I love it when you come on my cock," he whispers into my ear.

I swallow, trying to remember words.

"You're fucking dirty," I say, still panting for breath.

He's still fucking me, and it still feels *good*.

"Only for you," he whispers. "You *make* me dirty, *zloyushka*."

"Come inside me," I say. "Let me feel you."

His arm tightens. I kiss his shoulder. He growls something in Russian, and I grab him by the hair.

"Fucking come for me," I whisper.

He does. He pushes me against the couch, his arm tightening across me and I can feel his cock explode deep inside me as he groans in my ear. The only word I can make out is my name but he keeps saying it, rocking back and forth until he finally stops coming.

Then he leans his head against mine and wraps his other arm around me.

"*Yeah bluetube*," I think he says.

I put my hands over his and turn my head to kiss his shoulder. He nuzzles my neck, and after a moment, he finally stands, only to collapse back onto the couch where he pulls me up after him and then wraps his arms around me. I let myself feel safe and warm and happy, despite everything.

On the wall, Maksim is still staring at us, his crazy eyes almost the only thing visible in his face.

"I think the beheader gets off on watching," I say.

There's a moment of silence.

"What?" Kostya asks, sounding totally puzzled, so I point at Maksim.

"He saw everything," I say.

"Pervert," says Kostya.

CHAPTER THIRTY-FOUR
KOSTYA

Every time I move, trying to get comfortable, the couch creaks. Finally I shift, trying to get a lump out of my backbone, and there's the unmistakable sound of very old wood cracking. Hazel freezes.

"We broke the couch," she whispers.

"You mean we broke *my* couch," I say, shifting again. "I'm the king. Ugly couches live and die at my whim."

Hazel laughs.

I can't help but grin, because I *finally* did it. She curls into me a little more, and then she looks up at me.

She stops laughing immediately and looks suspicious.

"What?" she asks.

"I can't smile?" I ask.

Hazel just narrows her eyes.

"I told a joke and you laughed," I explain.

Now she looks puzzled.

"You make me laugh all the time," she says.

"This time was intentional," I say. "We were standing right there the first time I tried to make you laugh."

Hazel looks at me blankly.

"Before the dinner when I got really drunk and you had to come feed me bread?" she finally says.

"I told you I believed putting heads on spikes was frowned upon," I say.

There's a long pause.

"Oh," she says.

"It wasn't funny," I admit.

She draws her legs onto the couch and then moves around some, trying to get comfortable.

"It's a terrible couch," I say, and pull her against me so she's half lying on my chest, half off the damn couch. "We should just go get in my bed."

Hazel leans her head against me and blows a hair out of her face.

"Everyone will know if we do," she says.

"Let them," I say. "We can worry about that tomorrow afternoon."

She turns and gives me another weird look, like she's about to ask me something, but then doesn't. I think she's given up asking what I'm hiding from her.

It's for the best, because I'm not going to tell her. For the first time since my father died, I'm finally certain that I'm doing something right. I'm not even nervous, just satisfied.

We stand after another moment. I find my clothes and pull them back on, not bothering to tuck in my shirt, because I'm pretty sure the whole palace heard us and I couldn't care less.

When I turn, Hazel's topless, frowning at her bra.

"I didn't break it, did I?" I ask.

She bites her lip, like she's trying not to laugh.

"Kostya, do you know how to take bras off?" Hazel asks softly.

We look at each other for a long moment.

"I understand the principle," I finally admit. "It's harder to put into practice."

"So you're great at eating me out and you can't get a bra off," she says.

I put my hands on her arms and pull her in, kissing her.

"Say that again," I tell her.

She laughs and blushes.

"You heard me," she says.

"Come on," I say.

"Fine," she says, and drops her voice to a whisper. "You're great at eating me out."

I kiss her again.

"I prioritized learning certain skills over others," I say.

"Of course you did," she says, putting the bra on, clasping it behind her back with no problem. "You probably had a checklist."

"Not technically," I say.

She finds her shirt, and then we move the couch back, more or less, to where it was before. It's got a definite wobble to it, but we're not going to throw it out tonight.

I lift the bar from the door, but before we push it open, Hazel and I look at each other.

Tell her in English, I think.

I push the door open, and we leave the drawing room. If anyone else heard anything, they keep their mouths shut.

HAZEL'S WALKING toward a man I don't recognize, sitting at a table. I'm watching from fifty yards away, and we're all on a big flat outdoor space on top of a concrete slab. Some kind of factory that was never built. This must be the gray district.

It's hot, but she's wearing lots of gear: thick jacket, thick pants, helmet. The man stands.

I know what's going to happen before it happens, like I

read a few pages ahead, but I can't run. I can't move. I'm standing in glue, or maybe concrete. I can't even shout.

The scene shifts, and now there are trees where there was nothing before, interspersed with buildings. I still can't move, but something is scratching at the back of my brain, like it's trying to get in.

Hazel walks. She's almost to the table, but she can't get there, because if she does something bad will happen. I don't know how I know, but I do.

I feel like there's a screen between me and her, and I try to grab at it, tear it away, shout at her so she stops. She keeps walking.

The bomb is under the table.

Hazel and the man both fly backward, twenty feet, the flame blossoming and disappearing instantly. I watch her land wrong, her neck at a bad angle, and she's still for long, horrifying seconds.

I wake up shouting.

I sit bolt upright in bed. Next to me, someone jerks and I turn and catch a wrist on instinct, breathing hard, my body covered in sweat.

"Kostya," Hazel says.

I let her wrist go, yanking my hand back like she's a hot stove.

"*Prosti*," I whisper. "*Dermo, prosti.*"

She puts the hand on my shoulder.

"You're in the palace, in Velinsk, in your room," she says.

"*Ya sdelal tebe bolno?*" I ask.

"It was just a dream, you're fine, you're here," she says, her hand moving in wide circles on my back.

I look at her, and blink.

"Did I hurt you?" I ask, in English this time.

"No," she says.

"Are you sure?"

"Super sure," she says.

I look at the clock. 3:30. I shouldn't bother going back to sleep before I have to leave.

"I'm sorry," I say.

"Jesus, Kostya, quit apologizing," Hazel says. "I'm *fine*. You grab me all the time."

I lean on one hand and put my forehead against hers, and I stay there as I let the dream slide away, reminding myself over and over that she's here, she's in my bed, she's safe. She's going to stay safe.

I want to tell her not to be nervous about tomorrow morning, that she's got nothing to be afraid of. That if I can do one *fucking* thing as the King of Sveloria, it's protect her.

"*Ya lyublyu tebya,*" I say.

She just runs her hand through my hair, like she thinks I'm falling back asleep. I put my hand on her jaw, gently, my thumb across her lips, and she looks at me. Her hand in my hair goes still, and suddenly I'm bats-in-my-stomach, heart-in-my-throat nervous.

"What?" she whispers.

"I love you," I say.

Her lips move like she's about to speak.

"Don't say anything," I say. "Don't say it back. I just wanted to tell you."

After another moment, I move my thumb off her lips. My heart is still in my throat, and despite everything, I'm terrified of what she might say.

"I know," she whispers, and kisses me gently.

"You should go back to sleep," I say. "Before tomorrow."

"You know I'll be okay, right?" she asks.

"I know," I say.

We lie back down, and as we do, I feel her hand on the back of my neck.

"What happened?" she asks, and I reach behind myself.

"What are you talking about?" I say.

"You've got these long red streaks," she says, sitting up and getting closer. "It looks like somebody—"

She stops, then closes her mouth, looking sheepish.

"Looks like somebody raked their fingernails over my neck trying to get me inside her faster?"

My dick twitches, and I ignore it.

"Never mind," Hazel says, and I laugh, then lay next to her and pull her close.

"I learned my lesson," I tease, on my side curled against her, Hazel on her back.

She sighs.

"Give Hazel all the cock she wants," I say.

"I'm sorry," she says, but she's trying not to laugh. "Are you okay?"

"I survived this time," I say.

"Shut up," she whispers, and I kiss her.

I want to tell her *I like being marked yours*, but I don't. Instead she falls back asleep slowly, turning onto her side in my arms and snuggling into me while I watch the minutes tick by on the clock.

For the first time all day, I don't want to do this any more. I just want to stay in bed with her while the world goes on outside, but then I think of the dream again, of her head at that angle. She stirs in her sleep, and I realize I was holding her too tight.

I kiss her on the shoulder and slowly unwind myself. She turns onto her stomach but doesn't wake up.

"I love you," I whisper, kiss her other shoulder, and get out of bed.

At 4:15 I meet Niko in the Emerald Dining Room, the one we never use except for formal events. It's still dark outside, and he walks up to me without speaking.

"You're sure?" he asks, finally.

"I'm sure," I say, and he nods once, crisply.

"I thought so," he says.

At 4:30 we've made it to the east gate of the palace. Niko pulls out his phone and begins the security system updates, taking it offline, and he and I open the gate manually.

On the other side are four Humvees. American-made, nearly new. My father got them just last year. Dmitri waves from one window, and I wave back. Captain Ovechkin jumps out of a truck.

"Everything's in place?" he asks.

"Yes, sir," Niko and I say in unison.

The captain gives me a funny look, but doesn't say anything. He holds out one hand to Niko.

"Nikolai," he says, clapping his other hand over Niko's. "It's been an honor."

"Likewise," Niko says. The captain lets his hand go, and Niko's gaze washes over the trucks and the men inside them, full of naked, unabashed longing.

It must be hell to be the guy who has to stay behind while the rest of us get to go on a mission like this. It doesn't matter that he's got some of the most important jobs, or that there's no way it would be happening without Niko. There's nothing else like it in the world, and he knows that.

Captain Ovechkin nods again and turns back to his truck.

I turn to Niko and we embrace hard.

"Good luck, brother," he says gruffly.

I back up and we hold each other's shoulders at arm's length.

"I wish you could come," I say.

"I do too," he says. "I'd slow you down."

"You've got everything," I say.

He nods.

"You know the backup plans?" I ask.

This could go bad. I could die. We could all die.

"Of course," he says.

"Thank you, brother," I say, and we let go. He walks back through the still-open gate, his limp only just noticeable.

Then he watches us as we drive off, and the car is quiet for a moment. I look out the window at the barely-gray horizon, thinking about the hour and half between now and the meeting.

Finally, Sergei speaks up.

"What the hell happened to your neck?" he asks.

CHAPTER THIRTY-FIVE
HAZEL

I'm almost too wired to sleep, too nervous about the day ahead. I wake up again at 5:30, look at the clock, sigh, and roll over.

Then I sit up in surprise. The bed's empty. Kostya's gone. I put my hand on the mattress.

Cold. He's been gone a while.

There's a heavy feeling in the pit of my stomach as I roll out of his bed.

This is the thing he wouldn't tell me about, I think. *I fucking know it is.*

I yank on my pants and a bra. I can't find my shirt in the dark so I grab a t-shirt of his off a chair and it's barely over my head before I'm leaving his room, still barefoot, adrenaline spiking through my veins.

Maybe I can find him and stop whatever the fuck he's doing, I think.

I come out of his apartment into the hall and try to think. He's probably leaving, and if he didn't want to get caught he'd go out a lower level—

I round a corner into the broad, tall main hall and stop.

Niko's standing there, arms crossed, staring out a window. He looks over at me as I enter.

"I was about to come wake you up," he says.

"Where's Kostya?" I ask, doing my best to make my voice not shake.

"Already gone," he says.

"Gone *where*?" I ask.

I feel like I'm seconds away from losing my shit.

"Come on," he says, and starts to walk away.

"No!" I say, then look around.

I take a deep breath and lower my voice.

"I am fucking done with people not telling me shit," I say. "I'll come look at whatever you want me to look at but would you *please fucking tell me what is going on.*"

"He's meeting Pavel," Niko says, crossing his arms in front of his chest.

"I knew it," I say, pinching the bridge of my nose with one hand. "I fucking knew it."

I take a deep breath.

"What the hell *for*?" I ask.

"Because he's the King, and he didn't want to send a defenseless foreign national to do his work for him," Niko says, then lowers his voice. "And because neither of us trust the *volki* not to try something, even with an American."

"So *he's* going?" I ask.

"He's got half the Royal Guard with him," Niko says.

I exhale, crossing my arms in front of me.

"That's the first thing you've said that's made me feel any better," I admit.

"He's in very good hands," Niko says, and looks back out the window.

"When's the meeting?" I ask.

"Six," Niko says. "Thirty minutes. We have dashboard cameras, if you want to watch."

"Can I talk you out of this?" I ask quietly.

Niko shakes his head.

"You sure?" I ask.

My mind is racing. *What if I called the state department? The military base in Turkey?*

I'm pretty sure that's all stupid. Sveloria is a sovereign state. They were only involved because I was, and now I'm not.

"I'm sure," he says.

"Why didn't you tell me?"

"Then it wouldn't be a secret," Niko says.

"Come *on*," I say.

Niko almost smiles.

"Because you're also stubborn and argumentative, and he was afraid you'd do something like call the State Department, and then he'd have to argue with them for another day," he says. "His words, not mine."

It *was* the first thing I thought of.

"I don't have to like it," I say.

"No one thought you would," Niko says, and tilts his head toward the door. "Come on."

WE'RE in the same office where we have all our meetings, and we're projecting a dashboard camera onto the screen. Every so often Niko switches to a different one, but right now all four show the same thing: a wide open concrete slab, buildings in the distance. There's no sound, but we can see men carefully patrolling, checking the ground, keeping watch.

I have no idea which one's Kostya. The camera's not that good, and it's simultaneously boring and tense, like a nature documentary that could become a horror movie at any moment.

Right now, in the room, it's just the two of us, and we're not talking.

Finally, after a long stretch of silence, I speak up.

"Can I ask you a nosy question?" I say.

"Americans only ask that when they've made up their mind to ask it already," Niko says.

I sigh.

"Yes," he says.

"Are you watching from here instead of with them because of your leg?" I ask.

"Yes," he says again.

I wait for him to elaborate, and finally he looks at me, like he realizes I'm waiting.

"Land mine on a road in the mountains," he says.

I can tell there's more. I glance at the screen, then wait.

"It killed two other men instantly," he says. "I was ten feet away and just got a legful of shrapnel."

He folds his hands on the table and looks at them.

"It was a trap, and they started shooting the second I went down," he says softly. "Kostya and Sergei came back and dragged me behind cover. I'd be dead if they hadn't."

I glance at the screen. Still nothing.

"I'm sorry you're not there," I say.

"It's that obvious?" he says.

"Only to people with eyes," I say.

He's quiet for a long time, watching the screen.

"It's a stupid thing to miss, but I miss it," he says. "We all do. The words were hardly out of my mouth before Sergei and Dmitri said yes."

I almost say some platitude, like *you're also being helpful here* or *this is also important*, but I keep my mouth shut instead. I've learned that's not the sort of thing Svelorians appreciate.

"They liked you, you know," Niko says, his eyes still on the screen. "After they met you at the bar."

"They weren't what I was expecting at *all*," I admit. "You guys are fun."

"There was beer," Niko says. "And you could have knocked everyone over with a feather when he came in with you."

"Me?"

He hits a button, and we switch from one camera to another. A clock in the corner is ticking down, my stomach twisting with every minute, and I try to ignore it.

"With a girl at all," Niko says. He hits the button again, toggling through cameras. I think he's getting antsy too. "Let alone one who actually makes him smile."

Then he looks at me almost slyly.

"And who kicked her attacker in the balls twice."

"I also clocked him in the face with a motorcycle helmet," I say. Talking with Niko is finally starting to make me unwind. "He tell you that?"

"He *bragged* about that," Niko says.

He toggles through the cameras again. It's nearly six, and for a long moment, the two of us watch. I think Niko's just as nervous about this as me, even though he's been through this with Kostya more than once before.

Suddenly, on a camera, there's movement where there was nothing before.

"Go back!" I say, but Niko's already there, and we both sit forward in our chairs.

The camera is a hundred feet behind a small wooden table, off to one side. On the other side of the table, probably two hundred feet from the camera, there's a small knot of people.

I hold my breath. One of them starts moving, hesitantly, with small steps. After a few more seconds I can see blond hair and a lithe frame.

"That's Yelena," I say, and Niko nods.

Together, we watch her approach the table, pass it, walk

toward the camera and finally disappear. A few seconds later, a radio beeps in front of Niko, and he talks quietly in Russian for a few moments, then nods at me.

"She's safe," he says, and I swallow.

CHAPTER THIRTY-SIX
KOSTYA

Once Yelena passes the table, the knot in my stomach unwinds a little. I'm still strung like a piano wire, every nerve pinging, but at least it looks like Yelena's going to be safe.

She's twenty feet away, then ten, and then she's between two of the Humvees and staring around, bewildered, before she looks at me.

"Kostya," she says, like she's confused.

I take her gently by the shoulders.

"Did they hurt you?" I ask.

She shakes her head.

"Are you sure?" I ask, looking into her bloodshot blue eyes.

"I'm okay," she says.

Someone else comes, takes her hands, and pushes her into a vehicle.

There. I've done one thing right, at least.

I look back at the table, and realize that Pavel is already there, standing behind his wooden chair. The whole setup is strangely formal — a table and chairs on a concrete slab? — But I wonder if they just want this to look as legitimate as possible.

We checked the table for a bomb five times, maybe six, even though I wouldn't tell anyone why. I'm not superstitious as a rule, but that dream was hard to shake.

Dmitri hands me a small, sealed bottle of vodka and a glass. I take a deep breath, my kevlar vest tight against my chest, and I walk to the table.

Pavel straightens as I get closer, then holds out his right hand. I place my bottle on the table then take his hand in mine.

"Pavel Vasilovich," I greet him.

"Your Majesty, Konstantin Grigorovich," he says, very formally.

I gesture at the vodka. We've both brought bottles and glasses. It's customary.

"A drink?" I ask.

"Please, you first," he says.

This is all politeness. No one's poisoned anyone with vodka for a long time now, but allowing me to pour first is a show of trust on his part, that I haven't poisoned my bottle.

I pour into our glasses.

"To the light on the mountains," I say. It's traditional. We drink.

Then, at last, we sit. He pours two more shots.

"To the fish in the sea," he says, his voice quieter now. Everything before now has been for show, but now it's just the two of us talking.

"You came instead of the American," he says.

"It's a pretty bad king that lets defenseless Americans do his dirty work for him," I say.

He just nods. I wonder if that was a test.

"I apologize about the kidnapping," he says. "It isn't what I wanted."

"It's a brutish way to make a point," I say.

He nods once.

"Yes," Pavel says.

We sit there for a long time, or at least it feels long. Slowly, Pavel reveals more and more of what his faction wants, and at the same time he tells me about the politics of the USF, the in-fighting. Everyone at each other's throats, and the *volki* happy to come in and tear everything apart.

Without exactly telling me, he's saying that there doesn't have to be violence. He's saying that most people don't want things to change too much.

Pavel lists reforms. I've already uncensored the press and lifted the ban on meeting places, and we volley back and forth over taxes, elections, representation. He seems surprised that I'm willing to consider those things at all, and I tell him I'm not my father.

He considers this, and in the distance, I hear a rattle.

There's something familiar about it, something that alerts the fight-or-flight, instinctual part of my brain, and I look around.

Nothing. I try to ignore it.

Pavel moves on to export tariffs, but the sound is getting louder and I can't ignore it. I watch the open space to my right, desperately searching. I *know* something is there. I *know* something is going to happen.

"Konstantin," Pavel says, trying to get my attention, but then it comes into sight.

It's an old Soviet truck, and it comes out from between two factories and the driver guns the engine at top speed. Everyone is shouting. There's gun fire, and the truck rocks from side to side, its thick steel body denting with pockmarks.

The driver just ducks and keeps coming, and Pavel is staring, open-mouthed.

I don't think. I don't plan. I just grab him by the shirt, pull him around the table, and we both run.

CHAPTER THIRTY-SEVEN
HAZEL

This is *boring*. Thank God, this is boring, and we're just watching two men occasionally drink vodka and sit at a table. Every so often, Pavel will wave his hands around a little, but that's about it.

Niko and I just watch. Every few minutes, we toggle through the cameras, but they all show the same thing: two men talking.

After about ten minutes, we hear an outer door slam open. Niko and I both jump, and then look at each other. I think he was hoping to have this finished with before anyone else found out what was going on, but he doesn't exactly look surprised.

"Damn," he says, sounding resigned.

Footsteps stomp toward our meeting room, and the door flies open. Chief Minister Arkady is already shouting in Russian as he comes through it, a long string of guttural sounds and sibilants that sure *sound* angry.

Niko watches him, politely, as if waiting for him to finish. I realize he was expecting this.

Finally, the Chief Minister stops shouting at Niko. Niko

responds with one sentence, then looks back at the screen, and the Chief Minister looks at me.

"And *you*," he says. His face is bright red from all the shouting. "You Americans, you tell us one thing and then you do another, like a pack of lying weasel-snakes—"

Just take it, I tell myself. *You can't say anything to make him less angry right now, so just deal.*

"—You go back on promises and then we're left here to sweep up—"

Niko leans forward in his chair, suddenly going tense.

"What?" I ask him, ignoring Arkady.

He doesn't say anything, just toggles through the cameras.

"—Leave a country in ruins—"

"I don't know," Niko says, but his voice is strained.

On the screen, Kostya's stopped listening to Pavel, and he's just watching the open space to his right. Something about it makes my blood run cold, my stomach clench. Niko speaks quietly into the radio, and Arkady stops shouting mid-sentence, then turns and looks at the screen.

He's just in time to see Kostya grab Pavel by the collar of his shirt and drag him around the table.

"*Chto on del—*" Arkady starts.

Kostya and Pavel run toward the camera, which means toward the vehicles. Niko and I are both standing, and I don't think either of us are breathing.

An ancient, gray-green armored truck with a faded red star on one side rolls into view and comes to a hard stop. There's something strangely casual about it, like there's a red light that we can't see, and for one second, it sits there as Kostya and Pavel run hell-for-leather toward the Humvees.

Then the truck explodes. There's no sound on the dashboard cameras, so it's totally silent, orange blooming out, the truck bursting, flames turning to thick black smoke.

I'm frozen. There's a layer of surreality over everything,

like I'm watching an action movie and not real life, but then something heavy hits the windshield in front of the camera and a spider web splinters across it from one corner, and that's what shakes me back.

Niko's already shouting into the radio in Russian. Someone's shouting back, and I grab the camera toggle and switch views, but there's nothing that shows what's happening behind the trucks.

Where's Kostya, I think. *Where the fuck is Kostya?*

Arkady starts yelling, and then another older man comes in, takes one look, and starts yelling. It's all in Russian, and it's all directed at Niko, who turns his back with one hand over an ear.

I toggle the cameras again. One of them is shaking, like the truck it's in is being rocked from side to side. I toggle. When I come back, that camera is suddenly moving backwards and then it sweeps across a long vista of gray slabs and buildings.

No Kostya.

Please, I think. My heart's in a vice. *Please. Please.*

"Niko," I say, leaning forward and touching his shoulder. Arkady keeps shouting. The other man keeps shouting. I can't fucking *believe* them, and I don't know if Kostya's okay, and I think I'm about to tear something apart.

Niko holds up one finger. Arkady switches to shouting in English, the other man still shouting in Russian.

"—Come here and ruin everything—"

"SHUT UP!" I shout.

No one shuts up.

"How dare you—"

"SHUT THE FUCK UP OR GET THE FUCK OUT!"

They both stop for a second. A voice on Niko's radio says something. I hope it says *Kostya's fine* as I slam both hands on the table.

"You can stay here and *fucking* help or you can get the fuck out of here, because I swear to Christ if I see any more of your goddamn dick-waving right now I will fucking *lose my shit*," I shout.

They both stare at me. Sweat rolls down the back of my neck. I'm shaking, and I already regret my outburst because I don't have shit to back it up besides fury and sheer terror.

A voice in Russian comes through the radio. I try to listen for Kostya's name but I don't catch it. The camera is still moving, the car going somewhere, and I touch Niko's shoulder again and point at it.

I *want* to shake Niko until he tells me that Kostya's okay, but I don't. He knows what he's doing.

Arkady sits, slowly. The other man turns on his heel and leaves.

"*Da*, Hazel," Niko says into the radio, then looks at me. "Pavel was badly hurt. That truck is taking him to the hospital and bringing Yelena here. Kostya's going to have a nasty bruise but he's fine."

I exhale and sit again. My t-shirt sticks to my back. All the cameras show is a burning truck in the middle of a concrete slab.

Just leave, I think at the camera. My insides feels like lead.

Leave, just fucking leave.

CHAPTER THIRTY-EIGHT
KOSTYA

I lean against the back of the Humvee. I'm breathing hard, adrenaline is surging through my veins, and my side hurts like hell where the explosion threw me into the truck about thirty seconds ago, but I'm okay. Bruised, but fine.

I'm better than Pavel. I watch the other truck drive away, thumping over concrete and then dirt. He's in the back, a piece of steel the size of my hand sticking out of his leg. His blood is still pooled and dripped across the concrete in front of me, but if they drive fast enough, he might make it.

And Yelena's fine. She'll be at the palace in an hour. At least one good thing happened.

Everything goes still. The truck in the center is still burning, but since it's in the middle of a concrete slab, I'm not particularly worried that anything else will catch fire.

Everyone's still talking through my earpiece, and everything from the palace is coming through a blur of shouting, but it's all status updates. They're checking in that they're okay, that by some miracle they all got behind cover in time.

Then I hear a woman's voice over the radio. It's in the background, but it shouts SHUT UP over the yelling.

I look over my shoulder and around the side of the vehicle, but I can't help but smile at Hazel, even as the shouting continues.

Then I hear her again. We *all* hear her again, a long, curse-and-threat-filled tirade that would probably make my mother feel faint if she heard it, because in Sveloria, women do *not* curse.

It's followed by silence. Crouched behind the vehicles, no one says anything.

"Was that Hazel?" Dmitri asks Niko through his radio.

"Yeah, that was Hazel," Niko says. Everyone looks at me, and I start to shrug, but then I hear the rattle again.

Everyone freezes. I feel another jolt of adrenaline race through me, and my brain kicks over into instinct mode, the *fight* part of fight-or-flight.

"Down!" Captain Ovechkin shouts as another truck rolls into the square.

I brace for an explosion, but there isn't one. I wait and wait, forcing myself not to look around the truck, because I know the moment I do my face could get blown off.

Just explode, I think. *Just fucking explode.*

The only thing worse than a bomb is an unexploded bomb, because once an explosive fails it could go off at any time.

"Niko," the captain says into his radio. "Eyes?"

"It's a truck, the same kind of Soviet truck," Niko says.

Silence.

"Bullet holes through the driver's side window," Niko finally says.

Shit, I think. We don't know how the last bomber set off the bomb. We don't know if the person inside this one is dead or alive. We've got no idea whether this bomb will go off or not, whether jostling the truck will hit a trigger.

We wait. I hold my breath until I can't any more, and then

let it out in a long sigh. Captain Ovechkin and I look at each other.

"There might be people on the other side," I say. "I'm going to go check."

"No," he barks, and signals to two other men.

They nod, stand into a crouch, and begin making their way around the big concrete slab.

"Let someone else do something for once," the captain growls at me.

I hear a faraway noise, and for a moment my gut tightens.

How many fucking times is this going to happen? I think.

Then I see a helicopter fly into view over a faraway gray cube.

I relax a little. The cavalry's here.

Ovechkin stands.

"Get in," he says, gesturing at the Humvee. "We're heading out."

CHAPTER THIRTY-NINE
HAZEL

One by one, the cameras in the Humvees swing around, showing the full vista of the gray district, then drive away. For a long, long time I'm still convinced that the truck behind them is going to explode, that somehow the explosion is going to obliterate everyone even when they're half a mile away.

It doesn't. They just drive, and my terror slowly eases.

I put my head in my arms, on the table, and take a long, deep breath. I'm still shaking, still roiling inside, on edge, like the unexploded bomb is behind me and I don't know it.

Niko's still talking in Russian. *Always* talking in Russian, and this whole time he's somehow managed to do it without sweating or getting a single hair out of place.

This probably isn't the most stressful thing he's ever done, but still.

He stands. I look up. Arkady's gone, God knows where. Niko puts his hand on my shoulder.

"I'm going to field command," he says.

I stand.

"No," he says. "You're not trained and I don't need American fighter jets up *my* ass."

I close my mouth, because as much as I hate the thought of sitting in the palace doing goddamn nothing, I know he's right.

"But you could run our tracking software," he goes on. "I don't think any of these old men even know how to turn a computer on."

"Yes," I say. "Please, *God*, give me something to do."

THIRTY MINUTES later I'm in a different room with an array of screens and two twenty-year-old Svelorian aides who seem equal parts annoyed with and afraid of me. There's a map on every monitor: radar, infrared, GPS, even a few satellite. Every military vehicle is marked, and I can watch them all move around.

There's no way I should be in here. There's no way that the movements of the entire Svelorian military isn't the highest level of classified information, and yet, here I am. Not even a citizen, just some girl who doesn't even speak the language.

My earpiece fuzzes to life, and I turn it down a little, making a face. I feel official as hell wearing it, but it's *weird*, like there's constantly someone standing just behind me who I can hear and not see.

"Sung," says a man's voice I don't recognize.

"Yes," I say.

"We've got two teams, eastern quadrant, Velchek and Orsiny. Outside a sealed factory. Anything?"

I pause for a long time, trying to find what he's talking about. The aides are whispering to each other and not fucking helping at *all*.

"Sung?" the man asks.

"I'm here," I say, and finally find what he's talking about on the infrared map. "Looks like... one large heat signature inside. Maybe one smaller. Neither movi—no, one's moving, a little. I don't know what it is."

Shit, I'm bad at this, I think.

"Thank you," he says.

I do that for an hour. The questions back up sometimes, and the aides get more helpful, but it becomes quickly apparent that they don't know what they're doing either.

We all turn when the door opens, and a woman pokes her head in. I recognize her as one of the palace kitchen workers.

"Yelena Pavlovna is here," she says softly, her voice thickly accented.

"Thank you," I say.

"She wants to know if she can help."

I look at the screens, all of them festooned with Cyrillic characters. As much effort as I've been putting into learning Russian lately, I'm still sounding out words like a three-year-old learning to read.

"Yes," I say. "Send her here, *please.*"

TEN MINUTES later Yelena comes in. She's wearing clean clothes, and she's washed her face and pulled her hair back, but I don't think she's showered. Her eyes are bloodshot and red-rimmed, but she looks *pissed.*

I've never seen her look anything but sweet, happy, or slightly confused before, and I force myself not to smile.

"Are you okay?" I ask.

She holds out her hands. Her wrists and forearms are bruised and purpled, and I suck a breath in through my teeth.

"They tied me, but that's all," she says, her voice soft. "The *volki* didn't have me long before they traded me like a bargaining chip."

She looks at me, and for the first time, there's something *fierce* in her eyes.

"One tires of being used to bargain with," she says.

Her voice has a bitter edge to it that I've never heard before. Both the aides are looking at us. I shoot them a glare and they turn around, acting like it was their own idea.

I hand Yelena a headset.

"We're tracking the remnants of the *volki* through the gray quarter," I say, and quickly explain what everything is. She slides her headset on over her head and tells me what everything says, and we quickly slide back into the rhythm that we developed together in the palace.

IT'S SLOW, methodical, almost tedious work as the military works its way through the gray district, following up on all the leads. They arrest people one by one, and though I keep thinking that soon they'll find the headquarters, the *big* hideout, they never do.

The *volki* are hiding in holes simply and by pairs. The end isn't glamorous or exciting, it's mundane, as angry-looking men and a few women are driven off in military police cars.

Yelena and I sit in the room and tell people what's around the next corner. We tell one unit where another unit is, where the helicopters are, whether backup is coming. She knows the language and the city and I'm good at taking in three maps at once and describing the composite to someone on the other end of the line.

At some point, the aides leave. The room doesn't have any windows, so I'm surprised when I look at the clock and it's almost nine. Most of the motion on the maps has stopped. Not all the *volki* have been rounded up, and there are problems besides them, but it's not a bad day's work.

We sit in silence and watch. I feel wrung out from the day, from the heart-stopping terror that started it to its long, slow descent into tedium. Not with a bang but with a whimper, that kind of thing.

But Kostya's okay, I think. *Everything could have gone so much worse.*

All day, in the back of my mind, I've been replaying the morning. The meeting, the vodka, Kostya running. The explosion, horrifyingly silent on the screen, flames expanding and then blackening into a column of greasy smoke.

A few blips on the monitors move, but nothing noteworthy.

I think of Kostya saying *I just wanted to tell you.*

I swallow hard and fight tears.

He knew he might die, I think. The thought makes me nauseous, even though right now he's at the hospital, visiting Pavel. It looks like Pavel's going to pull through, so that's good.

"What's that?" Yelena asks, pointing at the screen.

There's one blue dot, an official car, making its way along the seaside road and toward the palace.

"Sung here," I say into my headset. "Who's driving toward the palace in a government vehicle?"

There's a second of silence, then Kostya's voice.

"Niko and I," he says.

My toes tingle. Yelena looks over at me. I try not to smile and fail miserably.

"You mind if we come in?" he asks.

"You've got some explaining to do," I say.

"How many more times do I get to use *because I'm the King*?" he asks.

"Zero, and it was a bullshit reason in the first place," I say, but I'm smiling.

Yelena's looking at me. I clear my throat.

"Drive safe," I say to Kostya, and my headset goes quiet.

Yelena looks forward and bites her lip.

Say something. Just say something.

I take off my headset, then reach over and switch hers off. She looks at me.

"I'm sorry about Kostya," I say.

I'm not exactly sure what I'm sorry for. All they did was attend official events together. They weren't dating. Kostya never even asked her out himself, it was always his father.

All I did was start sleeping with someone who had been in the company of another woman. I don't think he and Yelena ever *kissed*.

But I still feel like I've done something cruel, because I think Yelena might have had higher hopes for her and Kostya.

She looks down.

"Thank you," she says. She taps her finger on the console. "In hindsight, I don't think it was going to work even if you hadn't come along."

No, I think.

"It was my father's idea to begin with, and Kostya can be very stubborn," she says. "He was nice to me, and I confused that with liking me."

"I've made that mistake before," I say. "God, have I made that mistake."

"It's an easy mistake," she says, and I just nod. She looks at the screen, where Kostya's car is getting close.

"I'll stay here in case something happens," she says. "Go say hello."

"You're sure?"

"*Go*," Yelena says.

I don't ask again.

CHAPTER FORTY
KOSTYA

I hit the button on the SUV's console and the gate slides open, my headlights shining through to the dark shrubbery behind. Niko and I are silent. I think we've said everything we have to say to each other, and now we're just out of words.

The palace is up ahead, and in front of it, a roundabout with a fountain in the middle. There's a person sitting on the edge of the fountain, and as we approach, she stands, squinting into the headlights, her arms folded across her chest.

I smile like a moron. Niko glances at me and then almost smiles.

"She's good for you, you know," he says.

"I know," I say.

I stop the car in front of Hazel. She shades her eyes against the headlights so I cut them and we both get out.

"I'll walk," Niko calls.

He nods at Hazel.

"Good work today," he says.

"You too," she says, nodding back.

He disappears behind the fountain and then it's just me and Hazel, standing in the driveway. She takes a deep breath.

"Are you fucking crazy?" she whispers.

"Maybe," I say.

Then she's in my arms, squeezing me as hard as she can. I'm holding her against me, her head right under my chin. I kiss her hair. She squeezes harder.

"What the *hell*," she says.

I smile into her hair and don't answer. It's not a real question, anyway.

"And you wouldn't even tell me," she mutters.

"You would have tried to stop me," I say into her hair.

"Well, yeah," she says. "I was afraid someone would try to kill you. Which they fucking *did*."

"I'm harder to kill than that," I say. I stroke her hair, and she snuggles into me harder. "Even Pavel is harder to kill than that."

I don't say *you're safe and sound so it was worth it*, because I know I'm not supposed to base huge decisions like this on one person who's not even a citizen.

But I finally feel like I did something right, maybe for the first time since my father was killed. The *volki* are mostly rounded up. I'm in talks with the other side, and they're reasonable people.

We'll make progress. We'll move forward.

Best of all, Hazel's still here, in my arms, totally unhurt. For that, I'd face down ten more car bombs. Hell, twenty.

I don't tell her that either.

We stay there for a long time, holding each other. Every so often I kiss her head or stroke her hair, but mostly I like being here, with her, even if we're just standing still.

"I should go park the car," I finally say, letting her hair slide between my fingers.

Hazel swallows.

"I love you," she says.

I smile into her hair, even though she can't see me.

"I know," I murmur.

"I thought you were gonna die and I wasn't going to get to tell you," she whispers. "And I was *so* mad at you."

"Are you still mad?"

"No," she says. "Just don't do that again."

I pull back slightly and take her chin in my hand, tilting her face up.

"*Zloyushka*, that wasn't the first dumb thing I did to protect you and it probably won't be the last," I say.

"Kostya, you don't—"

"I didn't do it because you're fragile, or because you're helpless, or because I think you can't take care of yourself," I say. "I did it because I love you, and I want to protect you, and you can't say anything to change that."

I kiss her before she speak again.

I PULL into the garage and park in an open spot next to the old Soviet troop transport, the one we made out in the night we took the motorcycle to the gray district. It feels like it was a month ago, even though I think it was maybe two weeks.

I cut the engine with my left hand, because Hazel's still holding my right.

I know the second I'm inside the palace, I'm going to be hit with a barrage of people wanting to talk, shout, chastise me, ask me what to do next, but the truth is that right now I don't *care*. I'll care tomorrow, and the day after that and for the rest of my life, but for the next eight hours, I just want to sleep.

Hazel unbuckles her seatbelt.

Well, first I want Hazel again. *Then* sleep.

I run my thumb over the back of her hand.

"So pie-eating contests and beer pong are real," I say.

"Yes," she says, lifting her eyebrows in a question.

"Do American teenagers really take their cars to scenic overlooks to have sex?" I ask.

She laughs.

"There's not usually a scenic overlook, but yes," she says, and lifts my hand to her lips, kissing it as her eyes light up. "European teenagers don't fuck in cars?"

"Our cars are smaller," I say.

"So you never got it on in the back of your mom's station wagon?" she says.

"The Queen doesn't drive a station wagon," I tell her.

Hazel rolls her eyes.

"I *know* I told you I lost my virginity in the back of a Range Rover," she says.

"You did," I say.

A small, stupid twinge of jealousy twists in my stomach, and I try to ignore it. She's mine *now*. It doesn't matter who she slept with nine years ago.

"All these cars and you never used one to impress a girl?" she asks. She slips her shoes off and tucks her legs under her, leaning over the center console.

"I don't need cars to impress girls," I say. "I'm *royalty*."

"Yeah, you bring that up sometimes," she says, grinning. "All those girls threw themselves at your feet and they never got to ride the royal Maserati?"

I hesitate for a second. I really haven't had sex in one of these cars, but I also don't think we're talking about cars any more.

"Is the royal Maserati my dick?" I ask.

Hazel laughs so hard that for a moment she can't even talk. Then she kisses the back of my hand.

"Yes," she says.

She climbs over the center console until she's straddling me in the driver's seat. I'm still wearing fatigues, and she grabs my collar and leans over me.

"I was trying to be coy and flirtatious," she says.

I grab her ass with both hands and squeeze.

"English isn't my first language," I tease. "You have to be very literal with me."

She kisses me hard and I pull her in until she's right against my already-throbbing erection.

"Okay," she says, pulling away. "Let's fuck in the car."

"*That* I understand," I say, and slide my hands under her shirt, kissing her again. She's warm and soft and even though it's barely been a day since the last time, I think I craved her this whole time.

"Is this my shirt?" I ask. It's at least five sizes too big for her.

"I got dressed in the dark," she says, and starts unbuttoning my shirt. "Oh, and in a panic because you were gone."

She gets the buttons undone and slides her hands between my camo and my undershirt, looking at me with that heavy-lidded look she gets sometimes.

"It looks good on you," I say, then pull the shirt she's wearing over her head. "But better off you."

I pull her forward again and kiss her, my tongue snaking into her mouth.

"How was that for coy and flirtatious?" I ask.

"Better," she says, and bites my lip as she pushes my shirt over my shoulders and then yanks my undershirt off, too, running one hand down my torso and grabbing my cock through my pants.

I groan and dig my fingers into the dimples in her back.

"The Maserati's up and running," she says.

"We're not calling my dick that," I say, and push one thumb under her bra.

She laughs, then takes both my hands and puts them on her back, over the clasp. I sigh, fumbling.

"I can't even see," I say, but her head's on my shoulder and she's laughing too hard to respond.

A hook pops open.

"Something happened," I say.

She puts her hands over mine, shooing me away, and one second later her bra's off. I roll both her nipples between my fingers while I kiss her, and she makes a noise into my mouth that makes my cock twitch.

I move my lips to her jaw and then her neck, her hand in my hair. I'm pushing her backward and she's yielding, soft and warm and pliant beneath me, so I suck one pebbled nipple into my mouth and bite it gently.

Hazel gasps and I undo her pants with my mouth still on her. I push my hand inside and run my fingers across her clit quickly, just to feel the way her body tenses when I do.

She's already wet as hell, and it's not surprising but *god* I like it, and I slide two fingers into her and flatten my palm against—

A horn sounds, incredibly loud in the quiet garage and Hazel yelps, then hits her head on the roof.

"Shit," she says, and then starts laughing.

"Are you *trying* to tell everyone that we're fucking in an official government vehicle?" I tease.

"Sorry," she whispers.

"I can't get your pants off in here anyway," I say, and open the door. She pushes it and hops out, her pants already half off her and pulls them off herself before I'm even out of the car.

Now she's naked in the garage, between the car we were in and an ugly old Soviet truck. I can't stop grinning, and especially not as she pushes me against the SUV, kisses me with her tongue in my mouth, undoes my pants and grabs my cock.

She strokes it and I hear myself growl at her and she laughs, biting my lip.

"What?" I ask, my voice hoarse and rough.

"You're an animal," she says.

"You have no idea," I say.

She strokes my cock again. I growl louder, and she presses her lips to my neck then nips at me, and I sigh.

"I'll be gentle," she says, her voice buzzing against my skin.

I chuckle.

"You already marked me once," I tease. "I had to hear about it all day."

"Sorry," she says.

"I don't mind," I whisper. "I like being yours."

She kisses my collarbone, my chest, and then she's on her knees, tugging my pants off. Then her tongue is on the underside of my cock and she's looking up at me with a wicked look in her eyes.

Fuck, it's sexy.

She closes her lips around me and I lean my head back against the SUV and groan as she moves her mouth down my shaft and then pulls back, her tongue flat against the underside. I put one hand on her head gently, forcing myself not to grab her hair even though I've got the urge.

"Fuck, that feels good," I say as she does it again and then again, moving slightly faster and harder with each stroke. I look down and watch her, moving her hair out of her face as the heat pools inside me and I hear myself groan.

"Slow down," I say.

"Hmm?" she says, and her voice vibrates through my cock and straight up my spine. It makes my toes curl.

Hazel pulls back until her lips are just around the head of my cock, her hand around the base, and she looks up at me, swirling her tongue around it for a deliciously long moment before taking me back in her mouth. With every stroke I get closer and closer to the brink, my breath coming in gasps, and just as I'm about to tell her to stop before I come she pulls back slowly and looks up at me, grinning.

She stands and I push her backwards before I even know what I'm doing, until she's up against the ugly Soviet truck. My hand's behind her head, in her hair, and I'm kissing her hard.

"You taste like me," I murmur.

"You're probably dirty enough to like it," she says, her fingers on my spine, dragging upwards.

"Probably," I say, and kiss her again, her body moving against mine as she presses her hands into my lower back, urging me closer.

That's it. I need her *now*.

I grab her and lift, and in a moment her legs are wrapped around my hips and my length is pressed against her as she squeezes and I bite her neck because it's there and she's driving me wild. Then she wriggles and relaxes, grabs my cock and guides it to her entrance.

"Slow, right?" I tease her.

"Goddammit," she whispers.

I know what she wants. What we *both* want. I've got the claw marks to prove it.

I slide into her with one hard stroke, and it feels so good it takes my breath away.

"*Fuck* yes," she whispers into my ear.

I bite her earlobe and fuck her again, listening to her moan.

"I wanted to do this the night we took the motorcycle," I murmur. I'm driving into her, hard and deep, trying to control myself but it's hard. It's hard as hell.

"Push me against a truck and fuck me?" she asks.

I thrust again and her eyes slide closed, her head back against the green paint.

"Yes," I say.

"Good," she says.

She's slowly falling, because as fun as it is, this isn't a long-term position. I put her down, and then we're around the back of the truck and she's up on the tailgate. I shove the canvas out of the way, and some of it rips, but Hazel kisses me hard and I don't give a shit about anything else.

I push her gently and she lies back in the truck, one knee over my shoulder and I slide into her again, even deeper than before and Hazel gasps.

"That good?" I growl at her.

"Yes," she whispers.

I lean over her and try to go slow, one hand on her shoulder. I can't quite kiss her but I can watch her as she moves, like some kind of beautiful sex goddess.

A sex goddess who I'm balls-deep inside of. I can already feel her muscles clenching and releasing around me, and it's intoxicating. Even here, in a garage, I feel like I'm utterly lost in her, the only thing that even matters.

"Kostya," she murmurs.

"Yes?"

"I like saying your name when we're fucking," she says.

I thrust again, hard and deep, and she arches into me.

"I like hearing you say it when I'm inside you," I say.

"Kostya," she says again, but this time she moans it, and holy *fuck*. I keep going and she keeps saying my name, and soon there's fire pooling inside me and I know I can't last much longer. Not like *this*, but she's starting to clench around me, harder and harder.

I slide one hand down until I'm stroking her clit with my thumb. Hazel gasps.

"Fuck, Kostya," she whispers, and explodes. She clenches around me so hard I see white and I hear her moaning *oh fuck yes Kostya* as she comes and it feels so fucking good that I go right over the edge, like I'm falling into her endlessly.

Everything goes white for a second and my mind goes totally, completely blank except for *this* and how fucking *good* it feels to be here, with her, and how good she feels and how perfect this is.

When I finally stop I've got one hand on her stomach and Hazel puts her hand over it, still breathing hard. She swallows, and then we look at each other. I push her knee off my shoulder, kiss her, and climb into the truck next to her as she snuggles against me.

"You bit my knee," she says.

I pause, blinking.

"Just now?"

She laughs.

"Sorry," I say.

"Not hard," she says. "But you definitely bit my knee when you came."

I kiss the side of her head.

"Sometimes I get out of control around you," I murmur.

"Good thing I like it," she says.

We're quiet for a long moment, Hazel curled against me, my hand stroking her shoulder.

"We should go in and pretend that it normally takes two people half an hour to park the car," she says.

"I'm not keeping you secret any more," I say.

"I don't particularly need to announce that we had sex in the garage while people were waiting for you, though," she says.

It's a good point.

"I don't want to leave," I say. "Back there are people who want things and have questions and demands and suggestions and I just want to sit here with you in this horrible truck."

She nuzzles against my shoulder.

"We could get on the motorcycle and run away," she suggests.

"To where?" I ask. "We don't have passports, or a change of clothes, and I don't even have my phone with me."

"Kostya, you're terrible at this," Hazel says.

"At running away?"

"At co-authoring a fantasy that's not going to happen," she says.

I lean my head back against the truck.

"I don't understand any of what you just said," I say.

She laughs quietly.

"Okay," she says. "I say, 'We could run away on the motorcycle,' and you say, 'We'd go to the beach and drink champagne and watch the sun come up and it would be very romantic.'"

"Where are we going to get the—"

She puts one hand over my mouth, gently.

"We're not going to do it, just talk about it," she says. "Your turn."

"We could…" I trail off and look at her.

She raises her eyebrows.

"Go to another town," I say.

Hazel closes her eyes and bites her lip, laughing silently.

"We'll work on it," she says, and kisses my shoulder.

"I love you," I say.

"I love you too," she says.

We should go back. I should face the people back at the palace.

"Stay here," I say.

"In the truck?"

"In the country," I say. "If you can. I can get your visa extended."

Hazel shakes her head and looks up at me.

"Kostya, you're too much," she says. "You're the fucking king, of course you can get my visa extended. You could outlaw visas if you wanted."

"Not really," I say. "There's a—"

"I'll stay," she says, and pauses. "I'd like to. But only if you can extend my visa, of course."

"I won't if you keep making fun of me," I say.

"You like it," she says, and pushes me.

We climb out of the truck and find our clothes. Then we walk back to the palace through the gardens, holding hands.

I know everything could be shit again tomorrow, but right now, it might be perfect.

EPILOGUE
HAZEL

One Year Later

"But what do I *call* him?" Courtney asks. "Like, to his face."

"Kostya," I say.

She sighs over the phone.

"Don't make it weird," I say.

"He's the king of a whole country," she says. "It's already weird."

"They've got a parliament now," I say. "I mean, we've got a parliament now? Fuck."

Courtney laughs over the phone.

"At least becoming royalty hasn't stopped you from swearing like a sailor," she says.

"I'm not royalty yet," I say. "I can misbehave my ass off for another week."

"I'm *really* sure you'll change your ways after that," she says.

I just laugh, and Courtney laughs too.

"Okay, I have to go to work," she says. "God, the time difference is impossible."

I'm watching the sun set.

"You'll be here and jet lagged in a couple of days, though," I say. "We'll feed you good caviar and okay vodka."

"As long as it's at least okay."

"And as long as you don't tell anyone the vodka's just okay," I say.

"My lips are sealed," Courtney says.

I THINK I was almost as nervous about the rehearsal dinner as I am about the wedding, but it's gone smoothly, so smoothly I'm almost suspicious. I haven't forgotten anyone's names, I haven't gotten too drunk, and I haven't accidentally called someone a raccoon anus in Russian.

It's almost like I've finally learned how to do all this shit right.

Around ten, people start to trickle out. My mom and dad both got slightly drunk, and they each hug me twenty times and tell me that they're beyond thrilled and over the moon that we're getting married, and my mom *insists* that she knew it from the moment she introduced us, though I'm pretty sure that's bullshit.

Sergei and Dmitri are both drunk, and they both say polite things to me and then clap Kostya on the back and shout.

Niko's less drunk, and he gives me a warm hug when he says goodbye.

"Take care of him," he tells me.

Even Kostya's mom is nice. She's still wearing black, as if she's in mourning for his father, but Kostya thinks she's only doing it out of guilt that she's so much happier now.

Misha, his brother, just disappears. No one seems surprised.

Afterwards, we walk back and sit at a table with my college friends, Courtney, Alice, and Vivian.

"Kostya," Vivian says immediately. "I can call you Kostya, right?"

Already off to a great start, I think.

"You met earlier," I say. "Like, three times. You hung out."

"I'm just *checking*," she says.

"You can call me Kostya," he says.

"How does that even make *sense*," Alice says. "Konstantin doesn't shorten to Kostya."

"James doesn't shorten to Jim," Kostya points out.

Alice looks at him intently.

"Huh," she says thoughtfully.

"John doesn't shorten to Jack," Courtney says.

"Jack is a nickname for John?" Alice says.

"*Guys*, focus, please," Vivian says.

She turns to Kostya.

"I have it on good authority that you thought beer pong was only in movies," she says.

Kostya looks at me.

"This leads me to believe you've never played it," she says.

"I haven't," Kostya says.

Vivian reaches into her very large handbag.

She pulls out a stack of red solo cups and a package of ping pong balls, and I just start laughing hysterically.

"Tell me you brought those from the States," I say, barely able to breathe.

"Of course," she says, looking pleased with herself.

"Did you bring a ping-pong table?" I ask, still giggling.

"No," she says.

Now she looks *very* pleased with herself.

"I told some of the palace staff that I'm in training for the World Ping Pong Championships, and I really needed to practice my craft," she says. "Turns out there was a ping pong table in a rec room somewhere, and now it's in the living room of our suite, along with lots of shitty Ukrainian beer."

I've never seen three women look happier.

IT'S NOT like we have a choice. We head back to the suite they're sharing in the palace and invite along all the Americans, mostly family and a couple other friends, because if they managed to set up beer pong, I think we *have* to play it.

They even have a playlist for this, full of Springsteen, Johnny Cash, Bon Jovi, Old Crow Medicine Show, and all the most hyper-American music they could think of.

We set up the cups as Vivian explains the rules. The adults decline beer pong and mill around, wandering from the balcony to the living room, drinking wine.

"*I* drink if you get the ball into a cup on my side?" Kostya says. He's frowning at the table, his arms crossed over his chest.

"Right," says Vivian.

"Why don't you drink that? It would make more sense," he says.

"Because I'm trying to get *you* drunker than me so I can win," she says.

"The loser gets drunkest?"

Vivian stops and looks at me, standing on the sidelines.

"Cultural thing," I say.

"I still don't understand why you don't just drink the beer," he says.

"Drinking is *not* a game in Sveloria," I say. "They take it very seriously."

"I can hear you," Kostya says.

"Just go with it," Vivian says.

"These cups aren't even full," Kostya says.

"Remember the time a couple months ago that your brother was visiting and I got so wasted on three glasses of wine that I spent half an hour trying to talk him into adopting a kitten?" I ask.

"Right," Kostya says. "Americans."

"For the record, Misha should *not* have a cat," I say.

"No, he shouldn't," Kostya agrees.

"Okay!" Vivian shouts. "It's my turn until I miss, then it's your turn until you miss. Got it?"

"Got it," Kostya says.

Vivian wins the first one, and I play her. She wins again, then Courtney beats her and plays Alice. People wander in and out of the room. If they're surprised that the king is playing beer pong, they manage to keep it to themselves.

"They take this seriously," Kostya says. He rubs his knuckles down my back.

Beer splashes on Courtney, and she yelps, then laughs so hard she snorts.

"They do?" I ask.

Alice beats Courtney, and it's Kostya's turn again, and he wins by one cup. Then he beats me, and Courtney, and Vivian. My aunt Esther pokes her head in, shrugs, and leaves again.

"Is he even drunk?" Vivian whispers to me with the world's loudest whisper, watching Kostya play Alice.

"These people can fucking *drink*," I whisper back. "I don't know how they have livers anymore. Just goddamn vodka all fucking day."

"I hope you're ready for a royal rumble!" Alice shouts at Kostya.

Kostya throws a ping pong ball into her beer, and Alice grumbles.

Courtney giggles, then side-hugs me, her head on my shoulder.

"I can't wait until you're the world's filthy-mouthest queen," she says. "Filthiest-mouthed? Yeah."

"You're gonna wear a tiara, right?" Vivian asks.

"God, no," I say.

"Come on," she says.

"What happens to your title if Kostya dies?" Courtney asks.

"Courtney!" Vivian says.

"I become the dowager queen until I remarry and then I receive my new husband's title," I say.

"Oh," Courtney says.

"I asked all the questions already," I say.

"If you have kids, does succession go in age order or do boys go first?" Vivian asks.

I sigh.

"Right now, boys go first," I say.

"She says the baby factory's not open until that changes," Kostya says, then throws another ping-pong ball into Alice's cup.

My friends look at him.

"What? We talked about it," he says.

I shrug. Kostya beats Alice, and she flops dramatically on a couch.

"This is unfair," she says.

"I've never even played before," Kostya says. "How is that unfair?"

It's my turn to play him. He makes a big show of rolling up his sleeves, and I roll my eyes at him.

"You're going *down*," he says.

"Are you trash-talking me?" I ask.

"I'm gonna take you to beer pong *school*," Kostya says, and I giggle.

"Tell me more about beer pong school," I say. "Do I get grades? Is there recess?"

"I think beer pong school was Alpha Chi," Alice says from the couch.

An older couple wanders in. I'm pretty sure they're diplomats my mom invited, but I don't know.

"I didn't know there was beer pong," the woman says. "You know about the stoplight thing, right? When there's three cups left, arrange them like a stoplight. It makes it harder."

"Thanks," I say.

"That's the kind of thing you learn at beer pong school," Alice says.

I throw the ball way too far, off the table, and Kostya catches it.

"I have to stop after this one," I say.

"Oh, come on," Courtney says. "Be *fun*."

"I'd prefer not to be hung over during an hour-long ceremony in Russian," I say.

"It's gonna be an hour?" Alice says, still in exactly the same position she flopped in.

"You just have to stand there and look pretty," I say. "I have to do all the right stuff and say all the right stuff and not look like an idiot."

"You'll be fine," Kostya says.

I throw the ping pong ball. It bounces off the rim of a cup, off the table, and Kostya catches it again.

"Fucking stop catching it," I say.

"What, I should just let it fall on the floor?" he says.

"No, stop having hand-eye coordination," I say.

He throws it into one of my cups. I drink it. We've both only got one cup left, and he throws again, but I bat the ball away across the room.

"That's cheating," he says, very seriously.

"I can't play any more," I say. "Someone else play."

"Come at me, bro," Kostya says, and he sways a little.

Alice just giggles from her couch.

"You teach him that?" she asks.

I slump next to her.

"Sadly, yes," I say.

Kostya finishes the last solo cup of beer, and no one comes to play him, so he sits next to me on the couch.

"Guys, we're not twenty any more," Courtney says. "How did I ever do this all night?"

"I don't know," Vivian says, her head back on the couch.

"That was fun," Kostya says. "Anyone else wants to go I'll still take you on."

We all groan.

He nuzzles the top of my head and tries to slide his arms around my waist, even though we're on a couch with another person.

"You are *drunk*," I say.

"I'm tipsy," he says.

My friends are grinning like the cats that caught the canary.

"Guys, it was a success," Vivian says. "We should ask them embarrassing questions now."

"No," I say.

"Has he ever told you to call his dick 'Your Majesty'?" Courtney starts.

"What? No," I say.

"I never told you not to," Kostya says, and they giggle hysterically.

"Have you had sex on the throne?" Alice asks.

"There's no throne," I say.

"Is it weird that you're gonna be a queen?" Vivian says.

"It's weird as shit," I say.

"Is your brother single?" Alice says.

"Yes, and he'd probably have sex with you," Kostya says.

I giggle. I can't help it.

"He's eighteen," I say. "And please don't."

"Oh, ew," Alice says. "I don't fuck babies."

"What about your hot military friends?" Vivian says.

"I thought you and Chuck were moving in together," I say.

"He's not *here*," she says. "And I can look, okay?"

"I'm not moving in with anyone," Courtney says.

"Dmitri and Sergei are single," I say. "Niko's engaged."

"They like Americans?" Vivian asks.

"They like Hazel," Kostya says. I think he's falling asleep, half on top of me.

The girls raise their eyebrows.

"Not like *that*," he says. "Like normal."

The rest of the party is starting to die down, and people are meandering through the living room, leaving.

"We should go before you sleep on this couch," I tell Kostya. "I can't carry you."

"I should buy a royal golf cart to drive through the halls," he says.

"Fuck, I would love that," Courtney says.

"We could race," Kostya says.

I push him off me, stand, wobble, and hold my hand out. He takes it, and I brace myself to pull him up.

"Night, guys," I say as handsy, drunk Kostya stands behind me and puts his arms around me. "See you tomorrow. Kostya, *stop* it. Come on."

"Byeeeeeeee," Courtney says. The other two just wave.

WHEN WE GET to our apartment, as soon as we close the door Kostya grabs me and pulls me in, and then just holds me tight for a long, long time.

"You okay?" I finally ask.

He kisses the top of my head.

"I was gonna do this tomorrow but I think I'm braver right now," he says.

"The hell do you need to be brave about?" I ask.

"Stay there," he says.

I sit on the couch and listen to him pawing through something. I'm drunkish, but mostly sleepy, and I know I have to be up early tomorrow for a full day of ceremony and regalia.

Kostya comes back. There's something in one hand, and he just looks at me for a moment. He swallows, like he's nervous. I pull my legs up and sit cross-legged on the couch, getting a little nervous myself.

Then he sits down on the couch and turns toward me, still holding whatever it is in his hand.

"I still get nervous about you," he says.

"Don't," I say.

He looks at his hand and thinks for a moment, while I lean against his shoulder and he puts his arm around me.

"I found this when I was kid," he starts, his voice going quiet. "I kept this box of these little treasures I found, and even after everything got better and I grew up, I kept them and I never told anyone. And sometimes I take them out, still, when I feel like I'm getting too comfortable. Because I want to remind myself that it wasn't always this way."

I take his hand in mine and lace our fingers together.

"I'm not explaining this well at all," he says.

"You're fine," I say.

He exhales hard, looking at the wall opposite us.

"That's not what I'm trying to say," he says. "I'm trying to say that all that, the secret box, the being afraid that this will all fall part again, it's all part of me that I never told anyone until I met you. And I think it's easy to love a king with a palace and harder to love a dirty, scared kid who hoards trinkets because he always thinks everything might fall apart."

I squeeze his hand and he takes a deep breath.

"And tomorrow is all king stuff, but I wanted to give you this first, alone, from a dirty scared kid who has nothing, but he loves you and would do *anything* for you."

I'm crying, and I bite my lip hard, a tear running down my face. Kostya opens his hand and there's a dull, dark gray ring inside. He turns it over in his fingers.

"It's an iron wedding — don't cry," he says.

"It's good crying," I whisper.

"You sure?"

"Yes," I say, rubbing the tears off my face. "Tell me about the ring."

"It's an iron wedding band that I found in the chapel when I was five or six," he says. "I think it's a couple hundred years old, and it's pretty ugly, and you don't have to wear it, but I wanted to give you something with no pomp and circumstance. I wanted to give you something that's *mine*, not the king's."

He's flipping the ring around in his fingers, rubbing the outside along his thumb.

"I always thought that all that would be a weird, secret part of me forever, and I'd never share it with anyone. But then you came along, and I *wanted* to share it with you, and you love me anyway and I don't know why but I'm glad you do," he says.

I hold out my hand. He takes it, kisses it, then looks at me.

"Put the ring on me," I whisper.

"Oh," he says.

It doesn't fit on the ring finger of my right hand, but it fits on my middle finger, already warm from his hand. He wipes tears off my face with one thumb.

"I didn't mean to make you cry," he says.

"It's okay," I say, and swallow. "I'm glad you love me even if I'm a fuckup who fucks up a lot. I didn't get you anything. I'm sorry."

"You moved across the world," he says. "You volunteered to get married in a language you don't know

I just burrow my head against his neck and look at the iron ring on my finger.

"I love you," I say. "And I love you better because you were a scared dirty kid once, not despite that."

"I love you better because you met my family wearing spandex," he whispers.

"I really thought you hated me," I say.

"Not at all," he says, leaning his head against mine. "You made me feel funny and I didn't know what to do."

He strokes my shoulder, and I take his other hand in mine.

"We should go to bed so we can get married tomorrow," I say.

"This is nice, though," he says.

"It is," I say. "This won't change, right?"

"Not at all," he whispers. "I'm yours forever."

"*Ya lyublyu tebya*," I say. "A lot."

"I love you more," he says.

"It's not a contest," I whisper.

"I'd win if it were," he says.

I laugh, and he kisses me.

"No way," I say.

Kostya stands, still drunk, and pulls me up after him. He slides his arms around me and squeezes my ass.

"You've got one night left as a commoner," he says, pressing me against him. "Let's make it count."

"Are you saying that once I'm Queen all the fun stops?" I ask, teasing him.

He pulls my skirt up and then slides a hand under it.

"Hell no," he says, his voice getting lower. "I'm saying I'm drunk, I love you, you're the sexiest thing I've ever seen and I want you to ride my cock on this couch right now, and I love you."

"Dirty," I tease.

I kiss him and slide my hand along his cock. He growls into my mouth.

"Just honest," Kostya says, and kisses me back.

THE END